"Trouble you can [...] turning into trouble you can't," Pastor Zane said. "If you let us know what's going on, we'll figure a way out."

"The only thing going on here is I'm trying to figure a way to pay my debts, buy a horse and be on my way," Journey said. "The only thing going on here is a pastor who thinks he can fix every problem. Well, there are some problems you can't fix."

Zane bent his head, but his stance held no anger. "We'll play this your way for now, but watch yourself. And let us know when you need a hand."

She was determined not to skitter from him, no matter how her thoughts pleaded with her to. Why wouldn't he just go away?

Zane slid his hat back from his face and looked at her. "Journey, we have a saying here in the West that you might not have heard. But it's good sound advice."

"What's that?"

"Watch your back."

How little he knew. She was already backed into a corner.

Books by Kerri Mountain

Love Inspired Historical

The Parson's Christmas Gift

KERRI MOUNTAIN

grew up surrounded by books and storytellers, and credits her family for instilling in her the love of a good story in any form. An avid reader, the idea came to her that she ought to try writing a story of her own, but it didn't take her long to realize it was easier said than done. So when she had the opportunity to pursue a master's degree in Writing Popular Fiction, it seemed a natural fit. She tries to write the kinds of stories she would want to read. *The Parson's Christmas Gift* is her first novel.

Kerri lives in rural western Pennsylvania with her parents on their small family farm, and teaches in the district where she attended school as a child. She enjoys the quiet pace of country living and spoiling her niece and nephews on a regular basis.

KERRI MOUNTAIN

The Parson's Christmas Gift

Steeple
Hill®

Published by Steeple Hill Books™

STEEPLE HILL BOOKS

Steeple
Hill®

Recycling programs
for this product may
not exist in your area.

ISBN-13: 978-0-373-82802-9
ISBN-10: 0-373-82802-0

THE PARSON'S CHRISTMAS GIFT

Copyright © 2008 by Kerri Mountain

www.SteepleHill.com

Printed in U.S.A.

This is what the Lord says: Stand at the crossroads and look, ask for the ancient paths, ask where the good way is, and walk in it, and you will find rest for your souls.

—*Jeremiah* 6:16

To Mom and Dad—there aren't enough words to say thanks for all the love and support you've given in any adventure God allows. Love you both!

And a big thank-you to all the critique partners, mentors, friends and family who have helped develop and improve this story far beyond anything I might have imagined it could be. I praise God for putting each of you in my path at just the right time.

Chapter One

September 1870, Montana

She'd pay ten dollars for a hot bath if she had it.

Journey wiped the grit from her eyes and slid from her horse. She felt as if she'd been born in the saddle—and spent all of her twenty years there.

She checked her saddlebags. Eight dollars and some hairpins.

She scanned the town as it started to wake. Slowly the sun stretched over buildings, quiet and fresh as the barren peaks surrounding the settlement. Nothing like Savannah, still fighting to recover from the destruction of the War Between the States some five years past. Nothing like Independence, always bustling with folks coming from and going to parts unknown.

"It looks like we may be in luck, Gypsy," she whispered to her horse.

The shop she was looking for sat near the end of the street—one with a plain, honest front, a quaint little porch and a worn sign proclaiming General Store in faded blue letters. Underneath, smaller letters spelled out a wide variety of items.

Journey slipped along the shadowed side of the building and pulled a small silver mirror from her satchel. Dust muted the freckles over her round cheeks, and she debated as to which was the worse. Her skin had darkened over the miles, despite the broad-brimmed hat she wore. But no amount of color hid the exhaustion from her dark brown eyes. Pulling the hat from her head, she ran strong fingers through the curls that coiled around each other until she could feel the tangles before she touched them. She remembered the brilliant red of her mother's silky waves and wondered what had happened that it had translated to her as a dingy auburn, uncontrollable mass.

She tugged none too gently at her tight locks and poked hairpins in strategically. "If they catch me talking to you, Gyp, I guess it won't matter how civilized I look." She tugged the horse toward the front of the store.

Her dress barely showed its original flowered print and she didn't know how much shorter she could cut her petticoats to reinforce the material. But she brushed the dust off as best she could and looped the horse's reins around a post. With a deep breath she pulled on her shapeless hat and mounted the steps to the open door.

A cloud of grime swept over her worn skirt.

"Sorry, ma'am! I didn't see you there."

She drew her lips up in a gracious smile. So much for looking civilized.

The man stopped sweeping and leaned against the broom, nodding her through the doorway on his way out. "My wife'll be with you in a little bit, ma'am. Take a look around." Journey watched a grin peek from below his full mustache.

Whitened walls gave the store an open feel, much as the landscape did for the little town. An inviting stove glowed in the center near the back. Canned peaches, harness fittings and an odd conglomeration of pans and kettles rested on shelves and pegs behind the counters on either side. Barrels marked Flour and Sugar sat in front.

She tried not to notice the curious stares following her as she browsed her way along the bolts of yard goods, but still started when a young woman asked her, "Anything I can help you with?"

Pulling a bolt of navy broadcloth from the wall, she responded with a flash of smile, determined to be calm. "I'd like a dress length of this, please." It would cut into her meager funds, but a purchase always made an impression when she needed information. She'd need a new dress before winter anyway. Tattered hems made only wrong impressions.

She stepped toward the counter. Though she'd always been short of stature, the shopkeeper's wife dwarfed her by a good eight or nine inches. The woman must've been about her own age, judging from the smooth skin and bright green eyes. Honey-blond hair hung in a low tail down her back.

"I haven't seen you around here before," the lady said as she measured the cloth. Journey nodded when the woman glanced up. "I'm Abigail Norwood—Abby to most. Have you met my husband, Sam?"

"Yes, she did, I'm afraid," the low voice called from the porch. He wedged through the door and made a show of putting the broom in its corner space. "I gave her a right unfriendly greeting, though."

The woman shook her head in mock despair. "The one time I get him to sweep up in here." A sheepish grin drew across her lips. "Anyway, it's always nice to see a new face in town."

"Thanks," Journey said. She hoped her smile didn't waver.

"You visiting family?"

She shook her head, making a show of fumbling with the latches on her saddlebag.

"Just passing through, then?"

Sam Norwood stepped back into the room from what Journey guessed was a storage area. He smiled under his thick mustache again, and his eyes twinkled at his wife. "You'll have to forgive her," he said. "She has a soft spot for the curious cat."

A blush lit Abby's cheeks. "I didn't mean to pry. I just like to meet new folks. My apologies if I've overstepped, Miss…?"

"Smith…Journey Smith. Actually, someone with a little curiosity could be exactly the person to help me." She breathed deeply, gathering any poise and confidence she could muster. "I wondered if you know where I might find work around here."

"So you're planning on staying? Most folks pass through on their way to Virginia City. What type of work are you looking for?"

"I've done a little bit of a lot of things. Tended children, waited tables—"

"Ever done housekeeping?"

"My own."

Journey stood steadily under Abby's gaze. She thought if she held her breath she could probably hear the gears whirring in the woman's brain.

Abby turned to her husband then, looking down slightly to meet his eyes. "What about Miss Rose? She's been hoping to find someone to help out around her house. I'm not sure what arrangements she's thinking on, but I could take you out there if you're interested."

"I'm not sure how long I'll be in town. I was thinking—"

"Nonsense. Miss Rose is a fine woman. Once you meet her, you'll never want to leave."

"It's not that…" Journey stammered.

Abby looked up from where she was cutting the thick cloth. "At least speak with her. You never know how well things might work out."

Journey searched for an inoffensive excuse. "I don't want to be a bother. If you'll direct me to her house, I'd—"

"It's no bother at all. She lives on a ranch outside of town. Let me get my things and I'll take you there," Abby said, tying a string around the fabric Journey had purchased. "If you like, you can leave your trunks inside until you return."

Fear fluttered like a moth in her throat. "I'm traveling rather light. All I have is my horse tied out front. I'm certain I could find the place on my own."

As Abby patted the package and pulled her coat from a nearby hook, Journey caught her questioning glance but noticed it didn't stop her motion. "It'd be easier to show you. Sam knows I need to get out on days like this, anyway. He can handle the store for a few hours until we get back. I haven't had a chance to visit Miss Rose in a while myself. We'll take some sandwiches and have a nice little picnic. It'll give you a chance to get to know her."

"You can tether your horse around back, if that'll suit," Sam offered. "My wife's a natural guide, born and raised right here in Walten. Montana grows them pretty, that's for sure."

Journey forced her arms and legs to relax. There seemed no way around it, short of racing out the front door and galloping away on Gypsy. "If you're sure."

Sam moved back toward the storage room. "I'll hitch up the team. Oh, and, Miss Smith—"

"Please, call me Journey."

A dimple joined the grin on Sam's face. "Journey, if things don't work out with Miss Rose, come back here. We can't offer much more than a cot, but we might be able to find some work for you."

She nodded once, turning her head in time to catch the knowing smile Abby directed his way. Journey wrinkled her brow, wondering what these people expected from her.

"Thanks. I'll just go and tie my horse around back."

"Wait! Take your cloth—on the house." Abby thrust the neat package her way.

"I don't need charity." Well, that wasn't exactly true.

But she heard the insistence in Abby's voice. "Not charity. I guess Sam owes you for the mess he swept over you. We can't be treating our customers that way or we won't have them long."

She studied Abby. She seemed sincere enough, and she had made a point of not noticing the tattered seams in her dress. "I appreciate your kindness," Journey said, looking away as she slid the wrapped cloth into her satchel.

"I'll meet you around back," Abby said.

Journey nodded. Their kindness overwhelmed her a little. Maybe Hank's training had become more ingrained than she thought. They were just the type of people he had always sought—helpful and unsuspecting. Fortunately for them, she'd rid the world of at least one of his kind.

Journey slid farther into the corner of the narrow wagon seat. Abby had peppered her with a dozen questions before they'd even left sight of town. The sparse grass crackled under the wagon wheel, and she considered her odds of surviving a leap of escape.

"How far to the ranch?"

Abby paused. "Oh, probably three or four miles. Did you live—"

"It's easy to get caught up in the scenery here," Journey said.

"It is beautiful. Some folks complain about it being drab, with all the browns. They don't pay attention to the shades of the mountains in the light, or the pockets of sage tucked in everywhere. I've never wanted to live anywhere else. But listen to me jabber about myself. Where'd you hail from?"

"Back East."

"Yes, of course. I suppose most folks around here do, what with all the families settling in the area. What part?" Abby turned a smile her way.

Most folks took the hint when she answered in such an obviously vague way. "Well, I…I traveled quite a bit before coming here."

"I've never been out of Montana," Abby said. "But my pa's family came once to visit…"

Journey's attention wavered as she tried to ease her pounding heart. She considered making up something but hesitated. Lies had cost her plenty in the past. Weren't lies part of the reason she found herself here now? Hopefully the woman would lose interest.

"I'll bet you have a lot of stories about your trip west," Abby said.

"I suppose I'm one of those who'd rather hear the stories of other folks," Journey countered. She eased her lips into a smile, but it didn't come so easily to her eyes.

"Then Montana's the place for you. Plenty of storytellers around, waiting for a willing ear."

Journey nodded. She'd met grandmothers who adored their grandbabies less than this woman adored her home.

Tension quivered down her limbs. How could she end this line of conversation? "You—y'all do seem real friendly. I do appreciate your kindness."

Abby's thin fingers tapped her knee. "Oh, let me guess—you're from the South, right? Maybe somewhere in Georgia? My aunt Beth lives there. I remember when I was little and she came to visit us. She had the most delightful accent. I just recognized a little of it there in your voice. Am I right?"

"I, ah, I am from the…from the South, but—"

"You'll have to describe it all for me sometime. I always hoped to go back and visit my pa's family, see where he grew up. He and my ma moved back last fall, so to hear about it would make them feel a little closer."

The wagon lurched to the right and climbed steeply, bringing a large two-story ranch house into view. Journey breathed in the dry air, glad for the break in Abby's too-friendly curiosity. She had to stay alert. If something so minute as a tint in her voice could connect her back to Georgia, she wouldn't be safe even through Christmas.

She examined the ranch. A sturdy barn with an empty corral faced the broad porch of the home, with about thirty yards of grass-pocked dust between. The bluff they'd crossed boxed around one edge of the property, but the view beyond scooped across the wide valley. Sage and scrub brush were the only thriving plants she could see across the landscape. The property was secluded from the casual traveler but not closed off.

A pounding hammer echoed and drew her attention to a broad-shouldered figure on the roof.

"That's Zane—Reverend Thompson. He'd said he was going to see about patching some leaks for Miss Rose," Abby said. "The last time Zane visited, it rained, and he said he had to move three times when water started dripping down his back. Each time Miss Rose just pulled out another pot to catch it."

Journey knew what it was like to have to make do with what you had. She watched the man kneeling along the roof, sleeves rolled back over deeply tanned arms, shirt clinging between his shoulder blades despite the cool day. His dark brown hair glistened in the midmorning sun.

"You know him well?" She licked her dry lips.

"Oh, Zane and Sam grew up together. Their families came west together. I knew Zane long before he became our pastor. They say a prophet isn't honored in his hometown, but somehow Zane has made it work. He's a wonderful pastor, a true man of God. And of course those gray eyes of his don't hurt him, either." Abby patted her knee with a light laugh. "You'll get to hear him tomorrow." Journey forced another smile.

Tomorrow? She'd be long gone by then. She didn't need any pastor to make her see her guilt. She knew it well enough already.

"Journey? Is everything all right?"

She nodded, swallowing hard. Everything would be perfect—just as soon as Walten and all of its fine and overly welcoming citizens were miles of trail dust behind her.

Chapter Two

Everything moved so fast—too fast. Abby's chattering wearied her. She couldn't keep up. Journey rubbed her aching temples.

The wagon rolled to a stop beside the porch. "Hello, the house!" Abby called, climbing down over the wheel. Journey did the same and stood close to it.

"Thought I heard a wagon," a deep baritone answered. Reverend Thompson.

She watched Abby dig a sandwich out of the picnic basket and hand it to him as he stepped down the ladder and drank a dipper full of water. "We've come to share a lunch with Miss Rose."

"And this is?"

Journey felt his gaze as he unwrapped his sandwich. With a deep breath to steady her shaking, she tilted her head up to introduce herself. "Journey. Journey Smith."

"Now there's an unusual name. Pleased to meet you, ma'am. I imagine Abby's introduced me already." She stared at the hand he held out for a moment before shaking it. He smiled, crinkling his eyes at the corners and revealing a wide row of straight teeth and a cleft in his cheek. A shock of dark brown hair ruffled off his forehead, and a small thatch tufted at the back, making him look more like an unruly schoolboy than a minister. His square jaw proved more convincing, though his lips curved into a smile that seemed etched onto his face and had a depth she doubted lessened in many circumstances. "I'm Reverend Thompson to most folks, plain Zane to Abby. What brings you all this way?"

"Journey's new to the area, looking to settle in for a while. I thought maybe we could work something out with Miss Rose. She's been talking about hiring some help around here."

"That so?" Zane bit into the sandwich and nodded once slowly as he chewed, as if considering the idea. He swallowed. "Could work fine for you both. Miss Rose is inside. I'm sure she'll be glad to talk with you."

He gazed directly at her, his gray eyes alight in the sun. "So how'd you come by a name like that?"

Breath caught in her throat, choking her. One of the few questions Abby hadn't thought to ask.

"It's a family name."

His eyebrow tilted in a question, one she couldn't read. "Well, that's nice," he said. "I— We'll look forward to having you in our town."

Had they all assumed she'd decided? She wasn't staying here. She couldn't. She scanned the landscape again. Could she?

The young pastor continued. Before she could force a sound from her dry throat, his attention spread to both of them. "I expect we'll see you tomorrow at church. Hope everything works out for you, Miss Smith."

"Reverend Thompson."

"Please, feel free to call me Zane," he said, seeming not

to notice her wavering voice. He grinned, glancing up to the roof. Sunshine burnished the planes of his face a deep bronze. "If you'll excuse me, ladies, I have a few more boards to replace. I'll leave you to your visit. Thanks, Abby," he added, waving the sandwich. He snatched another bite as he headed up the ladder.

Journey watched him climb to the roof before following Abby.

An elderly woman with white-gray hair opened the door before they could knock. Her round blue eyes lit with a warm smile for Abby, and with a question for Journey.

"Who do we have here? Come on in, and bring your friend. My, but I haven't seen you in a spell," she said. "What's brought you ladies out today? Come in, come in."

Warm sunlight streamed in two wide windows on either side of the far wall, making the room bright and airy with a view of the distant mountains. A few delicate vases sat on shelves below them. Two daguerreotypes stood on a high shelf, shrouded with a layer of fine dust. Otherwise the room held little adornment beyond the ornate couch and a simple wooden rocker.

The fireplace in the middle of the house glowed with faint embers. On either side, a doorway opened. One led to the kitchen and Journey guessed the other led to Miss Rose's bedroom. Simple in design and decoration, it was so unlike the garish and cluttered rooms she'd lived in up until now. She liked it, quiet and unobtrusive.

They followed the tiny figure into the kitchen. Freshly baked bread steamed through cloths on the sideboard. The scent filled the room to the farthest corners.

"I was about to slice some bread for lunch," the woman said. Journey noted her slow, sure step and the steady voice.

Abby rested the basket she carried on the table. "Then we're just in time, Miss Rose. I've brought some chicken sandwiches for all of us. Zane already took one, and there's plenty more."

Miss Rose sat, then slid out a chair and nodded Journey into it. "I'm assuming your friend has a name you just haven't got around to sharing."

Abby's light laugh held none of the nervousness Journey felt. "This is Miss Smith. She wandered into town this morning, looking for work and a warm roof to sleep under. Journey, this is Mrs. Rose Bishop."

Journey forced her hand forward in greeting. Something about the woman reminded her of the ladies who would pass by the saloon on Sundays, all fine and proper. Except that this woman seemed to possess a kindness, a fairness—confidence born of something more than money and position. She tried to hold her fingers and voice steady. "Pleased to meet you, Mrs. Bishop. Please, call me Journey."

"Only if you'll call me Miss Rose," she said, getting up to set a kettle to heat. "Everybody does. Make yourselves at home, and I'll get the settings."

It seemed Mrs. Bishop—Miss Rose—could well handle the affairs of her own home. It didn't appear as if much needed to be done on the grounds that Miss Rose couldn't find a nearby rancher to lend a hand. She moved slowly but with a fairly steady step. While the house wasn't spotless, it wasn't unlivable, either. What would she want with hired help?

But Journey needed to find a more stationary hideout, and after months on the trail, eyeing every shadow, she was tired. The warmth and comfortable feeling this house offered could seep right in. She'd be inclined to let it.

She couldn't afford to let it.

Abby sat down across from her and placed sandwiches on the three plates Miss Rose brought out. Journey clasped her hands together, squeezing one thumb. Her knee bobbed as her mind raced to come up with a way to bring this meeting to a close before she agreed to something. She wanted to stay. She wanted to think she could belong in such a home. But where had her instincts taken her in the past? She was no longer fit for these fine people.

Miss Rose smiled, skin pulled paper-thin over her round cheeks. She seemed about to say something when Zane's hammer interrupted. Journey caught her motion to take a plate and pass a cloth-wrapped sandwich her way. Then the ladies bowed their heads without a word while she twitched in her seat.

"So you'd be willing to help out an old lady like me?" Miss Rose said when the pounding stopped. "You might find I'm too ornery for your liking."

"I'm not the easiest person to live with, either, ma'am." Hank had shown her that often enough. "I wouldn't want to obligate you."

"Nonsense. I've been looking for someone to move out here and help me some. My old bones can't go like they used to. I've been praying the Lord would send just the right person. To be honest, I'm looking for the company as much as the help."

Journey nodded and drew her eyebrows together. "You really think I could do that?"

From the corner of her eye, she saw Abby's own furrowed brow.

"Now that's hard to tell from this side of it," Miss Rose said. "Can you clean? Wipe windows?"

"Yes."

"Muck out a few stalls?"

"Sure."

"And you're in need of a place to stay?"

"Yes, ma'am."

"Well, then it seems like we're in a position to help each other. I can't believe it's a coincidence that you'd wander into town, into Abby and Sam's store, when here I am looking for someone like you."

"Like me, ma'am?"

Miss Rose looked her over, and Journey sensed the woman knew there was something more than met the eye. "Yes," she said. "Someone just like you."

"What about the preacher? He seems handy enough." Why argue the matter? She couldn't stay. She couldn't.

"Pastor Zane's been helpful to a lot of folks around here. He considers it part of his ministry. But he has plenty ministry beyond playing ranch hand. I found myself expecting it of him, and that's wrong. So I told God He'd have to send someone else along, so I could let Zane focus on more important things."

"You don't even know me." The steadiness of her voice surprised her. "I could only be looking for a handout from you."

A dignified sniff from the woman punctuated the air. "You might find you've gotten the harder end of the bargain. I'm set in my ways and terrible stubborn about some things. My Lord's had many a year to help me improve, and I still struggle with it—" she interrupted with a grin "—so that tells you what I was like at your age. I'll be after you to do some things both here in the house and around the property, but something tells me you're heartier than you look. Pay's not much—maybe a dollar a month, plus room and board, and of course, Sundays off. I'm figuring we could both win on this gamble, if you're willing."

Journey nodded. There was no way this could work. Who was she to involve this woman—this community— in her mess? The pounding on the roof matched the pounding in her head.

"So what do you say?" Abby's voice rose over the din.

Journey's muscles grew stiff. She needed to think. What would it matter if she darted for the door and never looked back? She waited for the hammering to stop.

"I appreciate your kind offer, Miss Rose, but I can't—"

The ring of the hammer interrupted again. It stopped, breaking the rhythm they'd grown accustomed to with a rough scrape. A heavy thud punctuated the instant of silence. For a moment, all three of them sat stock-still. Journey's heart leaped and she grasped the edge of the table, ready to push herself up and away.

"Zane…" Abby voiced Journey's own thought. They jumped from their seats as one.

"Go!" Miss Rose said, her voice calm and firm. "Make sure he's not hurt."

Journey thought that her very tone insisted that he was fine. Somehow that tone was comforting in itself. But that thought didn't keep her from flying out of the house, close at Abby's heels, wondering why it should matter to her.

Chapter Three

Journey turned the far corner of the house to see Zane struggle to his elbows. His gray eyes searched the skies above, unfocused. She watched as Abby knelt at his side, and followed her glance to the old woman. Miss Rose stood with a white-knuckled grip on the corner porch post, peering over the edge.

"Zane? Zane, are you all right?" Abby grasped his shoulders in both hands, holding him steady.

"What happened?" Journey asked. Zane's head jerked back, focusing his gaze on her. She fumbled for a handkerchief from her pocket and tapped it against Abby's shoulder but couldn't draw her gaze away from his. The woman took it to dab at the wide scrape on his right cheek with the limp cloth.

He blinked several times in his daze, thick lashes fluttering, but a small grin appeared. "Wasn't being careful enough, I suppose. I must have stood too heavy on a loose shingle board."

"If the pupils of his eyes aren't even, he could have hit his head," Journey said. Someone had told her about that once, after a rough bout with Hank.

She looked across the landscape. Even in the months and miles since his death, she couldn't shake the sense that he waited out there. She shivered in the cool mountain air.

A soft groan drew her attention back to the man on the ground as he tucked his feet and stood, taking the handkerchief from Abby. A wince crossed his face when his full weight rested on his ankle. He wobbled a little, but laughed. "Shows how great the wisdom of the Lord is, calling me to preach instead of to become a carpenter."

"Take it easy, there, Zane. Are you sure nothing's broken?" Abby inspected his elbow.

Journey wondered what the congregation might think of their pastor showing up with a nice shiner for Sunday service. He'd no doubt have one.

He pulled the thin cloth from his eye and examined it. "I'm fine, ladies. Really, I rolled right off, nice and gentle-like onto my hammer. Won't look too pretty for a while, but then, I don't reckon any of my parishioners come to see a pretty face."

Journey imagined his handsome face and strong build drew more than his share of coy glances. How could he not know it?

A rattled wheeze sounded behind her. Miss Rose had been forgotten in the excitement. "Well, he's standing and his tongue's working along with his brain same as usual. My goodness, Zane, you might have considered the rest of us. I declare, you took a good six months off my life. Now come inside a bit and rest yourself."

"I'm fine," he insisted, waving the offending hammer toward the roof. "There's only a little more to do before I'm finished. This time I'll pound an extra nail or two in this one." He tapped the fallen shingle with his boot and moved back to the ladder.

"Be careful this time!" Abby smiled at his retreating back.

Journey studied his broad form until he turned, catching her off guard. He shook out the mangled handkerchief to find a clean spot before touching it again to the cut.

"I'll wash this up and return it to you Sunday, ma'am."

"You needn't go to any bother, really."

"I appreciate it all the same, Miss Smith."

She thought to remind him to call her Journey, but then she realized it didn't matter. It would be just as well if he forgot her name altogether. He wouldn't be preaching to her on Sunday. She turned to follow Abby.

"Pardon me, ma'am. You prefer *Journey*, right? A name that pretty, I don't blame you. I'll keep that in mind."

He made her name sound like a complete sentence. But he seemed to look past her, over her. The wind blew his dark hair from his forehead, exposing the length of the hammer's cut.

The faint rustle across the porch drew her attention, reminding her that the others had already returned to the house. She nodded her leave. He smiled again and began pounding.

A job, a place to stay, and nothing more. Lie low for the winter, and be gone with spring thaw. What could be wrong with that? Right now, Walten, Montana, felt a world away from Georgia. Maybe it was.

"I declare," Miss Rose said, her voice puffing as they stepped into the warmth of the house, "sometimes I think that boy won't be happy till he's knocked his fool head off."

Journey couldn't help but smile at her exasperated tone. "Anyway, where were we?"

"Maybe Journey would like to see the rest of your place?" Abby suggested.

She flinched, startled at the tug on her sleeve. Before she could protest, Abby drew her across the sitting room to the stairway directly opposite the door. Her brow curled, but thankfully, the woman didn't voice any question. Journey flushed with embarrassment as she followed her up the narrow stairs.

"Well, what do you think?"

Journey peered around. "It's...light," she said. "I've never seen an upstairs so bright."

Instead of being divided into tiny, airless closets, two smaller rooms beckoned with open doors on either side of the hall. Light wooden boards made the rooms appear large and inviting. She walked toward the far end of the hallway, and the space broadened to the width of the house, windows bright with reflected sunlight. The cobwebby corners and dusty floors didn't dim the cheeriness of the room. How could four walls feel so unconfining?

"I haven't been up there in some time." Miss Rose's voice strained to reach them from the bottom step. "You'd be welcome to use the space. We cleared a lot out after my husband passed on."

She felt Abby's hopeful smile on her. "So? What do you say?"

"I think... Well, I just arrived in town, and here I am with a job offer and a roof over my head. It—it's all happened so fast." She glanced around the room and back over her shoulder. "I think I should catch my breath and consider it before I agree to anything. It's all so much kindness."

"It's you who'd be doing the kindness. It's a worry to me, knowing she's alone out here. I know she's lonesome, too. But what with the store and all… Oh, listen to me. You have to do what you feel is best, Journey."

She sounded sincere. Maybe she did want to help them both—Miss Rose and her. But that's not how people worked. A few folks might look out for a dear friend, most would take up a cause for family but no one cared for a stranger. So what did Abby really want? What did any of them want?

"I'll have to take your offer into consideration." She hoped she gave the impression there were other options.

"We've been praying for the right person to come along to help Miss Rose. Then you come along, looking for work." Abby sighed, her hands fluttering. "It's so exciting. Maybe I'll be proven wrong, but the Lord has blessed me with a pretty accurate sense of character. I'd be willing to take the chance. You seem like someone who needs a chance used on you."

Journey stared back, unsure of a response. She forced out a tense breath. "I am obliged for the offer, either way. You've been most kind."

"Will you at least go down and talk with Miss Rose awhile? It can't hurt, right?"

"I suppose not." She hoped not.

Abby stretched her arm toward the stairway. "Let's go, then."

Miss Rose waited in her rocker. Journey noticed she patted her hand over her heart until she saw them.

"Have a seat," she said. "I imagine you have some questions of your own to help you decide whether this would work for you."

Journey sat in the ladder-back chair near the door and tried to keep her breathing even. How could this woman treat her so well? She didn't even know her and yet had offered her so much. What would Miss Rose think if she knew what brought her here?

"It seems you keep the place well enough on your own." She didn't accuse, but she couldn't understand, either.

"I'm not completely feeble yet, but I can't get after this place like I used to. Still, I can't bear to part with what few animals I have left, either."

"You could hire someone from town to clean a few times a week and hire a ranch hand for the animals. Then you wouldn't be bothered with a boarder in your house," Journey said.

Miss Rose's laugh caught her by surprise. "I reckon you're right. It shows you have common sense. But the truth is, I need someone around more than that. It gets too quiet for my liking anymore. But town is too big and busy. I wouldn't be able to hear myself think."

Journey considered that. "I'm not one to chatter much."

Again the laugh. What a shame Mama never laughed like that. "So I've noticed."

Journey found the corners of her mouth curling up in spite of herself. "Please understand, I can't decide a thing like this before I think it through."

"Take all the time you need, darlin'. It's not like there's a flock of people knocking down my door for the job, Lord knows." Journey felt cool, wrinkled skin pat her hand.

"So when will your nephew be able to visit?" Abby asked. Journey figured the topic must be settled until she decided on her next move.

"Not soon enough for me, but I received a letter from him last week. He's going to try to make it for Thanksgiving, Lord willing."

Journey tightened her grip on the chair. A dollar a month plus board would help her save a little. If she held her purse strings very tightly, she'd be ready to move on by spring with money to get her to Oregon. Or even California. She scanned the warm wooden walls, the solid mantel above the all-but-dead fire. A certainty filled her. Yes. A good, safe home to rest in and regroup. Surely no one would look for her through a Montana winter. She'd be gone with spring thaw. Or, if things worked out well enough, maybe she'd stay on in the spring. Who could find her in a town as small as Walten?

"...some of the cases he works on, I declare. I wish he'd find a safer way to make a living." Miss Rose waved her hand before smacking it down on her knee.

Cases? Her nephew was a lawyer?

"Does he live far from here?" she asked. Her heart skipped a beat.

"Over in Virginia City," Miss Rose said, turning to face her with a smile. "He's a lawman there."

Chapter Four

Zane dismounted without his usual ease. That fall would have him stiff tomorrow but no lasting harm done. With a pat to Malachi's flank, he took off his tack and led him into his stall. After taking care of his mount, he moved to check on the other two horses he kept.

When he had heeded the Lord's call to the ministry, he thought his dreams of owning his own horse ranch were gone. It was a trade he'd been willing to make, but it didn't mean he wouldn't miss it. Sarah had been the one to encourage him to do both.

It hadn't been easy on a pastor's wage to get started, but he and Sarah had both made sacrifices enough to give them a start. He looked around now at the barn with the three horses. Not a grand beginning but room to grow. Without the horses to focus on after the fire and to fill those few hours when he was forced to be alone, he might've lost sight of their dream altogether.

He rubbed his tired eyes, wincing when he nudged the lump on the side of his head. He'd gladly trade it all to be rebuilding his dream with Sarah, rather than continuing it without her.

Zane made his way into the little house he'd built for himself. The Lord had called him to the ministry, and he had believed at one time that Sarah had been the one to be his helpmate in it. But hadn't the Lord shown him otherwise by taking her so soon from him? He'd failed somehow—failed to protect his family when they needed him most.

He rubbed his face and moved his hand back to his neck. He needed to wash up and finalize his sermon notes, then make a visit to the Culpeppers' and see how Agnes was faring with her gout. Then he'd ride upstream a bit and practice his sermon before turning in.

It would be a productive day. It had been a productive week. But it didn't change the fact that he'd come home to an empty house tonight.

Journey gave the ropes a final tug, securing her bedroll to the saddle. The horse sidestepped and pranced. Journey watched the evening sun drip into the horizon behind the peaked hills. She pinched her lips and let go a long breath, then nudged Gypsy toward the west.

Her cheeks ached from holding a tight smile for the better part of the afternoon. It took a firm hold to keep her horse at a walk tonight. They crossed the bridge leading out of town.

"I thanked her for the offer, of course, Gyp." She used low tones to calm the skittish horse. "But there's no way we can stay here. It wouldn't be right to drag her into our mess. Besides, her nephew is the law in Virginia City. We can't risk being caught. I'm not the fool I was when we first left Georgia." Her horse skittered and neighed. "Well, not quite."

Gypsy tossed her black mane and whinnied. "I know. I

liked the lady, too. I think we might have gotten a fair shake from her."

She felt guilty taking supper with the Norwoods, but Abby had all but tied her to a chair. Besides, she knew she'd do well to fill up before hitting the trail again. She excused herself before Abby brought out the pie, saying she wanted to explore the town before dark. But the wide, friendly streets and small, boasting businesses didn't attract her as much as the gurgling river and mountain views. They gave her space to breathe. She could appreciate Miss Rose's desire to be away from Walten's streets. There was no way she could stay. But she thought again of Miss Rose's ranch. Was there?

"We'll try the next town," she said. "We can't expect comfortable. Maybe when things have settled down more, we could come back. Everything is too messed up now."

She stroked the horse's brown neck. There was no time to be looking back. She'd had her chance. Stupid, stupid, stupid… Leaving Hank at the start would've been so much smarter. There'd been no reason to stick around after that first slap. There probably hadn't been much of a reason to stick around before it, for that matter.

She shivered, rousing herself back to the moment at hand. With the glow of the sun in the twilight sky being all that remained of the day, the cool of night drew up a breeze. It would be cold sleeping out on the trail tonight. She thought a moment of the airy upper floor of that ranch house. She could picture Miss Rose poking the fire, banking it for the night.

Journey buttoned her coat up to her chin and shifted in the saddle. She'd cut through toward the bluff and camp in the stand of pines there, then keep heading west at first light. Quiet sounds of the night echoed over the bluffs—

the hoot of an owl, soft wind from the hills. Her arms and legs lost some of their tenseness. The trail narrowed, but the trees brushing overhead gave the comfort of shelter.

Her eyelids drifted closed until her horse balked, refusing to move on. "A little farther, Gyp, and we'll bed down." She dug her heel into the flank.

But the horse reared back, snapping her fully awake, fingers tensed over the reins. She grabbed the saddle horn before she slid too far. Just as quickly, the forehooves clapped the packed dirt. It jarred the breath from her. The horse raced farther into the trees, heedless of the commands she bellowed. She stretched her arms as far as they'd reach around the horse's neck, muscles pulling as she hung tightly.

She bounced, her vision rattled as she tried to stay mounted and, at the same time, watch the direction the animal was taking.

The horse squealed, then lurched to a stop. Stars, leaves and dirt tangled before her. She felt weightless for an instant, then all of gravity's force came back to her with a crunch. The dimness of sunset faded to dark.

Chapter Five

Zane reined his horse to a stop, breathing hard. "Feels good to stretch the legs, eh, Malachi?" He patted the steamy neck as he dismounted by the stream. Closer to town, the brook broadened and slowed into a river. But here, it still gurgled and bounced over rocks.

He hunched down by the edge and trailed his fingers in the water a moment, then scooped a handful to drink. It ran fresh and cold down his throat, and he smoothed the back of his wet hand over his lips and chin. He'd need to shave before service.

Stretching out on the stubbled grass with his hands clasped behind his head, he stared up at a night sky of the deepest blue, covered with stars high above. Miss Rose would have a piece of his hide if she knew he'd come out without his coat.

For as long as he'd lived here, the beauty of the land had never failed to awe him. "Lord, I thank You for Your hand I see in all creation. It's a comfort to know things are in the order You made them to be." The scent of sage carried on the wind. He traced the swollen lump around his eye with his fingers.

"I pray, Lord, that You'll bless the folks here. Make sure I preach the words You give me to their benefit as well as my own. And thanks for watching out for me today when I fell. It could've been worse, I reckon. Turns out just my pride got hurt. Keep a special eye on Miss Rose, too, Lord. She's a dear old soul who's loved and served You a long while. I'm asking You to send the right person to help her."

Journey seemed an unlikely choice. She reminded him of a colt his father had bought from a rancher known for poor handling of his animals. That colt never lost the suspicious gleam in its eyes. It always flinched when touched, bolted often and busted fences more times than he could count.

"Until You do, Lord, help me look after Miss Rose. And thank You for putting her here to take care of me like she has ever since—"

Since Sarah died. He scratched his chin and sat up, resting his elbows on his knees. A fire blazed in his chest. Sarah. Their baby she carried. The flame that took them burned in him still. Three years without them—where would he be now without Miss Rose's prayer and love and support?

"I still miss them. I know they rest with You, Lord. It makes it easier, but I still ache that they're gone. Help me, Lord."

He stood and brushed himself off, clearing his dry throat. "All these things I lay before You, in the name of Your Son, Jesus Christ. Amen."

He nickered to his horse, who trotted over and nuzzled his shoulder. "C'mon, Malachi. Let's get back. You can listen to my sermon before I turn in."

He'd always been a fair tracker, but when the Lord had called him to preach, he was sure he'd misread the signs.

His palms still sweat when he stood before his congregation. Sarah had always listened to the sermon twice—once the evening before so he could practice and again during Sunday service. Her soft laugh would echo through the tiny home he'd been able to provide, and she'd run her fingers through his hair. He could still feel her wide, moist lips on his cheek.

"Preach it with the fire God's given you for His Word, for others, and you'll be fine," she'd say.

Now he had Malachi. Captive audience, little response. He mounted up and spurred the horse to a trot farther along the stream before heading home. It was too nice a night to head back early.

A cry broke through the night. He grabbed the Spencer gun holstered behind his saddle. He hadn't heard any talk of bobcats in the area, but it sure sounded like a woman's scream coming from the stand of trees ahead. He edged Malachi closer, picking his way into the darker night of the woods. What would a woman be doing out at this time of night?

He slid from the saddle and readied the gun in case he'd guessed wrong. A whinny sounded to his right as he drew closer, and it didn't take the brightness of the moon to find the broad, crooked path of broken twigs. Zane followed.

The thrashing horse caught his attention. The mare's eyes rolled back to white in panic as she neighed and struggled to get up from her side. He ground-tied his own mount, then moved toward the frightened animal.

"Easy, easy there, girl." He slid the halter off, stroking her wide brown head. The horse seemed to quiet, kicking only occasionally with her hind hooves.

He patted the heaving side, continuing to comfort the horse in low tones as he slid his other hand along her right foreleg. He grimaced when the bone shifted beneath his touch. Busted.

A soft moan drew his attention to the still, small form lying nearby. Peering through the dimness, he found a floppy brimmed hat lying against a tree trunk. The same one he'd seen on the woman Abby had introduced earlier. Journey? What was she doing all the way out here?

If not for the unnatural angle of her left leg, Zane could've believed she'd fallen asleep. She lay on her side, head cradled on her outstretched arm. A few loosened curls draped over her shoulder. He dropped down beside her and eased her over to her back. A bruise formed near her temple, stark against her pale skin. She moaned again and he leaned back on his haunches, pulling her tattered skirt down from where it bunched at her knees.

"Journey? Miss Smith?" He tapped her cheek. "Journey, wake up."

She tossed her head once to either side as if to refuse him. "Don't touch me. I—I mean it." Her voice slurred.

"Journey? Ma'am, it's me, Zane—Reverend Thompson." Her eyes fluttered. "That's it. Come on now."

He watched her eyes slit open, and she struggled to sit up. He saw her grind her teeth rather than cry out at the pain the movement had to have caused her leg.

"Gypsy?"

He guessed she meant the horse by the way she searched about with her deep brown eyes. She blinked at him as if he'd just appeared. She moved to touch the lump on her head, but he pulled her icy fingers away and held them in his hand.

"Hold on, there." Zane stayed her with a hand at her arm, not quite touching. "Let's check you out, first. How many fingers am I holding up?"

Squinting, her head wobbled slightly. "Four. How's my horse?"

"Three. And she's not good," Zane said. He slid down and picked up her left foot in both hands. "Neither are you. I need to check your leg."

She didn't protest, only turned her head and squinted in the direction of her whimpering horse. He slid the tattered fabric back to just past the smooth knee. Moving his hands along the leg, he felt the bone move beneath the stockings, much as the horse's had. Fortunately for her, unlike with the horse, it wasn't a fatal injury.

She shivered. Wind blew through the trees. "Journey? Are you with me? Your leg's broken. We need to get you inside."

"My horse..."

Her white skin glistened in the moonlight, like some ghostly beauty from an old story. Her head bobbed with no particular rhythm as she scanned the space around them.

Zane grabbed a blanket from her now-still horse. He balled it up and placed it under her head.

"Ma'am, my house isn't far from here if we cut straight through the field. It seems best if I carry you there, then go for the doc in town."

"I need my horse," she said, as if that should be his only concern.

He moved his head, trying to keep himself in her field of vision. "We'll get you inside, I'll get the doc and then I'll come back and take care of your horse. Ready?"

She stiffened as he moved to lift her. "I'll ride Gypsy." Her voice fairly shook.

He settled back on his heels and slid his hat off to scratch his head. The horse panted behind them, and he knew she hadn't gotten a good look at the damage. But then, she didn't seem to register her own damage.

She scrambled to her feet, slender arms swinging to gain balance. The instant she rested her weight on her broken leg, a low moan ripped through her throat. Zane saw her eyes flutter closed and caught her as she collapsed.

Her breath puffed warm on his neck. He knew he needed to get her indoors but set her back to pull a coil of rope from the horse's halter. He patted the horse's head and she quivered at his touch. "Hold on, gal."

Journey moaned softly. He found a few branches nearby to splint her awkward leg before bending to lift her. "I hope you're as light as you look, ma'am," he said, peering through the pine boughs waving overhead to the starry sky above.

Malachi was a sturdy sort. Not fast, but steady. Zane was thankful now as he lifted Journey to the saddle. He held her head in one hand and pulled himself into the saddle with the other. Her teeth clenched as he reached for the bridle.

"I mean it, Hank. Don't you touch me," she said. He leaned forward, but her eyes never opened.

"Don't worry, lady," he said. He lifted soft curls of hair to check the cut on her head again. "You'll feel a whole lot better, soon's we get the doc to take a look at you. Giddap, Malachi."

Journey listened, straining to catch the sounds of the room beyond the pounding in her head. Creaking boards told her she wasn't alone.

She opened her eyes a slit, peering through her lashes. She could barely make out a window frame opposite where she lay. The glow at her right side could've been only a lamp, but the warmth made her think of a fireplace. How did she get here? And where was here? She couldn't think with this stampede running through her head.

Gypsy. She remembered the horse stumbling, going down.

A shadow crossed over her. She sat up with a gasp as pain flashed hot like lightning down her leg.

"Take it easy," a voice spoke from the shadow. She jerked her head and opened her eyes wide, but the ache forced her back to the softness of the pillow.

"Abby?" She blinked until her eyes adjusted to the light. "Wh-what happened? Where am I?"

Abby pulled a chair closer to the edge of the bed and smiled down at her. "You're at Zane's. He found you in the woods, thrown by your horse."

"Gypsy? How is she?"

Abby smoothed the blanket over her and leaned back in her seat. "Sam and Zane went to check. Doc Ferris was here. He said your head should feel better in a day or so. It's a good thing Zane was there."

Journey shifted, biting her lip against the pain.

"That leg'll take a while longer. Doc left something to help ease the hurt."

She slid her leg under the quilt, feeling the stiff binding around it. "How much longer?"

Abby's lips quirked to one side. "At least a month, maybe more, Doc said."

She could be snowed in by that time, if the chill in the night air held. Where would she stay? She wouldn't be able to afford a room longer than a week, and that's if she didn't eat. She knew enough to realize Reverend Thompson couldn't extend his hospitality to her that long. And the doctor! How was she to pay him?

She had to leave before that. She'd give herself the day and let Gypsy rest. Then she'd be ready to move on. If she went slowly, they'd make out fine. She could just take it easy, not push the horse too much and keep her leg bound.

"I'll need to settle up with the doctor before I leave."

Abby patted her arm. "Don't you worry. Once you get settled in at Miss Rose's, you can work it out with her. I'm sure she'll help you. You can pay her back when you're on your feet again. Let me get that pain medicine. You're about due."

Abby moved to the table behind her. It seemed this room served as kitchen, sitting room and sleeping area for the pastor. It must be his bed she lay on. Her leg throbbed in time with her head. She had to get out of here.

"Here you go." Abby nudged a spoonful of liquid to her. "This'll help you rest, too. You've had quite a night. I should've told you to stick closer to town."

She swallowed the liquid, but Abby's words burned her with embarrassment. What would she think if she knew there had been no plan to stay? Not that it mattered now. Did it? Was there any way to explain how grateful she was for the kindness they'd shown and make them understand that she couldn't allow it anymore? It didn't seem likely, not without telling too much.

"I'm not one to be hemmed in," she said. She fisted the blankets around her and slid down into the pillow.

"Believe me, I can understand that," Abby said. Her eyebrows lifted, and Journey braced herself for more questions. "I didn't expect you to ride so far out of town. We were looking for you to come back any time when Zane came pounding on the door. He'd found Doc Ferris at the Wilsons' and sent him out here, then came for Sam to help with your horse. I had Sam hook up the wagon and bring me along to see what I could do. I thought you might feel better if you came to with a familiar face around, instead of a complete stranger here."

Journey fought the gathering tears. She nodded and her throat felt tight. "You're right. Thank you." She didn't know this woman well, but it was better than waking up with an unknown doctor prodding around. "Where are they?"

"Doc Ferris figured you'd rest quietly awhile, and he needed to get back to the Wilsons' to check on their new baby before he headed back to town," Abby said. "Zane and Sam should be back any minute now, soon as they get your horse checked over."

Journey felt the bandage over her temple as she brushed a curl from her forehead. She smoothed the blanket at her waist with the other hand even though Abby had already done that. Her leg felt better since taking the medicine, and her head slowed its throbbing. She yawned.

"Did Reverend Thompson—Zane—say how she was?"

"Your horse?"

"Yes." She yawned again. "Gypsy."

Abby turned away, as if she suddenly remembered the spoon and bottle she still held. They clinked together on the table. "Zane didn't say. He was more anxious about Doc Ferris getting out here to see you. He said you were in and out, calling him 'Hank' or something like that."

Journey kept her eyes down, staring at her hands on the quilt. A chill fell over her. She no longer felt drowsy. What else might she have said?

But Abby chattered on, unaware that she'd struck a nerve. "If anyone can patch up your horse, it's Zane. He worked with his father raising horses before Mr. Thompson passed away. What he didn't know about horses wouldn't fill a thimble, and he taught Zane everything."

She slid back down on the bed, pulling the covers all the way over her shoulders, and Abby put another log on the fire. "Keep warm. Doc was worried you'd fall into shock, being out in the cold air like you were. But you look better already than you did when I first arrived. Your color's back."

Boots on the porch boards outside the front door roused her. She and Abby turned as the door swung open, revealing Zane and Sam. Journey caught the shake of Sam's head when he looked at his wife. The sharp whinny of the horse echoed in her memory. How bad could it be?

Zane looked haggard. The bruise around his eye from his fall at Miss Rose's was dark and swollen. He rubbed a hand over the shadow beard on his chin, and she felt sorry for the trouble she'd caused him. He shrugged her saddlebag from his shoulder and hung it on a peg near the door, then hooked the gun he carried above it. He turned and stared at her.

She grew uneasy, self-conscious, thankful the doctor hadn't needed to disrobe her to splint the leg. She felt bare toes scrape the blanket only on that foot, the other stocking still in place. Why didn't he say something?

He swiped a hand through his hair and cleared his throat, then placed his hand on his hip.

"How bad is she? I have to know."

Zane cleared his throat again and looked over to Sam and Abby. Then his gray eyes turned in her direction and he drew in a deep breath.

"I'm so sorry, ma'am—Journey," he said. "I had to put her down."

The coldness swept through her again, and this time her injuries weren't to blame. She covered her face with her palms.

Slender fingers squeezed her shoulder. Journey looked up to see Abby's teary face. She'd cry herself if she thought it would do any good. She'd come all this way. She couldn't let herself get caught now. But without Gypsy...

"Don't worry about a thing," Abby said. "We'll help you. Miss Rose has plenty of space and a good little riding horse she'll let you use, I know it. We'll work things out with her."

"I have nothing to bargain with. I can't stay here. I'm sorry, I should have said before, but I couldn't possibly—"

"Sure you can," Sam said. "I'm sorry about your horse. Believe me, I know what it's like to lose a good mount like that. It feels like you lost your best friend. But the Lord works in mysterious ways, right, Zane?"

Zane nodded. "Don't worry about anything, Journey. It'll work out." His voice rasped as he stood in the flickering light.

You don't know! How could you take my horse? She wanted to scream at him. She wanted to shove him out the door and demand he bring Gypsy back.

"I'll stay with you tonight, and we'll let you get some rest," Abby said. "Zane and Sam can stay out in the barn. Then in the morning they can ride over and talk to Miss Rose, let her know what's happened. After church we'll ride you over in our wagon."

"But how can I work for her now?"

"It's the company she needs most," Abby said.

"And we'll be around to give her a hand," Zane added. "I guarantee she'll not consider you a bother."

Her options had been shot out from under her. It was all decided. She'd stay in Walten until her leg healed. Until she could afford another horse. Until she paid all the debts this one night had cost her. She sighed. Or until the law caught up with her.

Chapter Six

Zane dragged his feet across the rug at the door. Journey lay across his bed on top of the quilt Sarah had made. He'd had it in his buckboard the night of the fire, and it was the only tangible thing he had left of her.

"Zane? What's wrong?"

Abby's voice drew him from the memories that never were very far away. "Nothing. I was just…nothing." He nodded toward the patient. "She ready?"

Abby nodded. "She's tuckered out. I helped her wash her hair, so between that and the laudanum Doc Ferris left her, she sleeps hard." She looked from him to the tiny form on the bed. "I get the feeling she hasn't had a good rest for a long time."

Zane remembered her wild-eyed fear the night before when he'd found her in the woods. Something about her tugged at him, and he didn't know himself yet what it was. "Well, maybe that's why the Lord led her here. He definitely wanted her to stick around awhile. What did Doc say?"

"Six weeks. By then the snow will be through the pass and she'll be here until spring."

"Did she say where she was headed yesterday?"

Abby shook her head. "I have a feeling she wasn't planning to be here long, though." Her shoulders rose with a forceful breath. "Does Sam have the wagon ready?"

"He's ready and waiting."

"Good. I'll go out and get the blankets ready, and you can bring her out," Abby said, pulling on her sweater from the back of the chair.

Zane started. He hadn't thought of how they would get Journey to the wagon, but looking at her now, he knew she wouldn't be managing it on her own.

"It'll be good if she stays asleep. I know from experience that leg will pain her these first few days especially." He didn't add the fact that she hadn't been too fond of him the last time he'd tried to help.

Abby grinned and patted his shoulder on the way out. "Don't be nervous, Zane. It's not like she'll bite."

"You didn't see her last night when I brought her in here."

Abby got a strange look in her eyes, the one that told him her thoughts were moving the conversation into a different direction entirely. "Maybe in time both of you will change your perceptions, then. You deserve to give some girl the chance to make you happy again."

He laughed softly as she swept out the door with a wink. Abby, the eternal matchmaker. She'd been the one to introduce him to Sarah.

Striding over to Journey's prone form, he adjusted his hat and bent down to pick her up. Instead of the tense fear that weighed her down last night, she felt no heavier than a new colt. He pulled her head against his shoulder before managing to get a grip under her knees to lift her up.

Her hair followed in a trail that swept past his elbow, a

fiery wave of still-damp curls. She smelled of lavender soap, and he knew Abby had been adding any little thing she could to comfort their newest resident.

Standing upright, he felt her shift against him, burrowing her face into his shoulder with a soft murmur. Thick lashes brushed her tanned cheek, which blurred a fine spray of freckles that could be seen only from this close. Her wide mouth parted open slightly, and he felt her soft breath at his neck.

Zane tightened his hold and focused on moving her out the door without jarring her bound leg. But had she been awake and not fighting against him, he knew she would feel his pounding heart in the hand that brushed his chest.

Abby needed to stop putting ideas into a man's head.

The rumble of pans being placed in a cupboard roused Journey. She ran her fingers over the heavy brocade of the couch where she lay. The fire crackled and cast a soft light over the room, which had grown darker since her arrival that afternoon.

Her throbbing head reminded her why she was there. A groan escaped before she could stifle it. She eased into the pillow as Miss Rose came into view, standing in the doorway to the kitchen with a drying towel in her hand.

"Did you sleep well?"

Journey stretched her leg, the one that wasn't broken. "I must've. I forgot where I was for a moment. What time is it?" Her whole body felt stiff.

"Nigh onto seven o'clock."

"I guess I slept the day away."

Miss Rose smiled. "It's the best thing for you. You had enough excitement last night to wear a body out. And I'll bet the ride here this morning didn't help any. Are you hungry?"

Her stomach rumbled before she could deny it. "A little." She mustered a small grin.

"Good. You dropped off before supper and we hated to wake you, so I saved you a plate. Let me warm it a bit and I'll bring it in for you."

Journey pulled herself up further with her arm. "Please, don't trouble yourself. I can come out." She paused as her vision swam.

Miss Rose had already moved back into the kitchen, but her crackling voice carried through. "You'll do no such thing. Doc Ferris said you're to keep that leg up."

"Yes, ma'am."

Doc Ferris's word carried a lot of weight, Journey already knew. Pain medication was given every two hours, no matter how she tried to beg off. No weight on that leg meant being carted to the house by Zane Thompson in his arms, much to her embarrassment. She'd slept through the move from his house, at least. But now here she sat, being waited on by the woman she'd been hired to care for.

The steaming plate placed on her lap aroused her hunger even more. She smiled her thanks and leaned forward as Miss Rose propped more pillows behind her. The chicken leg and green beans smelled delicious, and a thick slice of bread with a generous spread of butter and a drizzle of honey made her mouth water. She calculated the cost of such a meal and made a mental note to keep a ledger. But for now there was nothing to do for it. She'd have to eat if she was going to stay strong and mend quickly. She poked a bean with her fork.

Miss Rose must have been satisfied, because she smiled and said, "I'll leave you to your supper. I figure you'll want some time to ponder your situation." Then she moved back toward the kitchen.

Journey sat back into the cushions, grateful for the solitude. But ponder? There wasn't much she could do. Miss Rose welcomed her with open arms and seemed pleased with the arrangement. Tears fought their way into her eyes as she thought about the kindness these people had shown. How could she tell them why she had run? Didn't they deserve to know? What if they threw her out? What would she do then?

Her options had been cut off. She tried to think what had spooked the horse in the first place, but a fog surrounded all the particulars of the night before. Now here she sat. No horse. No money. No job. Broken leg. She tore a corner from the bread and chewed, trying to slow her jumbled thoughts.

Part of the reason she'd taken up with Hank back then had been because she'd felt she had no choice. But the day she had stood up to Hank was the day she'd realized she was never without options. Even now, looking over her shoulder, waiting to be caught for her crime, she was better off than she'd been with Hank.

Biting into the tender chicken, she thought about her predicament. She couldn't walk around, but there was nothing wrong with her hands. There had to be something. No great loss without some small gain, Mama had always said. Where was the glimmer of hope?

Journey licked the salty crisps from her fingers. Cooking meant standing. Tending children was out of the question. She drew in a deep breath. Something would come to her. The one thing she did have was time to think—a lot of time to think.

She silently thanked Abby for taking the time to help wash her hair before she had dozed off. She'd need some pins to put it back up. She yawned. Maybe it could wait until tomorrow.

The shuffle of feet from the kitchen drew her attention. "I thought you might want your saddlebag," Miss Rose said, nodding toward the floor by her side. "Zane left it there for you."

She glanced at the buckles. They didn't seem to have been opened since she'd fastened them yesterday. "Thank you, ma'am."

"You might as well get into the practice of calling me Miss Rose," the old woman said.

"I'll work on it." She squirmed under the blanket, trying to shift her aching leg into a more comfortable position. "I appreciate what you're doing, honestly I do. I'd be at a loss without your kindness. I'll make it up to you. I'll pay you back for everything, somehow. I hate to be beholden."

"Nonsense. I'm glad to help. And I don't want you fretting about it. This gives me my chance to play the Good Samaritan." She patted Journey's good leg and took her empty plate. "We'll even it out when you're able, dear."

"You'll find I'm not very 'dear,'" she whispered. "Please, just call me Journey."

"I think there's more 'dear' in you than you give yourself credit for." Miss Rose stroked a hand over Journey's hair. Like Mama used to do. Warmth for this woman grew no matter how she tried to stop it.

"Zane left this package for you. He brought it in with your saddle." Miss Rose handed her a lump tied in brown paper, then returned to the kitchen.

The fabric she'd bought at the store. She'd have a fine dress, plenty warm for winter. At least she could work on that.

She always could sew a fine seam. Mama had taught her to stitch and to sew in the afternoon hours before she'd go to work. If she could find sewing to do, it might not be much, but at least she could pay something toward her board until she was up and around again. She would ask Abby to post a notice in the store.

She turned her attention to the saddlebag, listening for Miss Rose to return. Looking over her shoulder, she fumbled the buckle open and hefted the bag to her lap to reach the bottom of the deep pocket.

The touch of cool metal brought a sense of relief. They hadn't found it. She pulled the Double Derringer gun from the pack and slid it into her skirt pocket. The smooth nickel barrel and walnut handle felt secure in her fingers.

Yes, there were options. Spring was a long winter away. She had to wait and not tip her hand. Because if they knew she had killed a man, her only options would be prison or a rope.

Chapter Seven

A knock at the door woke Journey. The final glow of sunlight slanted lower through the back window. At least she hadn't slept as long this time. She eased up and swiped the curls clinging against her cheek from her face. Miss Rose stood from the nearby rocker and shuffled to the door.

"Zane! What a nice surprise!"

She slid lower under the covers. Maybe if she closed her eyes…

But Miss Rose's voice called her. "Journey, are you awake? Pastor Thompson is here to see you."

Not Zane this time—Pastor Thompson. This must be a business call. She pushed herself up again but kept the blanket close. The room swam slightly and the pressure in her head felt as if it would push her eyes right out of their sockets. She nodded to Miss Rose, who continued to block the doorway.

"Come on in, Zane," she said as she opened the door wider. "Have a seat and I'll put some coffee on. Journey, I'll get that medicine for you. Your head's probably feeling rocky again by now. I'll be right back."

Miss Rose slid off to the kitchen, leaving Zane to stand in the doorway. He grabbed the Stetson hat from his head and shut the door but seemed to linger longer than necessary before he faced Journey. She watched him rock heel-to-toe once, his eyes scanning the room for a place to lay his hat before sitting in the ladder-back chair at her feet. He finally capped it over his knee and ran his hand over his thick hair.

"Miss Smith," he began, leaning forward. "Journey, I wanted to see you, wanted to tell you how sorry I am about your horse."

She stared at him a moment and he paused. His gray eyes held shadows but didn't flinch. He was looking for something. She rubbed her throbbing head.

"I'm sure you are." She smoothed unseen wrinkles from the quilt.

His broad shoulders sagged a little. "I know horses, been around them all my life. I hate to see that kind of thing happen, but I want to assure you, there was no other option. That foreleg was busted up good."

She bit the inside of her cheek. She would have liked to have made that call herself.

"Believe me, I'd have liked nothing better than for you to have given the order. If you'd been in any shape, I'd have let you. But the horse was suffering. I know you would have done the same."

She nodded. She knew it wasn't his fault, but that didn't change the fact that he'd taken the thing she needed most.

Zane sat up in the chair, crossing a booted foot over his knee. He slid his hat across the bridge of his leg and hung it from the heel. "Could've been worse for you. What were you doing out that far from town anyway?"

"Exploring," she said but refused to meet his gaze.

He tapped the brim of his hat. "If there's anything you need, anything at all, you let me know. Part of my job around here is to help wayfaring strangers…and explorers." He had the audacity to smile.

"I'll work it out." Her voice sounded gritty and harsh to her own ears. The day had been too long. She cleared her throat delicately and tried again. He'd only done what he had to. "It's good you were there to find me."

"Glad I was there. I wish there'd been more I could've done. How are you feeling?"

Miss Rose returned with a tray of steaming mugs. "I expect she has a headache the size of the Beartooths. Here, Journey." She filled the spoon from the tray with laudanum.

Journey swallowed the bitter liquid. "I appreciate you taking me in, but there's no need to fuss over me, too. I'm feeling fine."

But Miss Rose just waved the empty spoon. "Nonsense. You take advantage, missy. Once you're back on your feet, you'll wish it back. Now, what would you like, coffee or tea?"

"Tea, please."

She took the cup and saucer. The pastor was handed a steaming mug of coffee without being given a choice.

"You have to let Miss Rose fuss at you. Otherwise, she's fussing at me." He smiled and took a swallow. "And you do look much better than you did last night. But with the knock you took, I dare say you're not feeling all that fine just yet."

Journey said no more and looked into her cup. It made no sense to argue. Besides, he was right.

"So where were you headed?" Zane asked.

She stared at him over the edge of the mug she held to

her lips. She moved it stiffly to her lap, breaking eye contact to glance at the door. "It doesn't matter now, does it?"

He set his cup down on the little table beside him, keeping his fingers wrapped around the handle. She slid back against the armrest but tried to pull herself upright.

His eyebrows shifted and quirked. "I thought if someone was expecting you somewhere, I'd send a telegram for you."

"No!" She jolted forward and pain shot down her leg. Tea sloshed over the blanket that covered her lap. Zane moved to pull it away before the heat could soak through. "I'm so sorry! I'm forever making a mess of things."

"It's all right." He shook out the quilt and brushed at it with his handkerchief. "There," he said, laying it back over her. "Good as new."

"Thank you." He looked down at her, waiting for an explanation. "It's just that, well…there's no one expecting me."

His look told her he was skeptical. "You're sure?"

She looked away from him and Miss Rose. "I'm sure."

Placing his mug on the tray, he stood to go, and for a moment she thought he was angry. But his lips pulled into a smile, though his teeth didn't show.

"If you think of anything—anything at all I can do to lend a hand, you let me know. Like I said, I'm sorry for the way things worked out for you." He squeezed the old woman's thin shoulder. "But you couldn't be in better hands. Miss Rose is a fine woman and very good at taking care of folks."

"I appreciate all your help, Pastor." She shook her head. "Zane. Please don't think I'm ungrateful. It's just…"

"I know," he said, in a tone that told her he somehow did. "Life has a funny way of throwing us once in a while."

He turned to Miss Rose. "Thank you for the coffee. Hot and black, just how I like it."

It surprised Journey to see him bow and place a soft kiss on the old woman's cheek. "Let's pray before I go."

Pray? Mama said she had prayed with that skinny little parson at the end of town before she died. It hadn't changed her situation any, and Journey couldn't imagine it would change her own. But apparently the job of pastor required it. If it meant he was leaving, she'd sit through it. He asked questions requiring answers that would only make things more complicated for everyone. It wore her out. The less they knew about her, the better they'd all be. And she never could lie well. No, she'd have to keep her distance from Pastor Zane.

"…Lord, we thank you, too, for our visitor. She's hurting, and we ask that You heal her and help her to find a home here. Be with Miss Rose as she cares for her, and may they find comfort in each other's company. Guide us, Lord, to live lives pleasing to You. In Jesus' name, amen."

Miss Rose startled Journey by echoing his amen. So now he'd leave.

Zane put his hat on and ambled toward the door. The sky was a muted evening gray. He turned as he stepped onto the porch.

"Thank you, ladies, for the visit. And, Journey, I meant what I said. You let me know if you need my help. To tell the truth, I feel responsible for the horse."

Miss Rose nodded to her as if she expected a response.

"It's not your fault. And I'm not your problem," Journey said slowly. "I know it's not something you wanted to do, and I'm glad you were there to do what I couldn't. Gypsy was a good horse and we've seen a lot of trail together. I'll miss her." She paused to steady her voice. "But accidents happen." She tried to spout all the expected responses, hoping she'd get to the proper one quickly so he'd go. The only help he could give would be to provide her a horse.

He tipped his hat. "Glad you see it that way, ma'am. Take care of that leg, and let Miss Rose fuss at you some, like I said. Just so she stays in practice." He grinned and grabbed Rose's hand with a squeeze. "I'll check in on you," he told her.

And then he was gone. But as much as she wished it otherwise, Journey knew it wasn't the last she'd seen of Reverend Zane Thompson.

"Well?"

Zane turned at the bottom step to face Miss Rose, who had followed him out to the porch. "'Well,' what?"

"Is everything set to right between you two?"

He dropped his head to hide his smile. "I don't suppose she's any too fond of me, but she's not liable to shoot me anyway. At least, I don't think so. Why do you ask?"

Miss Rose leaned a shoulder against a post. "She's a sweet girl. You're a good man. Allow an old woman some hope."

"Now, Miss Rose, don't start. You know I'm not ready to think along those lines with anyone and definitely not with someone I know so little about."

"Caution is good," she agreed with a nod. "I just want to start you thinking along those lines."

They'd had similar conversations before. "Why are you so determined to play matchmaker with me?"

"Because you're too good a man to not allow yourself to make another woman happy. Sarah would not have expected you to live the rest of your life alone."

"I'm not alone. I have my friends, my congregation and

this town. That's plenty to keep me busy, and it wouldn't be fair to saddle another woman with that."

"Let a woman make that choice for herself."

He looked to Miss Rose, her eyes lit with the setting sun. She couldn't understand. "It wouldn't be fair. I'm too used to being on my own now. Besides, I'd always be comparing them to her."

"Then I'll be praying in that direction. Remember, you're not replacing Sarah to open your heart to new possibilities." She sighed and stood upright, wrapping her arms around herself in the growing chill of dusk. "Did Journey forgive you for putting down her horse?"

He tipped his hat back and shrugged his shoulders. "She claims she's not upset about it. She knows I wouldn't have put the horse down if I didn't have to, I think. But I'm still the one who did it."

"She'll come around."

"I hope so," he said. The smile on Miss Rose's face hinted at more than his words intended.

"Me, too, young man," she said, turning back toward her door. She stopped before opening the latch. "In more ways than one."

Chapter Eight

Journey's heart throbbed in time with the thud of her foot on the wooden floor as she made her way to the window.

Her request to be awakened before the women left for the church had been denied. The mantel clock chimed ten o'clock, so she guessed they'd return before long. Having been confined to the great room and a cot in the kitchen for the past four days, she was elated when Abby had reminded Miss Rose about the ladies' Bible study or some such midweek church meeting. But Miss Rose wouldn't dawdle in town.

The sunny breeze from the open windows was no replacement for a peek of the horizon. She paused to catch her breath at the door. Sweat broke out across her forehead. Perspiration, Mama would say. Not even pigs sweat.

The day was warm, as summer flaunted itself before giving in to autumn. Journey hobbled out to the porch and sank into the chair beside the door.

She inhaled until her lungs wouldn't stretch anymore. The scent of sage wafted in the air, and she remembered riding through it with Gypsy. It had filled the landscape as far as the eye could see, rolling along with the brown hills, climbing higher and higher. It was the first time she realized she was alone—no one following behind, no one waiting ahead. It gave her hope that she'd found her escape. But now…

She listened for approaching wagons and fingered the pistol in her pocket.

Journey leaned against the chair post, glad for the chance to rest her leg. Her head barely hurt at all this morning, and the ache in her leg was tolerable without the pain medication that she'd refused the past two days. Doc Ferris had been out yesterday to rebind it and check the lump on her head. He'd proclaimed both on the mend but recommended keeping the leg raised as much as possible for another week at least. And Miss Rose followed his recommendations to the letter.

The stable stood, weathered but sturdy, across the dusty yard. She remembered Abby mentioning a riding horse and felt a pang of loneliness for her own. She and Gypsy had traveled the whole way from Georgia together. The hostler had laughed at her choice, but the mare was all she could afford, and she took a chance on the intelligence she thought she saw in the fine dark eyes. Some of the conversations held with the gentle brown horse were more enjoyable and wiser than any of the ones she'd had with Hank. What kind of horses would Miss Rose keep? It wasn't so awfully far to the barn.

She stood and lurched to the edge of the porch, grasping the banister. It took a couple of false starts before she found a rhythm of dangling the broken leg before her, leaning toward the banister, then hopping down on her bare foot. She hadn't planned on treading out into the yard, but to go back now would cost precious minutes of fresh air. Her feet would be tough enough to handle the rough ground for the distance.

Hopping several feet at a time before stopping to balance, she made her way to the barn and tugged the door, which caught a bit before sliding open enough to slip through. She leaned against a railing to ease her breathing and let her eyes adjust to the cool dimness inside. A soft whinny to the right drew her attention.

Two horses stood in the stalls, one a broad chestnut with a black mane and tail, the other a smaller paint. She hobbled over and stroked the white blaze across the paint's forehead, holding the harness to steady herself. She blew softly on its nose.

"And what's your name?" she whispered.

"Homer."

She drew the revolver from her pocket, pivoting on her good leg. Reverend Thompson fell back against the open door frame, holding up both hands in defense.

"What do you mean by sneaking up on me?" Her voice came low, ragged. "Moves like that can get you shot."

His Adam's apple bobbed just above his shirt collar, but his voice showed no strain. "I didn't mean to startle you."

"It seems to me you don't mean to do a lot of things you end up doing." She thought her heart would pound out of her throat.

He lowered his hands. "I saw the barn door open and knew Miss Rose had gone with Abby to the Ladies' Mission Society meeting. I thought I ought to check things out. After all, you're to be inside resting, with that leg up."

"Why were you out here?" She didn't know why she continued to question him. Did she really think he'd lie?

He moved farther into the barn with a calm confidence. "I made a call on the Hamlers. Listen, can you put that thing away?"

She looked at the gun palmed in her hand and lowered it

into the folds of her skirt, hoping to hide the shake in her hand.

"You—you startled me. And…and, well, I've learned it never hurts to have a little help in backing up your words. I apologize, Reverend Thompson."

"It's still Zane." He shifted and ran a finger along his collar before stepping closer. "You must be feeling a little better if you're making your way outside."

The matter of the gun seemed set aside but not forgotten. "I couldn't resist the sunshine," she said. "I'm afraid we won't have too many more fine days like this one. Then I remembered Miss Rose said she kept horses and I wanted to take a peek at them."

He walked over to the larger of the two horses, and scratched its nose. "This is Zeb, short for Zebulon, and that's Homer."

"Funny names."

"Ah, but fine horses. Homer would make a great mount for you while you're here." He smiled and turned to face her. "That is, once your leg heals. You really should listen to Doc Ferris. It is what we pay him for around here."

She didn't need to be reminded about her debt to the kind, quiet man who had tended to the injury. "I could use a seat," she conceded.

"Can I help you?"

She tensed, wondering if he meant more than the leg. "No. No, I'm fine. I can take care of myself."

She stepped across the dirt, the thin layer of loose hay tickling her feet, then back toward the yard. Journey tensed when Zane reached toward her as she faltered. But he drew back and merely followed close behind.

Beads of sweat dribbled down her cheeks by the time she reached the porch steps. The thought hit her that going up wouldn't be nearly as easy as the trip down. It wouldn't do to have an audience.

She turned toward the preacher, grasping the banister in both hands. "Listen. About the gun… I— You startled me and I reacted too quickly. It won't happen again, I assure you. I'd appreciate it if we could forget about the whole thing."

A shadow crossed his face, as though his mind were a hundred miles from where they stood. As if he could see beyond her secrets.

"Zane? Can't we keep this between us? I'd hate to startle Miss Rose. Or worse yet, have her kick me out."

His attention jerked back as he looked at her, turning his head to either side. "Right. But look, if you're in some kind of trouble, she deserves to know. Let her make up her own mind. Besides, maybe we can help."

"It's no trouble I can't handle, I assure you, Pastor." She leveled her gaze to his.

He rested his hands at his waist and stared at her a moment, then out across the dust-colored bluffs to the east. His jaw twitched. She backed up onto the first step with her good foot.

"Trouble you can handle has a way of turning into trouble you can't," he said, still not looking at her. "If you let us know what's going on, we'll figure a way out."

Her face grew warmer but this time not because of the temperature. "The only thing going on here is I'm trying to figure a way to pay my debts, buy a horse and be on my way. The only thing going on here is a pastor who thinks he can save every soul he meets, fix every problem. Well, there are some problems you can't fix with a sermon." She clamped her lips together as a shiver of fear shot through her. What possessed her to speak to him like that? Hank would have wailed on her before she spoke out. Mama would have been appalled. "We must always be nice to the gentlemen," she would say, in that soft drawl.

Zane bent his head but his stance held no anger. "I'm only trying to help. You may need it more than you think."

His sincerity softened her fear as well as her anger, more than she would have liked. But aggravating him would only increase his suspicions. "I appreciate the offer, but this is my trouble and I'll handle it my way. Getting more folks involved will only make things worse. Believe me, it's not worth it."

He looked at her, his eyebrows quirked. "We'll play this your way for now," he said after a pause. "I won't mention the gun to Miss Rose, but you watch yourself. You have to let us know when you need a hand."

She pulled her shoulders back, determined not to skitter away from him, no matter how her thoughts pleaded with her to. She didn't have to do anything as far as she was concerned. Why wouldn't he just go away?

She gave him a short nod. "I'll tell Miss Rose you stopped by."

He strode to his horse and paused with his foot in the stirrup. "I'd appreciate it," he said, easing his broad frame into the saddle. He grabbed his hat from the saddle horn and clamped it over his dark hair.

She thought he would leave with a tip of his hat, but instead he slid the brown leather brim back from his wide face and looked down at her. "Journey?"

"Yes."

"We have a saying here in the West that you might not have heard. But it's good sound advice."

"What's that?" She crooked her neck to look up at him, squinting an eye to block out the sun, and tightened her grasp on the banister.

"Watch your back."

She stared hard at his retreating form. How little he knew. She was already backed into a corner.

Chapter Nine

"Whoa, Malachi!"

Zane leaned back in the saddle and pushed upright in the stirrups, pulling the reins at the same time.

His thoughts had unraveled from the moment Journey cocked her gun his way in the barn. Lost in a jumble of possibilities, each worse than the one before, he had nudged the horse into a full gallop by the time he'd made it halfway to town. He gave the horse its head until he found himself almost at Norwood's Mercantile. Sliding from Malachi's high back, he landed in front of Mrs. Decker. She stepped back with a gasp, her hand patting her heart.

"Pardon me, ma'am." He swept his hat from his head. "I didn't see you coming."

She tucked her hair back into place with a dainty sniff. "I should think it would be hard to see much of anything coming in that cloud of dust you raised, Reverend."

Zane swiped his face in the crook of his elbow. She would have to be the one to catch him in a moment of recklessness. "Forgive me, Mrs. Decker. I'm afraid my mind was distracted and I allowed the horse too much leeway. I never meant to startle you."

She walked off with a huff, but he heard her mumble. "What that man needs is a good woman to settle him. I should think a minister and widower would maintain greater decorum. Now, my Mary…"

Widower. He hated that word. All the love and joy he and Sarah had shared, all the hopes and dreams and plans, cut down into that one word. He sobered, stroking Malachi's mane a moment before tromping up the steps.

Lost in thought, he plowed into Abby as he stepped through the door, catching her by the elbow. "Whoa! I'm sorry, Abby! You're the second person I've done that to in as many minutes."

She slipped a stray hair behind her ear. "Where's the fire then?"

"I'm in too big a hurry, I reckon. I— Wait, weren't you to take Miss Rose home after the Mission Society meeting?"

"Yes, she needed to pick up some things in town. Did you want to see her? She should be back any minute. I thought I'd straighten up a little while she finished."

"I need to talk to Sam if he's around."

Zane forced his glance to the storeroom, avoiding Abby's level gaze. "He's out back. Is everything all right?"

He smiled at her raised eyebrow. "Nothing you need to pester me about. I just was hoping to catch Sam."

"Fine. But you know he'll tell me anyway."

With a smile and a soft squeeze to her wrist, he cut through the room and around the counter to the back of the store.

He found Sam outside unloading supplies hauled from his weekly trip to Virginia City. "Need a hand?"

"You know I never turn away good cooking or a helping hand." Sam slid a box at him from the rig where he stood.

He hefted the crate and lugged it the few yards into the storage room. After several trips back, the wagon was soon cleared.

"I take it this isn't a social call," Sam said.

Zane watched him hop to the ground, the stubby Irishman who'd been his friend through everything from leaving grammar school to entering seminary and beyond. "What makes you say that?"

"I made you do all the heavy lifting, and you didn't rail at me about it."

Zane laughed. "It's been a long time since I've railed at you. But I did have something on my mind."

Sam folded his arms across his chest and focused on the ground at his feet, a sure sign he was listening intently. "Figured as much. What is it?"

He opened his mouth and then shut it, only to start again. Now that he had Sam's attention, he didn't know for sure what to say. Or leastways how to say it. He scratched the back of his neck. "What do you think of Miss Rose's new boarder?"

The look of surprise on Sam's face was unmistakable when his head cocked up to look him in the eye. "Journey?"

"Yes."

Sam grinned and quirked an eyebrow. "I think she's a pretty lady—seems like a sweet gal that's hit a jagged trail." A sly smile spread beneath his mustache. "Why do you ask?"

Zane shook his head. This wasn't going the way he'd hoped. "Not for the reason you're thinking. I'm asking if you think it's safe to let her stay with Miss Rose."

Sam's mustache twitched. "Since when do we *let* Rose Bishop do anything? What are you getting at?"

He wondered himself. He couldn't exactly cast unfair suspicion. And he had startled her there in the barn. But not just startled her. She'd been downright afraid.

"You don't think she's, well…dangerous?"

Laughter rumbled out of his friend. "Dangerous? The lady's barely five feet tall. She has a busted leg, no horse, no home to call her own. How dangerous could she be?"

"I'm serious, Sam. Don't you think it's a little odd, her coming into town alone? No mention of family. Winds up way out of town on a little evening ride? None of that gives you any cause for concern?"

"It makes me concerned for her. Come on, Zane. I'll admit it's unusual but not enough to put her on trial. This ain't like you. There something you're not telling me?"

He paused. If Sam didn't find any reason for alarm, there was no point in pushing the issue. Sam's sense of character seldom fell short, and if Sam had no qualms about Journey, Zane would try to put his aside as well. "I guess I just wanted your opinion on it."

"You sure that's all that's bothering you?"

"I'm looking out for Miss Rose. I'd hate to see anyone take advantage of her."

"Right."

Sam seemed all too ready to agree. "What is it you're wanting to say?"

"I'm saying she's a lovely young lady in need of help. I'm saying you're in a place to help her. And I'm saying there's no need for you to feel guilty about that."

"Why would I?"

"You've been dodging every available female around these parts for the past year. It's been three years since Sarah died, Zane. She'd want you to go on." Sam turned to straighten a few boxes.

Zane's chest felt as if it were made of bricks, and he drew in a deep breath to ease the heaviness. "I know."

"You might know it, but you ain't been acting like you believe it. I'm not pushing. I'm just reminding." Sam clamped his shoulder, moving them both toward the rear door and through it into the whitened walls of the storeroom. "But if you're really that concerned, I'll keep an eye out with you."

"Thanks, Sam. I don't want to alarm anyone if there's no need. I just have this funny feeling about her. There's more than she's telling."

"Of course there is. A woman always carries that air of mystery, my friend. Part of the charm. Don't tell me you've forgotten that?"

Zane moved around the counter, but Sam stayed behind it, pounding a soft beat on the weathered wood. The sound of footsteps on the stairway leading to the Norwood home above the store got his attention. Abby smoothed her shawl around her shoulders and adjusted her hat as she stood at Sam's side.

"I'm glad I caught you before you left, Zane," she said. "Miss Rose and I thought it might be nice to have a little 'Welcome to Walten' dinner for Journey. Sunday after church at Miss Rose's."

"I'm not sure—"

"Nonsense. We'll see you there." She moved around the counter and out to the porch. Zane waved out the door to Miss Rose, who sat waiting in the buggy.

Abby stopped at the bottom step. "Dinner will be served hot and delicious if the minister doesn't get too long-winded." She smiled. "Oh, and, Zane—that blue shirt Miss Rose gave you last Christmas? I'm sure she'd love to see you in it again on Sunday." With a wave and a swirl of her skirt, she climbed into the wagon and headed out of town. Miss Rose winked and waved a hand behind her as they pulled away.

Zane turned in time to see his friend smother a laugh.

"You think Journey can be more dangerous than those two?" Sam said. "Wonder what color they'll have *me* wearing?"

Chapter Ten

The house creaked in the Sunday-morning quiet. Journey hobbled around the couch on the crutches Doc Ferris had dropped off the night after Zane had caught her in the barn. The slender old man with the slight stoop never mentioned the preacher but simply said, "You seem to me to be a woman who's hard to keep down, so I thought we'd better get you onto these. But don't be thinking you can traipse all over creation with them. No farther than the porch for the next couple of weeks, you hear me?"

His fuzzy eyebrows had slouched over his sharp blue eyes. But the crook of a smile added to the stern look made her agree. The fact that Miss Rose stood behind him with her arms folded over herself didn't hurt, either. For reasons Journey could not understand, the woman had made her a personal responsibility and would see to it that she complied.

Hunched over the wooden frames, with dish towels wrapped to cushion the arm supports, she made her way to the cot. Miss Rose had set it in the corner of the kitchen for her, around the doorway from the parlor and near the stove. She sank onto the thick blanket with little grace, wondering if the crutches were intended to make getting around a little more cumbersome to discourage her from moving around so much.

"I should be thankful it wasn't any worse. They could have laid me up the entire six weeks." Doc Ferris assured her it wasn't a bad break, and by keeping the splint and binding tight, she could maneuver around some. Given the rough-and-tumble boys she'd played with as a little girl and her time with Hank, it was more a wonder she hadn't broken something before now.

The injury did excuse her from church, but Journey knew it wouldn't be long, unless Miss Rose thought the verses she read every morning at breakfast from the worn black book were enough. She seemed especially fond of "But as for me and my house, we will serve the Lord." Her soft voice emphasized the *my* as if she couldn't help it. No, part of her job would be to attend services with her employer. But no mention had been made as yet, and Journey didn't bring it up, either. Church was no place for a woman like her.

She stretched a hand under the cot and dragged her saddlebag over, pulling out a tiny mirror. She'd gone the past several days with her hair in no more than a low, loose chignon. The first few days her head had ached to the point where she thought a brush would kill her. But she determined to have it up today by the time Miss Rose, the Norwoods and Reverend Thompson arrived. She moved the mirror around to catch the wild mass from various angles. She should've tried harder before this. Pulling out the brush next, she tugged through the thick tangle of curls.

This whole dinner had her on edge. Why would someone hold a gathering to welcome the new hired hand?

Well, not actually working yet, but the sentiment was the same. It didn't make sense. But then a lot of things about these people didn't make sense.

Miss Rose, for all her no-nonsense approach, had something very warm at her core that she couldn't explain. Even her own mama, whom she knew loved her dearly and had never been harsh to her, had been a hard woman. She'd had to be.

Maybe that wasn't entirely true. Those last few days before Mama died, even though she'd been sick, something soft and strong had taken root. Maybe it had something to do with her talk with that parson. Maybe it was just what happened to folks when they knew they were dying. Or maybe the memories had been brightened by her youth.

Journey pulled through the last knot of hair with a jerk when she saw Miss Rose's wagon top the ridge through the front window. Journey swept her hair up with her fingers and tied it in place before adding a few hairpins to hold it in a smooth coil at the back of her head. Then she stowed everything away and pulled up on one crutch so she could bank the fire with another piece of wood.

She heard Miss Rose and Abby being helped from their wagon seats by Zane and Sam and sank down into the overstuffed couch. It seemed rather out of place in this simple wooden house but beautiful nonetheless, with its rose-pink upholstery flecked with tiny blue cornflowers. She eased her broken leg onto the pillow, glad she had already set the table, then blew a wayward curl from her line of vision and rested.

Zane stepped through the threshold first and held the door for Miss Rose. His blue chambray shirt made his eyes look bluer than the stone gray she remembered. She shifted her focus to Miss Rose instead, rather than risk looking him in the eye.

"We're home," Miss Rose said. "How's your leg feeling? I hope you weren't up and around too much while we were gone."

"Not too much," she said. "I'd imagine Doc Ferris will let me out of the house when he stops by later this week."

"We'll see about that," Abby said. She stepped through the door with what looked to be a loaf of bread, wrapped in a cloth. "Let me see that knot on your head. How's that feeling?"

Journey touched the small lump that remained. "Not bad." She forgot about it unless she turned to lie on it in her sleep. The blue swelling had almost faded.

Sam stepped through the door last and wiped his feet on the braided rug, more out of habit than of need, she guessed. "I'd say she looks better than Zane with that hammer mark on his eye," he said, helping Abby with her shawl. "'Course, Journey was further ahead in looks before he had the bruise, too." He laughed as Abby pretended to swat him with her hat.

Journey flushed. She wondered what Zane thought. Miss Rose stood in the kitchen, tying an apron over her Sunday dress. "You gentlemen have a seat while we get dinner on the table. And, Journey, I appreciate your setting the table, but I don't appreciate the fact that you were wandering around on that leg to do it. You have to rest if it's going to heal."

She allowed a small smile to crease her cheek. Somehow that warm spirit of Miss Rose's overtook her words and soothed them down, like taking medicine with honey when she was a girl. "It wasn't much, really. I'm glad to help."

"Well, we'll take it from here," Miss Rose said.

Zane sat on the chair he'd sat to make his apology about her horse. Had it been only a week ago?

Sam remained by the door. "I should have time to unhitch the horses before dinner, right?"

"Here, I'll help," Zane said, moving to stand.

"Nope, I got it." Before the pastor could argue, Sam continued, "Even the Lord Jesus had things that had to be done on the Sabbath. I figure preaching is yours. Besides, no sense in both of us smelling like the barn. It won't take me long. You can give Journey the highlights of your message."

Sam slid out the door with a wink before Zane could protest further. He turned to her and eased back in his seat. She twisted the blanket between her fingers.

"I hope you don't mind, Pastor, if I leave you on your own for a moment. I should help Abby and Miss Rose in the kitchen. There's surely something—"

"Oh, no, you don't." Abby stood at the back of the sofa, tying her own apron. "You've done plenty. Sit there and let that leg mend. We'll holler when we're ready for you all."

"I guess we've been sequestered to the parlor," Zane said.

Journey forced a smile and huffed a breath of air. She watched Abby return to the kitchen, leaving her to face Zane. Now what?

"Listen…"

"I need to…"

Zane gave a full grin, a row of fine white teeth showing. "I beg your pardon, ma'am," he said with teasing propriety. "You first."

She glanced over her shoulder to the kitchen, making

sure neither of the women worked near the doorway. The ring of the kettle lid and clink of tin plates confirmed their location near the far window. "I wanted to thank you for not saying anything about the other day. I need this job— well, when I can be up and working—and Miss Rose was very good to take me in like this. She doesn't seem the type to approve of my carrying a gun at all, not to mention pulling it on her pastor."

She licked her dry lips. "Please, believe me, I'm not out to hurt anyone. I'm looking after myself, and I'm counting on your honor as a minister to keep this quiet." She hoped her face carried her sincerity.

"I don't like the fact that you have it, let alone the fact that you feel the need to use it." He leaned forward with a huff. "I know we got off to a bad start when I had to put your horse down. But I have to tell you straight, I don't like the fact that someone with the kind of trouble you obviously have is hiding out here with one of the dearest women God made for this earth."

"There's no trouble here, Zane," she said, hoping she sounded more convincing than she felt. "There's no sense in creating problems where there aren't any."

He seemed to look through her. How much did he see?

"Zane, please—"

He held his hand up to stop her. "I don't like the fact that you won't let me—let any of us—help you." He kept his voice low.

"Most of all, I hate the fact that you're in this trouble, whatever it is. There's not much I can do about any of that, except pray. But let me tell you this," he said, pointing at her with one hand. He leaned even closer to put his other hand on the end of the couch. "I'm keeping my eye on you until I can figure out what kind of trouble you're into. I owe

Miss Rose a lot, and I'll not have anyone hurt her in any way if I have it within my power to stop it."

Journey realized she had leaned toward him in an effort to keep their conversation private, but she edged away as he pressed forward. She drew back from the fire in his eyes. Yet his voice held no heat, only concern. What would his sermons be like?

"Answer me this—who will come for you first? The law or someone else?"

"The less you know the better," she said, her voice soft. "You're the one who warned me to watch my back. I can do that fine on my own. All you have to know is that I did what I had to do to survive."

"I'm watching your back, too. I want to know what I'm looking for. I hope you'll come to know there's more folks to rely on here than yourself."

"I won't be here that long, honestly. You've all been so good to me. I'd never want to bring you into my problems."

"You might as well face the fact that you're here until spring. Do you really think your trouble is that far behind?" Zane leaned forward, his voice at a whisper. His gray eyes never wavered.

Blood pounded in her ears and she swallowed hard, drawing back as far as the arm of the couch allowed.

"Suit yourself. You've already answered my question."

Don't cry. Don't let him see you cry. She drew in a deep breath. "I'm warning you to stay as far away from my problems as you can. I can't be looking out for myself and for you as well."

He breathed deeply and the tight lines around his eyes eased.

"Don't you worry about me. I know Someone who can watch out for us both."

Steps on the porch ended any comment she would have made, if any had come to mind. Sam wandered into the room, rubbing his hands together. "It's getting mighty chilly out there. May have our first snow by Sunday next if this keeps up."

Journey shivered in the cold draft. Another reminder that Walten was where she'd be spending the long winter. Zane smiled and somehow she couldn't be angry with him. Wary, yes. Frightened even. But angry proved difficult.

He could ruin everything if he started meddling. And she didn't trust him not to. He was determined to involve himself in her trouble, but how could she stop him? She was thankful when Miss Rose called them to the dinner table, giving her mind a break from her tumbled thoughts.

Chapter Eleven

From Miss Rose's back porch, Zane watched Sam and Abby's wagon disappear over the bluff. He took another bite of apple cobbler and rocked his chair back on two legs. The tangy-sweet flavor on his tongue made him smile. "Sarah loved your baking."

Miss Rose laughed. "I know. She tried many of my recipes, but the poor girl couldn't get the hang of it. You married a good cook, Zane, but she had trouble with the sweets."

He nodded. He couldn't argue with that, though it seemed disloyal to comment. "She was sweet enough herself."

"That she was. But there's no harm in remembering her imperfections. They were part of the woman you loved, too."

True, he thought. But Sarah's imperfections were few and far between, and they lay buried in the ashes. He set his plate on the stand between the two chairs. "Journey still tires easily."

"Some. I have the feeling she uses it as an excuse to stay away from folks more than being truly worn out. That girl's got a lot on her mind."

Good. At least Miss Rose wasn't totally taken in by her new housemate. "She does seem rather secretive, doesn't she?"

"Oh, there's something bothering her. She's awful quiet most times, keeps glancing around at all the windows like she's waiting for someone to pop through them. I hear her setting the lock every night after I go to bed."

"Maybe it's not such a good idea for her to stay here. I'd hate to see her drag you into whatever problems she has."

"Zane Thompson!" Miss Rose jumped out of her seat and glared down at him, hands flapping. "I'm surprised at you. What would you have me do? Turn that girl out now when she has nothing? She lost her horse. She doesn't have any money. She had me talk to Abby about posting signs hoping to do a little sewing work until her leg mends to help pay for her keep. And you want me to turn her out?"

He held his hands up in a gesture of calm and protest. "Now, Miss Rose, don't get your dander up. I'm just saying maybe it'd be better if she stayed somewhere else, in town maybe. Sam and Abby might—"

"There's not room at Sam and Abby's. Besides, it's not right. They have a business to run, and Journey's under my own hire. She's my responsibility."

She was right. Dear Lord, forgive him, what was he to do? Journey's soft brown eyes and wary glance appeared in his mind's eye. He rubbed his face, hoping to wipe the image away. He had to keep his suspicions in mind. Otherwise it would be too easy to admire her determination.

"I'm sorry, Miss Rose. I know you can't turn her out. I shouldn't have even suggested it. But I worry about you."

Her wrinkled hand rubbed over his and her voice softened. "You can't take care of me any better than the Lord has all these years. You know worry's a sin and can't do you any good anyway. So pray, then stop worrying."

"I will. I have been, but my heart's not been in it. I guess even ministers don't get it right all the time." He smiled at the tiny woman standing over him.

"Being a pastor doesn't mean you're perfect. It means you have a greater responsibility, though. We have to do this for Journey. Whatever her trouble is, God sent her here for us to look after. I don't know what all that means, but we'll need to trust that the Lord knows what He's doing by bringing her to us." He felt the pressure of her thin lips on the top of his head followed by a warm flush over his ears. "But your concern isn't all for me. You care about her, too, Zane. I see it. I know."

He laced his fingers across his stomach and tipped the chair until it leaned against the windowsill. "Comes with the territory."

"I don't know. I've heard a lot of ministers pray with great compassion, but not one looked at me the way you look at her."

He laughed and turned away before she could read something else. "That's how rumors get started, you know."

She did not laugh. Instead, she set her knuckles on her bony hips and gave him a hard look. "That's not my style and you know it. And it's not going to change the subject."

"What subject?"

"The subject of when you're going to move on and give another woman at least half a chance to make you happy."

He rocked forward, both feet hitting the porch floor with a thump. "Hold on, now. I think it's a bit early to be hitching us up. She's not even a believer."

"Maybe not yet. Maybe it's too soon for us to know

much of anything about her spiritual life. But it's not like you have to marry her," she said, sitting down in the chair she pulled close to him.

"What?"

"Hear me out before you go jumping to conclusions. I'm saying you're young and handsome. I'm saying there are several young ladies around here who've offered you an invitation to Sunday dinner, and there's no harm in accepting. But Journey's the first lady you've shown that kind of interest in since—"

"Since Sarah died?" He closed his eyes as the remainder of the hammer-bruise on his forehead throbbed a little.

He felt the warmth of her hand on his knee. "Sarah wouldn't want you to be alone for fear you'll not honor her memory. It doesn't give her any honor for you not to go on living."

"All I feel for Journey is a sense of responsibility. It's obvious she needs help, and it's my duty to do that. The Lord has enough for me to do without thinking of courting again."

Miss Rose smiled. "I don't think you believe that any more than I do. The Lord didn't intend for any man to be alone. You need a helpmate."

"So you're trying to get rid of me?" He glanced her way from the corner of his eye and grinned.

"I love your company, Reverend Thompson," she told him, with a snap of her hand on his leg. "If I was younger, I'd be late for service myself, making that final preen. But I'm not, and it's not right that you should spend so much time with a crumbly old woman."

He leaned forward to kiss her soft cheek. "I'll be fine. Don't worry—it's a sin, remember?"

"I'm not worried. I just wanted to get you thinking.

After all—" she lowered her voice as if the sleeping patient could hear "—she is a beautiful and captive audience right now. That should make it easy enough, even for you."

She patted his cheek and wobbled a little until she steadied her feet under her. Zane watched her walk back into the house, catching the wink she sent his way before stepping through the doorway.

He rubbed a hand over his face before resting his forehead on his palm. What had just happened? He had meant to warn Miss Rose somehow. He knew Journey had more trouble than she could handle. As long as she stayed with Miss Rose, they could both be in danger. But Miss Rose had turned his concern into something entirely different.

He cupped his chin and stared out over the bluff as a small smile crept across his face. Leave it to her to suggest courting.

"Christians should find all the clean fun they can, show those unbelievers they don't need all Satan's wiles to have a good time," she often said.

He glanced back toward the door, thinking of auburn curls spilling over the arm of the couch and how she had felt in his arms as he settled her there weeks ago. He stretched to his feet, the smile slipping from his face. He couldn't waste his attention on such things as courting, especially now. There was definitely something more to Journey's story than she was telling. And until he found out what, he'd have no time for anything else.

Chapter Twelve

Journey paused at the top of the mercantile steps to catch her balance as she held her satchel and crutches at the same time.

In another week or so, Doc Ferris said he might allow her to start putting weight on her broken leg. She had taken that as having his permission to finally make a trip into town. Being stuck inside wrangled her nerves, like waiting for a firecracker to explode. So when Miss Rose went to visit Mrs. Hamler, she took advantage of the offer to use the horses.

"What do you think you're doing?" Abby's voice gave her a start and she froze. "I didn't think you were cleared to be walking around yet."

"I thought, with the crutches…"

Abby smiled and Journey relaxed a little. "I see. But I think that's what we call 'following the letter of the law.' Doc Ferris seemed to think it would be at least another week before you'd be able to come into town."

"I had a few shirts finished and wanted to get them to you." That was true enough. She made her way up the remaining steps and hobbled through the door Abby held open.

"I could've picked them up later this week. Sam and Zane are delivering an order, or I'd have brought them today. But since you're here, I've got a few more. Word is getting around about your work. The cowboys heading south through here are glad to find someone to take in their mending. But this'll probably be all from them until spring."

Journey nodded, trying to hide her disappointment as she deposited her satchel onto the store counter, fumbling with the strap. The sewing had held her through the past few weeks at least. Doc Ferris had never mentioned his fee, but she had been anxious to clear the debt. She couldn't let it lie unpaid.

"…post a letter?"

Abby's continued chatter floated back into her consciousness.

"I beg your pardon?"

"I wondered if Miss Rose had given you her letter to post. She usually sends one out the middle of the month to her nephew in Virginia City." As proud as she sounded, Journey would've thought the man was Abby's own kin.

"Uh, no, no letter today. Does she get to see him much?" She focused on the satchel strap, hoping not to sound overly interested. Her leg started to ache.

"Fairly much so, I guess. Of course, can you ever see enough of family? I know she wishes he were closer. He's the son of Rose's only sister, and the last of her family living. She knows he's doing what he's been called to do, so she doesn't complain. But she does spoil him all the more when he gets a chance to visit. I imagine you'll get to meet him over Thanksgiving." She wrapped the finished shirts in brown paper, fingers flying almost as fast as the words from her mouth.

"That'll be lovely, I'm sure." She'd cross that bridge when she came to it.

"Anything else you need, Journey?" Abby gave her the packet of shirts to be mended.

"No. I'll just take these next orders and head back."

Abby leaned over the wide wooden counter, its honey hues just shades darker than her braided hair sweeping across it. "You didn't tell her you were coming, eh?" she whispered, though they were the only ones in the bright storeroom.

"Not exactly, but—"

The woman waved her hands. "No need to explain to me. I understand as well as anybody how hard it is to be cooped up inside for very long. We're kindred spirits that way. So I won't keep you."

"I appreciate that," Journey said. "I figured it's easier to ask forgiveness than to gain permission."

Abby laughed, light and graceful. "I agree. You really must come for a visit—a good, long one—after you're all mended. Promise you will."

She nodded. "Zane tells me I'll not get beyond the mountains until spring now. I'm sure we'll have plenty of time to get together."

"Good. I'll count on it."

Abby moved to take the parcels out to the wagon. As much as she hated it, Journey had to admit she was grateful for the help. She wanted to be back before Miss Rose returned. It wouldn't be right to worry the woman, and she hadn't left a note.

"Have you made your own dress yet?" Abby asked.

Journey continued to make her way out the door. "I haven't been in any rush, what with working on the other mending and all."

"Well, you'd better get in a rush. You'll want to have it finished for the harvest party, and that's just over a week away. Lots of single, young ranchers from all over the area come into Walten for it." Abby fairly beamed with excitement.

Journey couldn't hide the nervousness in her voice. "Whatever would I do at a harvest party?"

She supposed Abby's excitement could be contagious if she'd let it. The woman smiled at her, hands moving as she described the town gathering. "People bring in some of their crops to share, kind of a way to see who has bragging rights, I guess. Men bring in sheared wool bales, their teams, those kinds of things. Ladies bring baked goods and sewing projects for display. There are games for the children, and the adults, too. Recitations by the school-children, and singing…" Her voice trailed off, apparently lost in memories of previous years. "It's great fun."

Despite herself, Journey found her curiosity growing. What must it have been like to grow up in such a place? Where children were safe and carefree and sent to a real school, where neighbors looked out for one another? The women who'd lived in one-room stalls above the saloon similar to Journey and her mother had formed their own type of neighborliness, she supposed, but it was nothing compared with what she'd experienced in the past few weeks.

While she hadn't missed a word of Abby's description, she must've adopted a rather bewildered expression, because Abby tapped her on the shoulder. "You will come, won't you? I'm sure Miss Rose will want you to bring her, and it'll be a great chance for you to get to meet all the folks around here. You won't get another chance like this until Christmas."

She allowed a tentative grin to pull her lips tight. "It

does sound nice." But the last thing she needed was to become acquainted with more people from Walten.

Sometimes the best place to hide is right in plain sight, darlin'. Folks never see what's right under their noses. Hank had told her that. Hank would know. He'd swindled more people in broad daylight than there were stars in the night sky.

She nodded her head once, firmly. "I'll think about it. Thank you for telling me. Maybe I should get started on that dress."

Abby's eyebrows rose as the smile on her face widened. "You let me know if I can do anything to help. Even if you just want to talk, stop in. I love to talk, but I'm not a bad listener, either."

Journey's heart skipped a moment. What had Zane told her? She drew a deep breath. Surely he wouldn't say anything about their meeting in the barn. But she couldn't afford to add to his suspicions.

Thanking Abby, she put her crutches in the wagon bed and hoisted herself into the seat with her arms and her good knee and was soon on her way out of town. She smiled with a small sense of satisfaction and drew her collar up around her as the sharp wind bit at her neck. It felt good to know she had a tight, warm house to go to, especially with autumn nearing an end. The whole town seemed determined to take her in, with or without her permission.

But an icy shiver shook her as she left the town's borders, one not caused by the winds of coming winter. She glanced over her shoulder. A tall shadow slid behind Norwood's Mercantile. Why it should make her uneasy she didn't know, but she urged the horses to a fast trot just the same.

* * *

"So what's put a burr in your saddle?"

Zane started, sitting forward on the wagon seat next to Sam. "What do you mean?"

"I mean you haven't said more than five words since we left Walten."

"I thought I was here for my strong back, not my conversational skills." Zane grinned at his old friend. "You could've brought Abby along."

Sam gave a wounded look. "I happen to enjoy her chatter. She's lively." He laughed. "Remember that first Sunday drive we took together, you and Sarah, me and Abby?"

Zane nodded. "I wanted her to stop talking in the worst way so Sarah'd be able to get a few words in."

"She was more quiet, like me." Sam gave a sidelong glance as he jostled the reins.

"Sure. And what was it we all called you in school? 'Magpie' comes to mind."

Sam laughed, a deep jolly sound, and Zane joined in. Then he quieted and asked again. "You seem to have something stuck in your craw, is all, and we have a long ride ahead, so you might as well tell me what's going on. Does it have anything to do with the lovely Miss Smith?"

Zane leaned back on the seat. "I suppose so. Something about that lady doesn't sit right with me."

"That's all it is?"

"Of course that's all it is. What are you asking?"

"It's hard not to notice how pretty she is. She's a smart one to have come all that way on her own, determined, kindhearted… No one would think any less of you for being interested in that."

"Don't you start. Miss Rose and Abby have both been hinting. I don't think she's even a believer," Zane argued.

"But if she were?"

Zane rumbled low in his throat. "You know I don't condone missionary courtship, Sam."

His friend slapped the reins lightly, silent for a moment. "After Sarah died, something changed in you—"

"What did you expect—"

"Hear me out, now," Sam said. "You've always been focused on your ministry. I think you had a sense of that even when we were kids. But that focus changed somehow. It's grown so large now I'm afraid it's keeping you from seeing anything beyond it."

"I'm fine, Sam." He leaned forward again, outside of his field of vision. "I'm doing the Lord's work, and that's enough for me."

"So you don't think she's pretty?" Sam asked.

Zane twisted his shoulders so he could look his friend in the eye. "I wouldn't go so far as to say that. But I can't let my judgment be clouded. I can't help but admire her courage, and she's got grit, I'll give you that. But unless she knows the Lord, and until I can figure out the missing pieces to her story, that's all it can be."

Sam nodded. "All the more reason for me to be praying for you."

"And for her, my friend," Zane said.

Chapter Thirteen

Over a week later and Walten's harvest party was in full swing by the time Journey and Miss Rose arrived. Journey carried a pan full of chicken, sizzled in bread crumbs just that morning, into the wagon-filled churchyard. Voices blended with the happy tune of a fiddle somewhere off to the right.

The sky cleared overhead and a strong breeze eased the sun's unexpected heat. The weather might be unpredictable this time of year, but it seemed it would cooperate for the day's festivities.

"Don't be fooled," Miss Rose said, fanning a handkerchief over her face. "Tomorrow we could wake to three feet of snow. Winter might tease us for a while, but it's coming. I've lived here long enough to smell it."

"How long have you lived here, Miss Rose?"

She feared she had crossed the line when the pause lengthened. Asking questions too often became a two-way street. Still, in sharing a house with this woman, she'd found her interest welcomed. The woman also was quick to take a hint, never pushing for answers beyond those she offered.

"I guess it's been nigh onto sixty years." Her voice carried a tone of disbelief, and she blinked with a look of amazement. "My Wallace and I were married when I was just sixteen, and we headed west the next day. I'll be seventy-six next spring."

They continued through the maze of booths and tables covered in vegetables and baked goods set in the grassy area behind the church. Children chased one another in the open spaces between. Men grouped near the horses, comparing harnesses. Ladies in bright dresses were busy arranging and rearranging displays.

It felt good to be outside and off the crutches, Journey thought as she placed the pan in a free spot on the table between a plate of crisp potato cakes and a tray of boiled ham. Doc Ferris had cleared her the day before. Even to be out among so many strangers it felt good.

"There you are!" Abby's voice could be heard over the general hubbub as she wound her way through the swarm of people. She took Miss Rose's arm and led them to another table crowded with still more picnic food. "You look lovely, Journey. You chose well for yourself in that color."

She smiled her thanks and fanned her hands over the navy fabric. Fashion was never a great concern, but she had made a point to finish the dress for this occasion. The fitted bodice clasped with simple buttons all the way up to a collar of the same color, but with a scalloped edge. She had been tempted to sew a split skirt for riding but hadn't noticed any other women wearing them in town, and so she resisted. It wouldn't do to stand out.

Besides the work dress she wore for everyday use, her sparse wardrobe was ragged. She had needed something decent to wear to meet the community. It might reflect poorly on Miss Rose if she came looking unkempt.

"Let me introduce you to our sewing circle," Abby said. Journey found herself pulled into a crowd of women before she could protest. She slipped her fingers along the curls that had already pulled from the low chignon at her neck and tried to tuck them back into the general mass.

"Ladies, I'd like you to meet Miss Journey Smith," Abby said. "She's new to Walten, staying with Miss Rose out at the ranch. Journey, this is Mrs. Phoebe Decker, Miss Sue Anderson and Mrs. Evie Wilson. Journey is quite a seamstress, and now that she's recuperated from a recent accident, I've invited her to join our sewing circle."

Mrs. Wilson shifted her baby from one hip to the other and stretched her right hand in greeting. Journey took it, forcing a smile to her anxious lips. "So nice to finally meet you, since Abby's been telling us about you. I'm sorry to hear you had such a traumatic introduction to our town. We're so glad you're up and about now." Something in Mrs. Wilson's soft grip reminded Journey of her mother.

Sue Anderson's carefully coiffed hair, dimpled face and glittering broach told her story.

The swooping feather of her hat brushed her over-pink cheeks and pointed to an over-wide smile. Her eyes were kind, but Journey had met women like her before. Society. Well-bred. She'd no doubt been born to a life of leisure and had no idea of how hard everyday labors could be. "So nice to meet you, Journey." She held out a gloved hand.

Journey stiffened when Phoebe Decker interrupted with her nasal tone. "After everything we've heard from Rose Bishop, the Norwoods and Reverend Thompson, we've all been anxious to meet you. You've been quite the topic of conversation."

She was not very old, not very pretty and not at all

friendly. Journey had a feeling Phoebe was not one to ignore those she could not tolerate.

"I didn't realize I had caused such a stir," Journey said, questioning Abby with a look.

"We're a small community," Abby said. "Anyone new creates a sensation."

"Traveling all that way on your own…" Phoebe clucked her tongue. *Chicken Lady.* The name popped into Journey's mind and she smiled in spite of herself. "I'm certain you'll have stories to share. Surely there are a few worthy of polite company."

Phoebe was not looking for tales of entertainment. This woman had already formulated a few stories of her own about her. But she somehow doubted she had imagination enough to get close to the truth.

Sue stepped closer. "I know I couldn't have done it— traveled alone—without an escort. And then to lose your horse." Sue looked dutifully distressed. "Well, I'm glad to see you're on the mend. We'll see you at sewing circle. Now, if you'll excuse me, I must speak with Mrs. Hamler about the Ladies' Aid Society." With a flounce of her bustle, she moved to the booths, waving a gloved hand.

"I think it'll be wonderful to have a new face in the sewing circle." Evie smiled, and Journey felt her anxiety ease. "We haven't been meeting real regularly through the summer, but now that harvesting is done, we'll start our weekly get-togethers. We talk about as much as we sew, but you'll have to excuse us. We're a bunch of harmless busybodies for the most part, so feel free to tell us to mind our own concerns if we get out of line. Right, Phoebe?"

The woman nodded, drawing a line straight down with the point of her nose. "We have to extend a welcome to you. Especially with all your sewing accomplishments

I've heard so much about. You take in mending for the cowboys traveling through town, I hear." She didn't smile. "Please excuse me, Pastor Zane has arrived. He has to have a piece of my Mary's apple pie."

"Never mind her," Evie said, patting Journey's arm as Phoebe hurried off. "She's been after Pastor Thompson for her daughter ever since his wife passed away, and she's jealous of any woman prettier than her Mary."

Journey bit the inside of her lip. "But I don't think—"

"Nonsense. With beauty like yours, who could blame him? Just don't let her get to you and you'll be fine. I'll let you know about our first meeting next week, ladies. I trust we'll see you in services now that your leg has healed, Journey. Well, I had better catch up with my Jimmy. I'm sure he's pestering his father something awful about now. See you on Sunday."

Journey nodded her off, grateful to be away from the inquisition. Her mouth felt dry as she searched the growing crowd, spotting Miss Rose with a group of older ladies sitting near the pie-laden tables, ready to serve.

"Come on," Abby said. "There are plenty more folks to meet."

"I'm feeling easily worn out these first days," Journey said. "I'm not used to so much walking around. Miss Rose has all but tied me down these past few weeks, especially since my trip into town last week. I'll find a shady spot to sit and enjoy the crowd."

Abby did not look convinced. "If you're sure, but everyone's anxious to meet you. We've been praying for you at church, so naturally folks are wondering who you are and how you're doing. I'll find you again later on?"

Journey relented, seeing that Abby wouldn't be content to simply let her be a wallflower. "Maybe this afternoon we can meet more people. I'm not very good with names, so it's easier to go slow."

Her breath left her in a gasp as Abby caught her in a tight squeeze. "That'll be fine. You find a good spot and enjoy the day. I'm so glad you're walking around and that you're here. You'll love Walten. I know it."

Journey watched Abby's tall form slide across the open space, toward Miss Rose. She breathed easier and started off in search of a quiet tree to hide under. There were few to choose from, but anyplace away from the crowd would be welcome. It was going to be a long day.

Chapter Fourteen

Zane arrived to find wagons filling the churchyard. He gazed at the wide expanse of sky, thankful for the clear weather. Snow could be here as early as tomorrow, with the way the wind blew over the mountains, but today the community could enjoy the picnic.

He raised his arms and stepped back, narrowly avoiding some children chasing each other between tables. How Sarah had loved to race with them. "Not dignified," Mrs. Decker had muttered so many times. He and Sarah had talked about having their own children one day. When Sarah had suspected they would soon become a family, Zane had never been a happier man. Sometimes it felt like yesterday. But it was years ago. Three years…

He blinked hard in the sun. Was that Mrs. Decker headed his way? She probably wanted him to have a piece of Mary's apple pie. His mouth puckered at the thought. He hoped Mary wouldn't have to rely on her cooking skills to snare a husband.

Where was Miss Rose? She made a good fence when it came to keeping Phoebe Decker at bay. He felt sorry for Mary. He doubted her mother gave the shy girl a chance to find her own beau. But he was not sorry enough to eat that pie.

He spied Miss Rose and her friends, sitting in the sunshine. Her silver hair shone, and Zane wondered what she must've looked like when she'd come to Montana as a young bride. He returned her wave when he realized he'd been caught staring, and moved to greet her.

"Hello, ladies," he said. "It looks like the Lord's blessed us with beautiful weather." He relaxed when he noticed Phoebe Decker stop short, then turn to the quilt display. He'd dodged the pie for a moment, anyhow.

Zane squeezed Miss Rose's shoulder as she patted his hand.

"Is Journey here?" he asked.

"Yes." Her smile warned him of where her thoughts were going. "She was with Abby the last I saw her."

"She went to find some shade," Abby said, walking up behind the group. "Meeting Phoebe wore her out, I'm afraid." Her voice lowered, but the gleam in her eye didn't dim.

"Hello. Where's Sam?" Zane asked, searching the crowd.

Abby flicked back her blond hair. "He'll be along. A shipment from Virginia City arrived this morning."

"I'll have to catch him later, then." He craned his neck. "It's good to see so many come out for the day."

"It won't be long until we're all fighting cabin fever," Miss Rose said. "No reason not to get out and enjoy the fellowship when we can."

"I'd better try to find Journey. She doesn't seem one for socializing. With so many people around…" He shrugged. What did he really think she could do? It's not as if she'd pull her gun in this crowd, would she?

"Right," Abby said. "It'd be a shame to have a pretty thing like her sitting alone with all these gentlemen ranchers and handsome trail hands wandering around."

"Especially in that pretty new dress she sewed for herself," Miss Rose said. He didn't miss the chime in her voice.

He fought with all he had to keep the heat from his ears. The outer ridge grew red enough to give him away every time, no matter how brown his skin turned in the summer sun.

Many of the women in the circle smiled; some even twittered behind gloved hands. Zane swallowed hard. "I'll stroll around a bit, introduce myself to some of the new faces. Ladies, if you'll excuse me."

He ducked his head and cleared his throat as he made his exit from the group. He walked quickly but couldn't miss Abby's voice.

"We really shouldn't tease Pastor Thompson so. He's only doing his duty." Her tone didn't sound very supportive, and several of the ladies laughed outright.

Thank the Lord he'd gotten away when he did. He couldn't decide who tried harder at being a matchmaker, Abby or Miss Rose.

Zane stared at the many unfamiliar faces wandering around the yard. The community had grown over the past year, and the harvest festival gave many new families their first opportunity to relax and meet their neighbors. He remembered how busy his folks had been when they'd moved to Walten.

A few haggard faces testified to a rough start for some. Zane hoped to make his way to all the newcomers and give them an invitation to Sunday services. He also hoped to check in with the cowboys he recognized from those rare

Sundays when they could make it to service. Most of them wouldn't be traveling through town again until next fall.

Zane's glance stopped at a shifty-eyed drifter. He looked as if he'd seen more than his share of bad trail and stared through the crowd as if he wanted to find someone in particular.

Zane passed by Evie Wilson, serving up cider.

"How do, Pastor Thompson?" She handed him a battered tin cup. "You look as though you could use some cool refreshment."

He took a sip. "Cold and sweet. That hits the spot, ma'am. Thank you." He set the tin back. "Good to see so many turn out."

"I know. It gives me the chance to see folks there's never time to visit in the busyness of summer."

"Especially with that new little one to watch after," Zane said.

Mrs. Wilson nodded, looking over the crowd.

"Do you recognize that cowhand over there?" she asked, nodding across the dusty clearing at the man who'd caught his attention a moment ago.

"No, ma'am. Why do you ask?"

She shrugged. "He seems lost, looks out of place. You know, I usually recognize the faces around here, even if the names escape me."

Zane squinted against the bright sun. "Probably some cowpoke decided to stop on the way back from Virginia City or somewhere, same as the others. I'll try to catch him sometime today and introduce myself, invite him to services. Right now I thought I'd check on Journey—I mean, Miss Smith. Have you seen her?"

Evie shaded her eyes and gestured to the edge of the yard. "She's under the aspen."

He spotted her, feet drawn beneath her on a quilt. She wore a navy dress he hadn't seen before, and he found himself admiring the narrow silhouette she presented. Her auburn hair shone brightly in the filtered sunlight, full and rich until tight ringlets fell from her temples to brush her flushed cheeks. He swallowed hard.

She seemed not to notice the milling crowd as she looked toward some undetermined spot in the east. Zane glanced around, trying to decide on what or whom she was focused. There was nothing but the open range.

"I see her. Thanks." He headed toward Journey.

As he walked, he noticed the drifter's focus on her. The man's eyes appeared cold and lifeless; the smile he wore looked as if he'd pasted it on moments ago—a smile that could be peeled off with his socks that evening. Zane forced himself to look away before he read too much into the scene. Between Journey's gun, Abby's warning and Miss Rose's insinuations, his mind had started moving independently from his common sense. Now his heart seemed to have taken a direction all its own.

He paused a moment, then moved toward Journey. Why did he feel compelled to guard her? He laughed at himself. He continued until he stood within her line of sight.

"Enjoying yourself?" he asked.

Journey looked up at him slowly, blinking in the shadow he cast over her face. He waited, wondering if he'd woken her.

"The picnic is lovely." Her crooked smile shook as her wide brown eyes twitched.

"Mind if I sit down?"

"Suit yourself," she said, sliding over on the blanket.

He sat and rested an elbow on his bent knee. Together they studied the people. The stranger still stood off to the side, away from the other cowboys. Zane watched as Journey's gaze traced a path to the man. Had she noticed the cowboy earlier? She seemed edgier than usual, and he figured that not much made its way past her.

"Nice weather we're having for the picnic," Zane said. "Last year a late storm blew in and chased us all into the church."

Journey nodded, chewing her full lower lip.

"Then we had relay races climbing into the steeple."

"Is that so?"

"Sure is. Miss Rose won and crowed like a chicken from the rafters."

"That sounds nice."

He blew out a breath and chanced a glance at her, then back to the figure that held her attention. He thought about pointing out the man's earlier interest but he didn't have the heart to tease her when she looked ready to bolt as it was.

They sat through the three-legged race in silence. He'd been asked to serve as judge for the pie-baking contest after the noon meal.

He nudged her shoulder with his. "Penny for your thoughts."

She started, eyes flashing with surprise as his arm brushed hers. "I beg your pardon?"

"Are you feeling better, Journey, now that you're up and around?"

"Yes." She turned toward him but glanced over her shoulder. "It feels good to be moving unhampered by those blamed crutches."

Her emphatic response caught him off guard and he laughed. "How are things going with Miss Rose? Is she working you like a mule?"

Journey smiled yet Zane saw her tension grow after a

few questions. Was she afraid she'd say too much? "It's more work for her thinking up enough to keep me busy. But she seems happy for the company."

"I know she is." He nodded. "She's not as spry as she once was."

"I couldn't imagine keeping up with her then," Journey said. Her auburn curls caught the sunlight, and he imagined what it would be like to wrap one around his finger.

"It's safer for you to be somewhere warm with winter beating down the door," he said.

She shifted on the quilt. "That's what I hear, but it feels awfully warm to me right now."

"The weather switches as hard as the trails through the mountains. You'll see, we'll have snow soon."

"So I hear." Again, her voice sounded as if her mind was far away. Zane searched her face. For what, he wasn't exactly sure, but hoped he'd know it when he saw it.

She struggled to her feet, and he stood quickly to offer a hand. She pushed curls into place and stood without assistance. "I'd better find Abby."

He stayed her with a hand on her arm. She flinched but didn't pull away. "There are a lot of good people here, Journey," Zane said, staring at her face. How could eyes so wide hide so much? He fought the sudden compulsion to draw her close.

A dimple appeared on her left cheek, one he hadn't noticed before. "I appreciate the company, Pastor. Now, if you'll please excuse me."

"Sure." He watched her limp in Abby's direction, then turn between two tables and around the side of the church building instead. This time, he made no move to seek her out.

Chapter Fifteen

Journey glanced across the circle of people huddled around the bonfire as evening settled on the group of stragglers at the end of the long day. She had hoped to leave hours ago. The strain of seeing so many new faces tired her. But when the fire was lit, and a violin brought out, Miss Rose settled in close, swaying to the music.

She had to admit that the music, combined with the thinned crowd, restored the sense of comfort she'd gotten used to at Miss Rose's house.

A cold breeze picked up when the sun went down. Journey pulled the heavy cape Miss Rose had insisted she bring closer around her. Maybe there would be snow before long. She'd been in the West long enough to know that weather changed quickly. Even though a circle of people blocked some of the fire's heat, the glow kept her nose from numbing.

She scanned the crowd, the faces almost familiar, though she didn't know their names. That thought comforted her, too. Actually, that word could be used to describe the entire town—comforting. She crossed her arms over her knees and stared at her boot tips. Maybe come spring she could afford a new pair before moving on.

Another pair of boots entered her field of vision. She stiffened. Fear shot like ice down her spine.

"Mind if I sit down?" Zane again.

Journey nodded, trying to breathe normally. He said nothing, just stretched his legs out before him and tapped his fingers across his knee in time to the music. Her tension melted as the comfortable silence grew.

The wind switched direction, driving the evening chill a little deeper.

"Bet the cold'll bother you for a while yet." Zane scratched his chin.

"I'm supposing it might." Journey rubbed her leg.

"It might help if you walked around some or sat closer to the fire," Zane said. His eyes were framed with shiny black lashes, and the firelight threw the planes of his cheek and jaw into strong relief.

"Zane, I—"

Loud, coarse laughter interrupted. A wagon drew near the bonfire. Journey recognized some of the men on the wagon from earlier in the day. She stood, smoothing her skirt, and gripped her shaking hands. A sense of dread filled her, but Zane moved and stood behind her, blocking the chill of the wind.

Three men tumbled off before the wagon even stopped. Their singing drowned out the soft violin.

A lanky cowboy with a tan hat strolled her way. His two buddies knocked into each other behind him, with whispers and crude laughter. She edged back, bumping into Zane's solid warmth.

The tall man laughed and only leaned closer. The smell of alcohol rolling from his mouth made her gag, and Journey pressed the back of her hand to her nose. "Hey, gal, don' be so shy now. I hear you're the right friendly type."

He made a grab for her, but the man tripped and fell as Zane drew her back farther. She stumbled over Zane's feet until his fingers tightened around her arm, as if he knew she would turn and run. Yet there was something in the rumble of his chest that stilled her. "You have no business with her," he said.

The three cowboys howled and slapped their legs, swaying into one another as they helped their friend to his feet. "Business is right, Preacher, from what I hear tell. Ain't that right, missy?"

The crowd grew quiet and the music stopped. Heat rushed to Journey's face, but an icy streak cut the air off at her throat and settled into her stomach. She couldn't breathe. "I'm certain I don't know what you're referring to."

Zane moved from behind to stand between her and the men. "And I'm certain that when you sober up, you'll realize you're mistaken about the woman." His tone left no doubt. "I'll ask you to leave now, before you make bigger fools of yourselves."

The tall one lost his easy smile. He swayed closer and Journey slid back farther, despite the fact that Zane held his place in front of her. "The only fool I see here, Preacher, is you for not knowing when to stand aside."

Cheers from his friends blended to a dull thud in her ears. Zane seemed relaxed, but his feet dug into the dirt. She looked over to the other side of the fire when Abby gasped. She and Miss Rose sat huddled together, hands clasped.

"Zane, don't," Journey whispered, scratching his shoulder with her fingertips barely touching.

"Hold up, fellas." The voice drew her attention to the shadow on the wagon seat. The dark figure didn't step down but let his gruff, sober voice carry his intent. The cowboy who'd been eyeing her all day, the one so familiar and yet…

Sam appeared at Zane's shoulder. "Listen to your friend," he said. "No reason to be stirring up a fuss. Go home, sleep it off. Let these people enjoy their evening."

The lead man half turned, grinning at his friends. "I was hoping to enjoy myself here," he said but turned toward the wagon and the others followed. Journey caught his final glare as he passed through the firelight.

The dark form hovering over the wagon seat tipped his hat in silence. Journey shivered, swallowing back the bitter taste of bile that flooded her mouth. She knew that shadow. Roy.

She shook her imagination back into place before it could run away with her. He was only that cowboy who'd been at the picnic earlier that day, not Roy. She sucked a breath in and heaved it out.

Any other possibility was too frightening to consider.

Zane rocked heel-to-toe on his feet, watching his parishioners return to their homes through the heavy snow that had blanketed the town overnight. Attendance had been down, but he never closed the doors if he could make it, no matter how high or thick the snow.

Conversations had naturally centered around the picnic yesterday, and he had to credit his faithful members for the effort they had put into not adding to the tale of the wild cowboys who'd made an appearance. But Journey sat through the entire service in misery, expecting someone to.

"Zane?"

Her timid voice caught him by surprise. He thought he'd missed her slipping out ahead of the others. "Glad to see you and Miss Rose could make it out this morning, Journey. I thought maybe you two would be snowed in."

"It was tempting to crawl back under the covers, I have to admit," she said. She gave a short, nervous laugh that made a choking sound. "But I figured I owe you for last night."

She bit her lip, hands fluttering together. Her brown eyes drooped with exhaustion, and he knew she had gotten little sleep after the events of the night before. But her hair gleamed in a wide roll that framed her face, with thick curls trailing from the nape of her neck, some sweeping over her shoulder—the effect disarming. "They passed on through and didn't stay in town last night," he told her.

"You checked?"

"Sam and I took a little ride before turning in. I don't know that they didn't stay close but not in town. Do you have any reason to think they'll be back?"

She shook her head, and he waited for her to say more but she didn't. Frustration built in him, a tight ball in his chest. Then he noticed a thin, wet trail across her cheek. She wiped it away almost before he noticed, and she steadied herself with a deep breath and looked him in the eye.

"Journey, please—"

"I need you to know that I'm not… That is, I never—" She breathed deeply and tried again, her hand shaking now and bunching the fabric of her skirt. "I've done a lot of things I'm not proud of, things that give me no right to be in this church today. But I never did what that cowboy hinted at last night. My mama, she worked as a saloon girl. That and more, you know?"

Her eyes pleaded for understanding, and he nodded without a sound.

"But that wasn't me. I didn't live that way, not exactly…" Her voice faded and her gaze searched the tiny vestibule where they stood. She drew in a breath to continue, but he placed his hand over both of hers, knotted together at her waist.

His other hand brushed the loose curls at her neck of its own volition. "You don't have to explain those men to me," he said. But his mind demanded answers to a thousand other questions.

"I just wanted to thank you, Zane. No one's ever taken up for me before, not like you did. I do owe you for that."

He scanned outside to judge the distance of the others shouting farewells to neighbors in the churchyard. "Then tell me what's going on."

"Oh, Zane," she said, pulling her hands from his grasp and brushing past him. "Not getting you involved is paying you back."

She went down the steps and hopped into the wagon, sitting next to Miss Rose, leaving him with more questions than ever.

Chapter Sixteen

Journey woke at first light and stretched, then curled deeper into the quilts, studying the ceiling. She rubbed the sleep from her face and sighed, stretching the stiffness from her leg.

With the scene in the churchyard one week past, the days had returned to a comfortable routine. She turned to the frosty window, where sunlight peered over the horizon, gleaming from the fresh snow that covered the ground.

The party had broken up soon after the cowboys had wheeled out of town that night. Tiny white flecks, determined dry crystals, had followed the crowd to their homes. Walten awoke to three feet of snow, with fresh coatings each day for the next week.

This morning the skies were clear, calm. Journey felt much that way herself. She hoped the forced seclusion around the community would stop any speculation about her and those men. Her only option was to stay, regardless. She'd never get through that mountain pass on her own now, even if she'd had a horse. But keeping her name out of the local gossip mill wouldn't hurt.

Circumstances held her there. Much to her surprise, she

enjoyed the routine that she and Miss Rose established. Clean. Wash. Care for the animals. Cook. Sew. Quiet evenings.

Journey dressed and twisted her hair into some semblance of order. She'd have to do better before going to Evie Wilson's to meet the other ladies in the sewing circle. If only she could get out of it. The weather had been her last hope. But as the sunlight grew warmer and brighter, she knew that was not to be.

She'd been judged before, and likely would be again, but that didn't erase the sting. But by now, nothing they guessed could come close to the reality.

That afternoon Journey realized the forced seclusion had served only to inflame the speculation about her.

"I thought for a moment Pastor Thompson might take a swing at the man himself." Sue Anderson retold the events in grand fashion to the ladies as they sat stitching.

"I don't believe it would have come to that. Reverend Thompson was defending the defenseless, as the Lord would have us do." Phoebe Decker seemed to talk without moving her lips. "It's not like Miss Smith could have known these men would single her out, I'm certain. Don't you agree, Mary?"

Phoebe's tone conveyed anything but certainty, and she flashed a penetrating gaze at her. Journey concentrated on the quilt, bound tight enough in its frame to bounce a thimble on. The only thing sure in this conversation would be Mary Decker's dutiful "Yes, Mother."

She stole a glance at Mary. Her pale skin and black hair created a striking contrast, and had her cheeks been fuller, she would have been a true beauty. Journey felt a stab of sympathy for her. Mary looked a little older than she, and

Phoebe's control over her daughter was as strong as Hank's had been over her. Maybe stronger.

With her attention wrapped in the quilt, Journey tried to hide from all the curious stares.

Next time I'll wait for Abby at the store. She pulled another stitch through.

Evie Wilson gave a friendly smile. "I'm sure it's not something we need to review for Journey."

Sue's eyes widened and her hands stopped. "Oh, my, I suppose not. It's just so romantic, I never thought…"

Journey flushed, yet she couldn't hold back her laugh. That laugh never worked right, always slipping out at the strangest times. What could be keeping Abby?

"It didn't seem very romantic at the time," Journey said, glancing around the circle. Blank looks and cool stares outnumbered the smiles that greeted her. She focused again on the quilt. The ladies intended this one as a Christmas present for Zane.

The Wilsons' door opened and Abby breezed through, shaking powdered snow from her bonnet and coat. Journey added her greeting to the others' and shifted her chair, hoping she would accept the invitation. Having Abby act as a buffer between her and Phoebe would make the afternoon much easier.

"I'm sorry I'm late." Abby smoothed her hair and dug a quilting needle and thread from a tiny sewing box as she settled into the space. "We had a late shipment and Sam needed me to watch the store while he unloaded. I hoped to catch you, Journey, but I'm glad you came along without me."

"Miss Rose cleared the afternoon so I could come." Not that there'd been much to clear. She managed a faint smile. "I thought you'd be here ahead of me." *Hoped.*

"I'm sure you've been entertaining the ladies with tales of your adventures." Abby caught the eye of each woman with her bright expression before turning her attention to the cloth.

Phoebe was the only one to reply. "We haven't gotten beyond Journey's adventures since arriving in Walten. If she brings about this much excitement everywhere, it will take several quilts to hear all the tales."

Most of the women giggled—a high, twittery sound that scraped Journey's ears. Her face grew hot, knowing there was more jibe than jest in the comment.

"If you're so very interested, you'll have to arrange a time to compare stories, I suppose." Evie's voice sounded low and cool. A seamless smile graced her face.

Journey raised an eyebrow to clear a view of Phoebe without staring outright. The flush that came to Phoebe's pinched face helped cool her shame. Several moments of silence passed.

Sue Anderson spoke first. "Please don't think us rude, Journey. We're just interested in all you've seen along your way to Walten." Silence hung for another moment. "At least, I'd like to hear about it."

She searched Sue's face. "Truly, there isn't much to tell. I'd be more interested in learning more about Walten. I haven't had an opportunity to explore."

"So you are staying, then?" Phoebe asked. "I'd heard you were considering it, but I couldn't believe it."

Journey ground her teeth. It wouldn't do to give Phoebe the satisfaction of rattling her. "I have no choice since I have no horse. And with the snow piling and the cold wind blowing, I'm very grateful to have found a job with Miss Rose."

She chanced a look at the group. Abby smiled at her,

with a nod so slight that Journey almost missed it. Her face grew warm again, but she turned her attention back to her stitches, a small smile on her own face.

"How is Miss Rose handling this weather?" Evie Wilson rose to her role as hostess, but her eyes never drifted far from her baby, sleeping in a cradle near the fireplace.

Journey thought for a moment. "Miss Rose is a strong woman. I'm sure she'd make out fine without me, but she's very charitable to take me in."

"She needs you more than you realize," Abby said. "There are many in this town who are thankful she has someone living out there with her. Especially to get ready for the holidays."

Sue twittered again and arched her eyebrows in a telling look. "Pastor Zane will definitely be indebted to you. He has a soft spot for the dear woman."

"He always has, and it's the same for her. Even more so since Sarah…" The sentence hung for a moment before Abby continued, this time with a scratch to her voice. "I don't know how he would've made it through without Miss Rose's help."

"He would've found his way," Evie said. "He's always been strong, and his faith even stronger."

Journey's hand slowed. She couldn't help but wonder about the relationship between the pastor and Miss Rose. And who was Sarah?

"That fire burned the heart out of that man. To lose your wife and baby." Abby shook herself, as if realizing she had spoken aloud more than she had intended, and turned to Journey. "Sarah was my best friend."

Journey barely heard her. A lump formed in her throat, but she swallowed it down. Everyone had their stories. This one wasn't her concern. She couldn't let it be.

"I suppose Reverend Thompson will be going to Miss Rose's for Thanksgiving? Is her nephew coming?" Evie asked.

"Zane will be there, and Sam and I are going. Has Miss Rose mentioned if Reed is coming?" Abby tied off a thread and snipped it free.

Journey didn't know. It was news to her that Zane had been invited. And now the nephew—the sheriff from Virginia City—might be coming?

"I— She hasn't said. I suppose I hadn't realized it was getting on that time of year." In truth, she'd never celebrated the holiday before.

"It's only a couple of weeks away. If Reed's coming, he'll ride in the morning before and ride out the day after. Miss Rose never expects him exactly, but she always prepares for him. He always manages to come." Abby clearly looked forward to the holiday.

Most people in Savannah thought it nothing but a Yankee holiday, since Mr. Lincoln proclaimed the first Thanksgiving after Gettysburg. Journey had always figured there was no harm in taking a day to be thankful, but she'd never had cause to before.

She wondered what it would entail. Turkey—she'd have to cook a turkey. Maybe Abby would help. But if Abby were an invited guest and Miss Rose's family would be there, she guessed not. And where would she go? It wasn't as if she could celebrate with other servants. Holidays were for family, and she had none.

Though she tried to squelch it, hope rose in her that she might be asked to stay. Yet how could she sit and share Thanksgiving dinner with a minister and an officer of the law? "I'll talk to Miss Rose when I get back."

The shadows lengthened and the women made their

leave. The afternoon had passed with discussions of canning, quilting and raising children, but there were no further comments concerning Journey's past. Mrs. Wilson was a kind and accommodating hostess, but as she stepped from the porch, Journey felt her ease return, one that had been lost when she was among the quilters.

She adjusted the cinches on her saddle, spinning around at a tap on her shoulder. Her hand moved to the pocket of her long coat where the pistol remained. Before she had a chance to pull it, Abby stepped back and smiled.

"I said, can you stay for supper?"

Journey caught her breath and her face grew hot as she glanced around at the other ladies climbing into their wagons. She turned back to Abby. "I beg your pardon. I didn't realize you were speaking to me. Supper?" She searched the sun's position in the sky. "I should be getting back. Miss Rose will be wanting me to get supper ready for her."

Abby sighed. "I told Miss Rose I might try to keep you longer if I could. Won't you come?"

The temptation was strong. If she weren't so different from Abby, they might have been good friends. But she couldn't risk it now. As much as she liked the place she found herself in, it wouldn't do to relax. She couldn't get too comfortable, because it would only be harder in the long run.

"I'm sorry, Abby. I have to go. Maybe another time?" She continued adjusting the reins.

"Can you at least walk back to town with me? I'd enjoy the company." Abby looked hopeful.

Why would Abby want company, having spent the entire afternoon in the midst of half a dozen ladies? Still, she could hardly refuse. Abby had helped her so much. She nodded, adjusted her hat and tugged the halter for the horse to follow.

"The ladies like you."

Journey's step faltered as she considered that. "I suppose someone new passing through is bound to garner some attention. It seems they have some rather exciting notions about me."

Abby laughed. "It's more than that. You have a grace that draws people. Are you really, though, just passing through?"

Melting snow slushed under their feet. "I'll move on come spring."

"We could help you if you want to stay."

Journey froze. "You've all helped me so much already. There's nothing more I need." She attempted to calm her fast breath and pounding heart. "Well, except for a horse and a short winter." She laughed, but it sounded false.

Abby would not be put off. "Are you worried about those cowboys?"

Not all of them, Journey thought. Only the one who should've been a few thousand miles away.

"I'm not worried, because I've never seen them before." She hoped it was nothing more than too much alcohol. Maybe Roy hadn't even recognized her. She'd been the wife of his best friend, if you could consider Hank a friend of anyone. But she never held that much faith in luck or coincidence. She'd never held much faith in anything.

Abby placed a warm hand on her shoulder. "Please, be careful. God sent you to us for a reason. Don't leave before we figure out what that is."

Journey chirped and tugged the horse into motion again. The town came into view as they topped the rise. She fought the urge to nod a promise. "I'll head on from here.

I should have that dress for Mrs. Fletcher finished by midweek, and I'll bring it into town. I think Miss Rose wants to pick up some things, too."

"Miss Rose is a hard one to keep down. She manages to finagle a trip to town once a week, no matter what the weather." Abby allowed the subject to be changed. "I'll see you tomorrow morning in church."

Journey guessed she would. She'd avoided it as long as she could, with her broken leg, and last week had been an obligation. She climbed into the saddle and adjusted her skirt around her—a split skirt would have been much easier. She turned to wave goodbye.

Abby waved back. Journey saw her lips move, but the wind had picked up, disguising the sound too much to be sure she'd spoken. But it sounded like "I'm praying for you."

Zane greeted his parishioners from the top of the steps of the church. The sanctuary was already cozy from the tiny woodstove and the heat from the seated worshippers, and it might have made more sense to wait there. But he held at the door, and watched for Miss Rose's buggy to appear from around the little grove of trees.

He checked his watch and thrust it back into his pocket, then stepped into the sanctuary to nod at Abby, her signal to start playing the battered piano. All the hymns sounded tinny, like music that spilled from a city saloon. If he could sell the yearling colt for a fair price come spring, they could get a new organ. Abby played beautifully, but she couldn't work miracles.

Zane shrugged and smiled at her raised eyebrows. He didn't know where Miss Rose and Journey were. Miss Rose hadn't been late since the time her wagon hitch broke. This delay had to be about Journey. About Journey not wanting to come to church.

She'd been less than thrilled when he made a special point to invite her. Now that she was up and about, without a doubt Miss Rose would have her in church, if at all possible. But if she weren't inclined to come again, he had thought a personal invitation might smooth the way. Something stirred in him at the thought of seeing her face in the pews, and it disconcerted him to know all the reasons for that weren't strictly pastoral.

Zane glanced again at his timepiece. Eight o'clock. He pulled the bell rope, and the deep ring permeated the air. Just as he turned to walk to the pulpit, he spotted them. The wagon fairly slid over the light coat of fresh snow. He gave the bell another tug and made a slow routine of dusting tiny snowflakes from his suit. He'd have time to greet them before he took his place at the pulpit—if they hurried.

The wagon pulled into the yard, and he stepped down to help Miss Rose. Journey hopped to the ground with a flash of navy skirt before he could offer assistance to the elderly woman. She took her responsibility to Miss Rose seriously. If he could fault her on that, he'd have a clear reason to take his concerns to Miss Rose. Not that she'd listen. Striking a balance between concern for Miss Rose and his overwhelming desire to protect Journey hadn't proved easy.

"Good morning! You ladies are right on time." He slid the old woman's arm through his to escort her into the church.

He thought Journey flushed, but perhaps only the chill in the air was to blame. Whatever the cause, he admired the contrast with her navy dress. She limped a little on the healing leg, yet a gracefulness remained.

"These old bones don't move so quick as they used to on mornings like this," Miss Rose told him as they climbed the steps together. "Now, get in there before Sam gets up to take your place."

He squeezed Miss Rose's gloved hand and slipped to the front of the congregation before Abby finished playing. He grasped the front corners of the pulpit his father had built for him when he first took over this church and could feel the smooth edges under his tight grip.

Scanning his congregation, he let his gaze rest for a moment on each member, taking a bit more time at the second pew on the left. He could almost see Sarah as she'd looked that first Sunday after her family moved to Walten. Beautiful, strong, full of life. He'd been only too anxious to make a call on the family that first week.

Her family had filed in beside the woman who still occupied that seat. But today another young woman caught his interest—very different from his wife, but still beautiful, still strong and still full of life. And in the same seat.

Zane snapped his gaze to the Bible resting before him. That wasn't right. His beautiful Sarah; no one could ever compare to her. He hadn't given anyone a chance to, he supposed. So how was it this strange woman managed to seep into his thoughts so often? Journey was pretty enough, with her copper curls and skin pale like china. Eyes of deep brown. But her long, pointed nose gave her a coltish look. And she was far too mysterious, perhaps even dangerous, to be appealing to him.

He smiled at his flock as the hymn ended. "Good morning, and praise God for it. Let's begin with prayer."

He'd have time to figure Journey out later.

Chapter Seventeen

A puff of hot air from the kitchen woodstove hit Journey. The smell of roasting turkey met her as she spooned golden broth over it, humming one of the hymns they'd sung at church on Sunday. She didn't know the words, but the tune was pretty.

She yawned and rubbed her cheeks into the sleeve of her day dress. Awake before dawn, she determined to cook this bird to perfection for Miss Rose and her guests. Then she'd take her leave to the church, certain it would be deserted at that time of day.

"It smells like Thanksgiving already."

She swung around with a gasp as the deep voice startled her. Broth dripped from the spoon and sizzled on the edge of the stove.

"Who are you?" She raised the clutched spoon in her hand and backed away.

"Whoa, there!" The man held his hands up in surrender, stepping back himself. "I'm Reed, Rose's nephew."

Air left her in a rush, and surely he could hear her heart thunder in her chest. She squinted, trying to make out his features in the gray morning light. Nervous laughter bubbled up in the relief of the moment, making it harder to steady her voice. "Then I guess you're safe from my spoon, sir."

His teeth stood out as a smile split his face. "You must be Miss Smith," he said, pulling a chair over for her. "I am so sorry I frightened you. Aunt Rose mentioned you in her last letter. I came into town late last night and figured I'd let myself in to surprise her this morning. Guess I'm the one who got the surprise."

She took the offered chair. "You're not the only one. Miss Rose expected you yesterday."

"I got tied up with some business. I expect my aunt's told you I'm a lawman in Virginia City. There's plenty there to keep a man busy these days." He paused suddenly. "Now, where are my manners? Please, call me Reed."

"And you should call me Journey."

"Right. Journey. How's the turkey coming?"

"I think it will be cooked in time. I'm glad Abby took care of dressing it and all. I've never done anything like that."

Reed turned to watch the rising sun through the windowpane. "From what my aunt Rose tells me, I'm sure you would've managed fine. She and Zane both seem to think you can handle whatever comes your way."

Journey cleared her throat, not knowing what to say to the older man. "They've been very kind." What else might Zane have said about her to this lawman? "Can I get you something for breakfast?"

"No, thanks. I think I'll pass this morning, save room for dinner." He ran a hand over his graying mustache and stubbled chin. "I'm going out to tend to the horses. It'll keep me from being underfoot. Even an old bachelor like me knows enough to stay out of the kitchen when a woman is cooking."

She smiled, wondering what kind of sheriff this man was. He didn't match the image she'd had of a Montana lawman. He seemed friendly, now that she'd had time to recover from her fright. She watched him put on his hat and head out the front door. Maybe he got more results that way.

The real fright was that she'd not heard him. She hadn't slept so soundly since she was a girl. She thought of the raucous music and giddy laughter of the saloon swelling well into the night and realized maybe not even then. And she'd been caught up in the preparations for the day and missed him coming in behind her. What if he had been Roy? It seemed that the scare of those men at the harvest festival and that feeling of being watched in the weeks following dropped off at the door of this house. She had to stay alert, though. What if Roy really was in town? She hoped not, but she couldn't rely on wishes.

"I thought I heard you up and about." Miss Rose's voice rasped with first morning use and interrupted her thoughts. She'd slept later than usual.

"Good morning. Your nephew has arrived, and I just checked the turkey. It's coming along fine. Would you like a little something for breakfast?" Journey asked.

"I saw Reed on his way out to the barn. I don't believe I'll have anything this morning, thank you. My goodness, as late as I've slept this morning, it'll soon be dinnertime! My Wallace and I never had breakfast on holiday mornings. We'd just have that big dinner meal a little early. It's mighty hard to sleep on a full stomach if we wait until the evening meal. No, no, you go on, do what you need to."

She wondered a moment if she shouldn't fry some eggs anyway, but then decided to take her employer at her word. If she'd learned anything these past two months, she did know Miss Rose wasn't shy about speaking her mind. She started for the stairs.

"Journey?" Miss Rose called after her.

She paused at the bottom step. "Yes?"

Miss Rose stepped closer, patting her hand as it rested on the carved wooden banister. "Why don't you wear your Sunday dress—that deep blue one? It brings out the fire in your hair."

"Ah, yes—yes, ma'am." Her eyebrow tugged upward in confusion. Was she to stay and serve? Miss Rose had never said, but she'd assumed that once the meal was on the table, she'd be expected to take her leave. But if the occasion called for it, she'd wear her navy dress.

She climbed the stairs and washed her face in the tepid water from the basin and changed from her everyday dress. Then she pulled the tiny mirror from her saddlebag and propped it on the stand Abby had loaned her.

Her thoughts turned to the day ahead as she tugged her brush through tangled curls. She and Miss Rose had been planning and baking for a week. "There's always reason to thank the Lord," she'd told Journey. "And it's real nice to think that all across this great land of ours, folks are stopping and bowing their heads in gratefulness to the Almighty."

She had never thought about being thankful, let alone considered God. She'd been happy to find this place for the winter, true enough, though it hadn't been her plan. But she'd run long and hard and made her way. She didn't blame God, but neither would she give Him any credit.

She stared out the window. The wind blew hard, but the sun felt warmer than the day before. It would be a good day for a ride.

"Journey? Is there anything you need?" Miss Rose's voice carried up to the room and into her thoughts.

"I'm coming," she called, fluttering her fingers up her back once more, double-checking the tiny buttons. It wouldn't do to miss one today especially.

"How can I help?" Journey asked, reaching the bottom of the stairs.

"You've done yourself proud, the way you got everything ready for this day. I wondered if there's anything left that I could help you with before everyone arrives."

She stretched a hand to pat Miss Rose's arm but withdrew it before she made contact. Leave it to Miss Rose to ask if *she* needed anything. "I've got things under control, I think," she said. "I'm going to set the table and lay out the pies. Everything else is ready. You go on and finish your primping. Your guests will be here before too long."

Miss Rose sniffed. "I never primp." But her slow smile took any bite out of her words. She moved toward her own room.

The clock on the mantel soon chimed eleven. From the kitchen window, she could see Zane and the Norwoods follow one another over the hill. Journey brushed her sweeping skirt for any unseen crumbs and patted the moisture from her face. A tangled curl worked its way free again, and she swept it back.

Journey watched as Reed greeted the men with a slap on the shoulder and leaned over to kiss Abby's cheek as they made their way to the house. Frosty breath hung before them.

Cold, fresh air blew in as they clomped wet snow from their feet. "Happy Thanksgiving," Journey said.

Abby swept her into a hug with a quick release. "Happy Thanksgiving! You look lovely, Journey. How did your turkey turn out?"

"I hope it's as big as Abby says," Sam said. His mustache twitched with a smile underneath it. "I believe I could eat the entire bird myself. If it's not burnt, that is."

Journey laughed. "I think your wife and your pastor may challenge you to it. If I didn't burn it, that is."

"I'll eat it, even if it is burned," Reed said.

Miss Rose made her appearance, wearing a deep green wool dress fitted around her narrow figure. Her hair was still mostly dark, with the gray framing her face in a wide roll that circled her head like a halo. Journey wondered about her flushed cheeks and hoped Miss Rose wasn't pushing too hard by hosting such a dinner. Though she'd prepared much of it, the woman had worked along beside her a good bit of the time.

"You look lovely, Miss Rose," Zane said. "Happy Thanksgiving."

Journey excused herself to get the meal set on the table. She smiled and took a deep breath as the steam from the roasting turkey puffed into her face. With Abby's help, she'd learned how to butcher and scald it. It surprised her to have been squeamish about it.

"Can I help?" Abby's voice startled her, and the lid slipped from her hand, clattering to the floor.

"I was about ready to set everything out. You'll want to get a good seat." She wiped her hands on her apron and pulled it over her head.

"That's why I came. We're one place setting short."

Her eyes widened and she mentally checked off the seating arrangement as she pulled plates from the stack. Surely she hadn't forgotten anyone. "I'll get another setting. I'm so sorry."

"I'll arrange it. You've been so busy getting the meal ready that it probably slipped your mind. Everything smells wonderful." Abby lifted the dishes from her hands and sauntered back to the parlor, where the table had been moved to accommodate everyone.

Journey followed with a platter piled high with stuffing.

Placing the steaming plate to one side, she slid the china and silverware to make room for the extra setting. Again she counted—Miss Rose, Abby, Sam, Zane and Reed. She knew she couldn't have miscounted when there were only five to begin with. Miss Rose must've forgotten to mention the other guest. No matter. It looked as if there would be plenty of food for everyone.

"The turkey is ready. Would you like me to bring it out now, or wait until your other guest arrives?"

"Other guest?" Miss Rose asked.

"The one you need the extra plate for?"

Miss Rose looked at each of her guests from where she sat on the edge of her rocker. "We're all here—Reed, Zane, Sam, Abby, you and me."

Journey's lips parted softly.

"Is there something wrong?" Zane asked.

"No, I thought… That is, I didn't expect…"

Miss Rose stood. "What do you mean? You didn't expect to stay?"

"Why, you have to stay!" Abby said. She laid a hand on her arm, as if to hold her there.

Journey smiled. "The hired help doesn't usually eat with the employer. I thought you had me sit with you at supper because you'd rather that than eat alone."

"Nonsense. We're not all that formal here. Not like it is back East. I should've made it plain." Miss Rose moved and motioned the others toward the table. "Besides, you're more than hired help, Journey. Zane, carry in the turkey and let's give thanks."

Journey was scooted into a chair to the left of Miss

Rose, at the head of the table. Sam seated Abby across from her. Zane disappeared into the kitchen and returned with the plump turkey, steaming from the platter. He placed it in the center of the table, amid an appreciative dose of sighs. He sat beside her, and Reed took the seat at the end of the table opposite his aunt.

"Zane, will you ask the blessing?" Miss Rose asked. Journey felt her hand clasped in the woman's wrinkled one, and saw Miss Rose stretch her other hand to Abby. Abby placed her right hand in Sam's.

Journey clenched her left hand into a fist. But no one seemed to notice. Zane's outstretched fingers waited.

Her own fingers loosened and trembled. Zane seemed to take that as permission to pull her hand into his. Journey found it warm and rough. He didn't clasp her hand but instead let it rest in his open one. She slipped it back into her lap before he could finish saying "Amen."

Journey reached forward to pass the turkey but stilled as Miss Rose cleared her throat.

"I'd like to take this opportunity to say how happy I am to have you all here," she began. "My nephew, all the way from his big job in Virginia City. Abby and Sam, who bring back so many memories of me and my Wallace. My pastor and friend, Zane, who's done so much for me. And, of course, my new friend and boarder, Journey, who grows dearer to me each day. Yes, the Lord has blessed me with so much more than I deserve. And I'm grateful to all of you for the part you play in that."

Abby squeezed Miss Rose's hand on the table. "I'm glad you invited us. I've been missing my family so much since they moved back East. But since we can't be with them, it's good to be with the next best thing."

"Since we're talking thanks, I have my share, too," Sam

said. He rubbed his thick fingers together. "God's been mightily good to me. He's given me a wife prettier than He should have to look at my face, a beautiful country to live in, good friends and a turkey that ain't been burned. Yep, I was doing well before the turkey, but that's an extra blessing."

Laughter rang around the table. Journey looked at each face. Everyone was so kind to her—perhaps the kindest anyone had been since her mother died. With Mama, too, so much of her time had been spent entertaining saloon customers that Journey found herself alone often. And the way decent folk thought of Mama and what she did, they hadn't looked very kindly on her daughter with no papa to lay claim to, either. Her pulse skipped at her temple.

Could she trust them?

She rubbed her hand over Miss Rose's cool, textured skin. "Thank you," she said, her voice straining to reach a whisper. She stiffened, suddenly wanting to say so much more and not knowing where to begin. "Thank you, all, for everything you've done. I'll never be able to make it up to you."

The voices quieted around the table, and her face grew warm under the sudden stares. Miss Rose blinked, emphasizing the wrinkles around her wide eyes. Journey tilted her head to check on her, but Zane drew everyone's attention.

"Making this fine dinner is a start in repayment, so let's not waste it." He stood to carve the large bird.

The meal continued with laughter and stories. Dishes had been cleared in anticipation of the pies that waited in the kitchen. Suddenly a heavy knock at the door drew everyone's attention.

They looked at one another a moment before Zane moved to answer. The light gleamed off the snow through the open doorway.

Something familiar in the voice that returned Zane's greeting froze Journey inside and out. She dug her fingers into the seat of her chair to hold herself still. She'd never forget that voice.

Blood rushed from her face, and her eyes felt too large. The room grew dark as she heard Zane's voice from a muffled distance. "What can we do for you, stranger?"

Stranger... Even in the shadows, she knew him. Recognized the way he ducked into the room. The way the man tugged on his greasy mustache. She jerked to her feet, sending the chair crashing behind her.

"Pardon me." She whirled, bent low, her breath heaving in sharp hitches, and staggered through the kitchen. Tiny black specks darkened her vision. She swayed and banged her hip into the sideboard. Unsteady already, she lost her balance, falling headlong toward the door. But she picked herself up and made her way outside.

She fell down the last step. Her stomach heaved and clenched as she knelt at the bottom of the porch.

Dead...dead...dead.

She'd been so sure. She thrust her hands into the snow that soaked into her dress, but nothing would wash away the blood. Why wasn't he dead? She had swung the iron and left Hank bleeding and still on the bare floor of their room above the saloon. It was her chance to get away from the drunken beatings and conniving schemes.

The law hadn't caught up to her yet and likely wouldn't have, as long as she continued to lie low and mind her own business.

Had Hank risen from the grave?

The landscape around her swirled and darkened. She swayed to her feet but couldn't find her balance. Terror and shock blurred her senses. She fell face-first into cold, wet snow as consciousness faded.

Chapter Eighteen

Zane knelt and rolled Journey to her back. Her skin
blended with the snow she lay in. He leaned down and
lifted her. Once inside, he'd find out what was wrong.
Miss Rose had sent him out to check on her sudden departure.

Journey struggled as he pulled her close, supporting her
in his arms. Her eyes fluttered under closed lids, and her
breath became swift and harsh again. She lashed out and
caught him on the cheek but too weakly to do anything but
brush him. "Hank," she murmured. "Hank, you get away
from me. You'll never—"

"Journey?" He squeezed her shoulders. "Journey! It's
me, Zane."

She shuddered in his arms. "No…no."

He looked into her upturned face, relieved to see a little
color returning. Her eyes fluttered open, a solid ring of
brown, and her nostrils flared slightly, reminding him
again of a wild colt. She gulped air as if she couldn't get
enough. A sudden fierceness rose in him to tuck her away
and protect her forever.

"Come on, now." He moved slowly, not wanting to

startle her. He eased her to her feet, grasping her waist as she swayed. Her hands fluttered over his outstretched arm.

"I'm fine," she insisted. "I—I needed some air, that's all."

Zane challenged her with a look. "There's more to this than feeling penned in. Who is that man?"

"Wh-who?"

He crossed his arms and rocked away on his heels. "Our new visitor. Who is he, Journey? Who's Hank?"

"Don't get involved in my problems," she whispered. "Please."

He drew closer and she ducked, raising her arm as if to ward off a blow. He ran a hand through his hair. "Why can't you let me help you?"

"Where is he?" She shivered as her eyes darted around the horizon.

"He left. He stopped to ask for directions to Virginia City." Zane eased his suit coat off and wrapped it around Journey's shoulders. He let his arm linger at her elbow, nudging her into a walk toward the barn. It might help for her to move around in the cold fresh air before going back indoors.

When she stopped wobbling and he decided she wouldn't bolt, he released her and stepped away before giving in to the desire to gather her close and sweep that one loose curl from her forehead.

"Feeling better?"

She nodded. "You're sure he's gone?"

He stopped and heaved a heavy breath. Instead of the paleness of moments before, Journey now flushed with a bright spot of color on each cheek. She looked embarrassed. No, scared. Vulnerable.

"He said he was headed farther west. I have no reason to doubt him. Should I?"

Journey's breath steamed out in one long puff, clouding her face. "Did he ask about me?"

"I don't know that he even saw you. By the time he'd stepped around the door, you were gone. Why?" He searched her face, hoping for a straightforward answer but not expecting one.

Zane stepped in front of her, forcing her attention toward him. "Who is Hank, Journey? You mentioned him twice now—today and the night you broke your leg."

"Hank's dead."

Why fear a dead man? The more he learned, the more questions he came up with.

"Who was he then?"

"No one who mattered."

Zane coughed, his breath catching in his tight throat. He followed her gaze across the horizon. The sky spread out blue and wide, but deceptive. The wind sliced along the rusty bluffs in the distance. "Let's get you inside. We'll sort it out later. It is Thanksgiving and pie's waiting."

She smiled and nodded, but it didn't ease his suspicions. Instead it only confirmed them, and a desire to help overwhelmed him. Just what that fear had to do with the man who'd wandered by, he didn't know, but he aimed to find out.

Miss Rose and Abby had looked forward to this for too long for this to be hashed out right now. He wouldn't ruin their Thanksgiving plans. Journey's past could wait one more day.

Chapter Nineteen

Journey scratched a hole in the frosted window and stared outside. Wind howled, blowing piles of powder snow into whirling puffs. The storm had hit hard Sunday afternoon and blew strong and steady well into midweek. The bitter cold sliced deeply. She shivered, pulling the shawl Miss Rose had loaned her closer.

Bundling up to face the biting weather as she made her way to the barn each morning and evening made her miss the balmy Georgia winters. Yet she welcomed the coziness of Miss Rose's house and the forced quietness. Journey couldn't hold back a smile. If time to think could solve her problems, she'd have none left to consider.

"No one will be out today." Miss Rose entered the room and interrupted Journey's thoughts. "I think I'll read a bit this morning. Care for me to read aloud?"

"If you like." She sat on the davenport, facing Miss Rose in her rocker. "I think the wind might ease up by afternoon. If so, I might take a ride into town and see how Abby fared during this storm."

The look on the woman's face told her what she thought of the idea.

"You'll freeze solid out on a day like this."

Journey could well imagine what she would think if she knew the entire story.

"I'll bundle up. The fresh air will be wonderful, and you'll be thankful for the break from me." She hoped to make light of her announcement, despite her pounding heart. "I won't be long."

Truth be known, she didn't relish riding out in the strong north winds. The chill settled deep into her bones; shivering was the only motion she could make until the warm fire thawed her. But it was time. Not to see Abby, but to face Hank, if he were to be found. Putting together the sense of being watched during the past weeks with Hank's arrival on Miss Rose's doorstep, she figured he would have sought her out.

The storm had forced her to wait for several days, giving her time to plan. She was thankful, knowing she'd have run if the weather had given her any opportunity.

She realized two things. First, Hank was alive. Hadn't she sensed him the night those cowboys accosted her? She was certain now that Hank's partner Roy had been the cowboy whose gaze she couldn't shake at the church picnic. He'd looked leaner and had shaved his beard, but having Hank turn up on the doorstep confirmed her suspicions. Hank was alive, and he and Roy were up to their old tricks.

Even more dangerous, Hank knew she was in Walten. No coincidence had brought him to the door that day. He knew where she was, and he wanted something from her. It was time to take control because she couldn't run forever. She had to find him first.

Miss Rose read from *Gulliver's Travels* for nearly an hour before her eyes drooped. Journey wasted no time in bundling up and heading into town.

Walten was not large, and Hank was not at all inconspicuous. Tall, with a deep Southern drawl that oozed charm and sophistication, Journey knew the appeal. Knowing how he truly was made her think of the stores she'd seen since coming west. Large and impressive looking from the front but small and plain inside.

Eavesdropping outside the saloon revealed he'd been working at an abandoned mine outside of town. From there Journey had only to ask for directions.

She slid from the horse into snow that buried her ankles and loosened her chinstrap when she spotted the abandoned miner's cabin at the bottom of the slope. It suited Hank, squatting in some tiny hovel so he could afford to maintain his wealthy veneer.

The frigid air stabbed her lungs as a gust of wind kicked and she moved forward. How was Hank handling a Montana winter? She hoped he sat shivering even now. He should've stayed in Georgia. He should've stayed dead.

Suddenly, Journey crashed to the ground, a heavy weight pinning her into a drift. Kicking into the layers of snow, she fought to free herself. She fumbled for the lead rope of the horse, but it slid from her mittens. For a moment she suffocated in the icy wetness. Then with a determined growl, she jolted back, smacking into a firm barrier that echoed her groan. There was a soft thump in the snow beside her as the weight rolled off and she was free.

"I surely do miss that fire!"

Journey whirled to face him, backing onto her feet. "What do you want from me, Hank?" Scared. She could hear it herself.

"Now, darlin', is that any way to greet your dearly departed husband?" He drew to his full height and brushed the snow from his long coat, then smoothed his limp mustache. "I suppose you want to know why I'm here."

"What do you want with me?" She struggled to catch her breath.

"Oh, my dear, don't take things so personally. I didn't know you were here until the night of that quaint little picnic. By the way, your gentlemen friends send their regards," he said. "Roy was quite surprised to see you. Almost as much as you were to see him, I'd gather."

Journey froze as Hank stepped closer. "I won't bore you with details of my premature obituary. But I'll share what plans I have for us here."

"I won't help you, Hank. I didn't then, and I'm not now. There is no *us.*" She edged back but not fast enough to escape Hank's grasp. Her arm twinged as he squeezed and jerked her forward.

"You've not willingly helped me, that's true, Maura." His stale breath hung close to her face. "Or should I say, *Journey?*"

"Journey Smith. Maura Baines died the day I thought you did. There's nothing I can do for you, Hank. Ride on and leave me be." She raised her chin, trying to look him in the eye. An icy glare met hers and she flinched. He'd been cruel, but generally his gaze had been dulled with liquor. Not now. His sobriety somehow made him more frightening.

Hank's hollow laugh echoed on the wind. "Oh, I don't think so. You have a delightful setup in this town. You owe me, Maura. You are still my wife, the woman who murdered me."

She jerked her hand from his grasp, stepping out of his reach. "They think you're dead, back in Georgia?"

"Didn't you?" Hank smiled. "Roy convinced the authorities that I'd met my untimely demise at the hands of my beloved. Alas," he said, his face a mask of feigned sorrow, "such a tragic story. It even made the newspaper. But then, you've made some papers of your own."

"I protected myself, Hank. If you were any kind of decent man, none of this would have happened. I never meant to hurt you but was never sorry I had, until now."

Hank shook his head. Waves of hair slid over his shoulders, longer than she remembered. "Such talk… I'm loath to consider what your new minister friend would think to hear you. It'd be a shame to change his perception, when he seems so fond of you."

"He's the preacher here, that's all. He doesn't trust me as it is," she said.

"What about that lawman? I'm thinking he'd be interested to find he had a wanted woman within his very grasp."

"He's the woman's nephew, and he's back in Virginia City. I'm not his concern now."

"Working for his dear aunt makes you his concern. Would Miss Rose enjoy the fact she employs a criminal? Would she keep it quiet?"

"There's nothing tying me here, Hank. I got away from you once, and I can do it again."

He stepped forward, open palm out. She flinched, but his coarse fingers only caressed her cheek, then smacked her lightly. "What a shame if this town lost their pastor and Miss Rose in one fell swoop. And so close to Christmas."

Journey bit her lip against the tension rising in her chest, glad for the cold that numbed her and kept her focused. Hank was out for blood.

"I understand." She inhaled, filling herself with the icy chill. "Tell me what you want me to do. But after this, leave and never come back. I have a chance at something good here, and you won't take that away from me."

Hank threw back his head and laughed. "Little lady, you are in no position to make demands. But we'll try to keep your part in this simple."

"What do I have to do?"

He shrugged, palms open. "You'll introduce me around town to these good people, find me a job to hold me over until things fall into place."

"How will I explain how I know you? They've helped me, Hank, but they don't trust me. Knowing me means nothing to them. You'd be better off on your own. Why do you have to do this here?"

Hank's hand snagged her coat, jerking her forward. "You'll do as I say." His voice thundered and his gaze flared only inches away from hers.

Journey's breath caught. Then his grip relaxed and his expression softened. "Actually, Roy and I were heading toward Virginia City. It's a wild town, darlin'. We could make a fortune before the law even knew what we were up to."

"So go there. Please, Hank."

He grinned. "But *you* are *here*. And a pretty face is always an asset in my line of work."

She couldn't look at him or get her feet to move. "I won't."

A sneer tightened his features. She retreated under Hank's advance, glancing about her.

"Oh, you'll not find a flatiron so handy as you did in Georgia, Maura. Now it's time to pay the piper. The way I see it, you owe me the two hundred dollars in cash you stole from me. Then there's that little matter of the land deal you ruined for me when I became deceased in the eyes of the law."

She fisted her hands in her coat pockets. Why hadn't she brought the gun and ended it here? "Hank, won't you listen—"

His temper flared. She knew it by the widened eyes, the sharp peaks that arched his eyebrows. She ducked on instinct, but no blow followed this time.

"There's nothing to listen to!" He drew in a deep breath and seemed to compose himself. "We'll start simple. You'll do as I say until we seal the new deal. Then I'll be out of your life for good. I only want my two hundred dollars back."

She shivered, silent, hoping it would be enough for him to assume her agreement.

"Good, good." He drew two fingers over his chin, his smile making her flinch. "So, who will I be, Maura? Uncle Hank, Cousin Hank or your dear old brother?"

It didn't matter to her. The only thing Hank could ever be was trouble.

Chapter Twenty

The ride back to the ranch was long and cold. Wind howled, announcing another dose of snow. Journey latched the door behind her as she escaped into the warmth of the house. Within the comfortable walls of Miss Rose's home, she hoped the blizzard would strike quick and hard. With any luck, Hank would be caught off guard and freeze to death in the abandoned shack.

She shook the tiny balls of snow from her coat and hair, hanging the damp coat by the door, and felt a certain sense of relief, knowing she hadn't killed a man. She wished he weren't here now, but she was innocent of his death, at least.

"Goodness, girl! Come by the fire and get warm. You'll catch your death out there," Miss Rose said. The woman came into the main room from the kitchen using her cane. Her hip must have been bothering her again.

Journey curled up on the davenport after removing her damp boots to dry by the fire. "The snow came up so fast."

Miss Rose drew her rocker closer and pushed her chair into a gentle sway with the tip of her cane. "That's the way winter works out here. Everything can change from sunny

and warm to downright blizzardlike within a few hours."
Her voice sounded raspy, but she smiled, leaning her head
against the high back of the rocker. "It makes me so glad
you decided to stay with me this winter."

"When the wind blows like that, I'm glad to be indoors."
Journey leaned toward Miss Rose. "Are you feeling all
right?"

"It's this winter air getting into my bones. I'll be all
right. How about you?"

Journey plucked a strand of thread from her dress.
"What do you mean?"

"How well do you know him?"

"Who?" She jerked her head to the door, as if she'd
heard something.

"I hoped you would tell me. Maybe I should ask, is he
the man you thought he was?"

Journey edged forward. "No," she said. "He's not the
man I thought he was. What did Zane tell you?"

"Nothing. He said you'd let us know if there was anything we had to worry about," Miss Rose said. "So you
don't know that man?"

She breathed deeply and stared at the woman, who had
stopped rocking to fasten her tiny round blue eyes on her.
"I didn't say that. I guess no one is really who they seem."

Miss Rose's expression said she didn't agree with that
statement. But instead of saying something, she closed
her eyes and began to rock, her lips moving slightly. It was
strange, not to mention disconcerting, the way the woman
would drop suddenly into these silent prayers and pleas.

"I'll work it out. Don't worry about me."

Miss Rose's eyes snapped open and the rocker stopped.
She smiled, that sweet smile that hid the strength of character beneath. "I'm not worrying. And neither can you.

God's looking out for you, dear, whether you want Him to or not. He sent you to me to help you know that."

"You don't know what a mess I've made of things."

"I don't need to," Miss Rose insisted. "He already does."

By the end of the week, the air had warmed enough to take Miss Rose into town. They rode without talking, soaking in the bright sun overhead, enjoying the chance to be out-of-doors.

She dropped off Miss Rose at Norwood's Mercantile for a visit and supplies. When she helped the woman clear the wagon wheel, Miss Rose gripped her arm. "Go on, Journey. I know you're itching to move about. I'll be a while." Miss Rose patted her arm and moved up the steps.

Journey smiled, eager to slip away and stretch her legs. The open spaces gave her a sense of freedom, but towns provided the reality—she couldn't forget that she wasn't free, not truly. She walked along the boards pounded into the slush, past the handful of businesses along the main street.

The wind blew, sending a shiver up her spine. She pulled the collar of her coat tightly about her neck and quickened her stride.

"I wondered when you'd make it into town."

She stopped at the gruff voice at her ear. "What do you want, Hank?"

"Darlin'," he said, snatching her hand into his own, "I thought I made that clear. This seems like the perfect opportunity for you to introduce me around town. Let's go."

She tugged her fingers free. Doc Ferris caught her eye and nodded a greeting as he walked by. She forced a smile in return and ducked her head. "Not now, Hank. Don't worry, I'll set things up. Give me some time to make the arrangements."

Hank bowed his long frame over her and she shrunk back. "There aren't any arrangements to be made. We'll go back to that quaint little shop, and you can announce your good fortune in meeting your cousin Hank in this speck of a town. What are the odds, really?"

"It would be best if—"

Hank laughed outright. "My dear, we both know you were never the thinker in this relationship. We'll do this my way."

She jerked as he whispered in her ear. "We wouldn't want your friends to suffer because you denied them a chance to cash in on a valuable business venture, right?"

She swung back but couldn't break his hold on her wrist. Grinding her teeth, she struggled, then relaxed before her tears fell. "I'll introduce you, but that's it, Hank. I can't lie to these people."

His heavy hand pushed her ahead. She stumbled but caught herself and tilted her chin as she walked on.

"That's it, Maura," he whispered. "Always the proud one. You just concern yourself with my presentation. We'll discuss how deep your commitment is to this deal as we go along."

He threw an arm around her shoulders, and she stiffened with memories. "It'll be like the old days, Beautiful. Who knows? We were always looking for that one big strike. Maybe this is it. A new beginning for us."

"There is no *us,* Hank. Not now, not ever. The only big strike I looked for was the next one coming from your fist. No, if I do this for you, we're through. For good this time." She strode ahead, wrapping her arms around herself. A few introductions, and she'd be rid of Hank Baines for good.

* * *

Zane watched the door. He had felt twitchy ever since Miss Rose walked in without Journey at her side. Ten minutes passed, fifteen—he slid from the counter where he sat and picked up his coat.

He breathed deeply when the door opened and Journey finally poked her head through. The bell jangled in announcement. But the ease lasted only until he saw the dark form saunter in behind her.

Zane caught Journey's glance as her brown eyes flickered around the room, and she started when she saw him. He leaned against the counter, arms crossed.

Miss Rose broke the silence. "You're back sooner than I expected, Journey."

The tall man standing behind her stepped forward. "Excuse her, ma'am. I believe she's in shock. We're just so surprised—"

"Journey?" Zane stepped closer, reaching for her.

She gestured toward Hank. "I—I'd like to, to introduce Hank Baines."

Zane's stomach clenched. "You know him?"

The tall man stepped forward, tucking long black hair behind his ear and stretching a hand toward Zane. "I'm Miss Smith's—"

"Old family acquaintance," Journey filled in.

Excited questions hummed through the store as Abby and Miss Rose swarmed Journey. Zane straightened his shoulders and took the offered hand. The man's mustache twitched and he glanced around the mercantile with a look that reminded Zane of a rabid wolf he'd tracked years ago. Cunning. Cold.

"Fortunate you should meet Journey here. Are you just passing through?" he asked.

Baines stroked his mustache. Zane wondered if he checked it to be sure it hadn't fallen off. "I'm here on business. It was sheer luck that put Journey in my path this day."

Zane wondered whose luck he meant. "I see. And how are you acquainted?"

Silence echoed as the women quieted. Zane stared at the man but felt similar stares from Abby and Miss Rose aimed in Hank's direction. Journey bowed her head behind Hank, unable to meet his gaze.

"I've known her family for years," he said. "I've been in a position to help Journey on a number of occasions. Why, most folk assumed we'd be married by now." He chuckled. "But I think of her as my younger sister. I hope you'll consider me part of her family." Hank stretched back and grabbed Journey, pulling her to his side. Zane tried to catch her eye, but she stared at the other women and held herself from his embrace.

"I'm sure Journey will be glad to have a familiar face here. What a shame you missed her when you stopped by the ranch for directions," Zane said.

A dark look crossed Hank's face, gone as fast as it'd come. "Why, to think that we might have been reunited all that much sooner!" Hank squeezed her shoulder, holding her like a possession under his control.

Not if he could help it, Zane thought. "Where will you be staying?"

Miss Rose raised her gloved hand. "You're welcome to bed down in the loft of my barn."

"He'll stay with me," Zane said.

Miss Rose quirked her eyebrow at him, but there was no way he would let Baines stay with them out there alone.

"My," Baines said. "So kind of you all to offer. But, as

I am here on business, I'll be staying out at the old Allen homestead."

"That place has been abandoned for years," Abby said. "Deplorable condition."

"True. But I own it now, so it's no longer abandoned, and I'm well-satisfied to stay there." Hank spoke to Abby, but his gaze didn't waver from Zane's.

"That's a large parcel," Zane said. "How'd you come by that?"

Hank smirked, hugging Journey. "An unusually boring chain of events, I assure you."

"Well, tell us all about it when you come for supper Friday night." Miss Rose made the offer before Zane could stop her.

Hank hadn't stepped out of the shadows long enough for Miss Rose to recognize him from Thanksgiving. It was the only reason Zane could think of for her to make such an offer. But couldn't she feel the tension in Journey?

"How kind. I welcome the opportunity," Hank said. He pressed his lips to Journey's head. "I'll see you Friday, then. Now, if you'll excuse me," he added, bowing to the ladies and nodding to Zane, "I must get back to my property. Journey, my dear, I can't tell you how glad I am to have found you out here after all this time."

Journey didn't acknowledge Hank's departure with anything more than a slight stoop of her frame. Zane slipped closer and laid a hand on her shoulder, softly, fearing she would bolt and run. He stared at her and noticed how her hair kinked tightly on either side of her part, regardless of how tightly she pulled it into the low chignon at her neck.

A strong yearning to lean in and kiss her bent head, as Hank Baines had done moments ago, possessed him.

Instead, Zane squared his shoulders and dropped his hand to squeeze her wrist.

Journey peered at him as if she were waking from some strange dream. Her eyebrows curled and tears glazed her eyes, and she blinked hard and turned. "I'll wait for you in the wagon, Miss Rose," she said, walking out the door.

Zane laid a hand on the older woman's shoulder to keep her from giving chase. "I'll go. You finish up here." From the expression on her face, he'd surprised her as much as he had himself.

Did he have any business stepping in? Journey had made it plain she didn't want his help. But that was before Baines made an appearance. Before she was more wary of someone else than she was of him.

Zane stopped short at the door. "Oh, and, Miss Rose—"

"I'll see you Friday evening as well, Zane."

He leaned down to kiss her tiny gray head. "I'll see you Friday evening, then. I hope you're making chicken. You know it's my favorite."

Journey knew he would follow. Not Miss Rose, not Abby, but Zane. She squeezed the reins and stared ahead, trying to control her breath. The smell of Hank filled her senses, and she rubbed her nose with the back of her palm.

Zane stayed on the sidewalk for a few moments, and Journey wondered if he waited for his sake or hers. She heard him walk toward her, knowing the easy, sure movements of his broad frame. He was nothing like Hank.

She stiffened at the thought. Could that be? She'd been so fooled by Hank in the beginning. His concern had seemed real, but now she knew everything he'd done for her had benefited him in some way.

But Zane had nothing to gain, and his offer of help

would only cost him. Yet he wanted to do something. She'd seen it in his eyes in the store. It's the only reason he'd be standing here now. Journey kept her glance strained forward, willing Miss Rose to join her so they could go back to the ranch.

"Journey?" Zane's voice was low, quiet.

She couldn't look at him. "Does Miss Rose need help loading her things?"

"She'll be out in a minute," he said. "Mind if I join you?"

Journey slid away from him on the springboard. She breathed in, trapping the cold air in her lungs and wishing the stale scent of Hank's cigar didn't cling to her clothing.

Zane said nothing for a full minute. She scratched her knuckles. "Is there something you wanted?"

"The Lord works in mysterious ways."

"Pardon?"

The wagon creaked and she turned. Zane leaned a shoulder on the high side of the box, facing forward. "Strong coincidence, running into your old friend in a place like Walten."

"He isn't a friend." She sighed. "I knew him a long time ago."

Zane's gray eyes scanned her face and she turned away. Let him think what he wanted.

"Do you like it here, Journey?"

She hadn't thought about it before, one way or the other. She smoothed the bunched fabric of her coat and loosed her hold on the reins, thankful to see Miss Rose easing her way out the doorway. It would take Zane's attention away from the tears that welled unbidden and clogged her view. She squinted and fumbled in her pockets.

"Journey?"

She gasped and bit her upper lip, searching the horizon. "More than I expected," she whispered. She felt a warm hand on her forearm even through her sleeve and turned to face him. "For all the good it's done me, Zane. More than I expected."

He squeezed her arm with a gentle touch. "We've been known to have that effect." He smiled up at her, winking in the glaring sun moving low in the sky. The light made his eyes reflect blue. "I don't pretend to know where you're coming from, Journey, or what kind of ghosts you've got hounding you. But here's as good a place as any to put them to rest. There's plenty of folks willing to help if you'll let us."

Journey parted her lips, wanting to protest, but he walked away before she could. Who was she fooling? Right now, all she knew is that it certainly wasn't Zane.

Chapter Twenty-One

Journey pulled the collar of her coat around her neck and replaced the pitchfork along the wall. Although the snow held and the sun shone, a bitter wind blew over the mountains from the northwest. The muted landscape and darkening skies had deceived her eyes, looking from the window of the fire-warmed house. Out here, the wind shook the stalls and whistled through the rafters of the barn. But the horses were fed, brushed and blanketed in the cozy darkness for the night. As a child, she would often sneak into the livery to stroke the horses' noses or treat them to a bit of carrot or apple she'd scrounged. She longed now to lie down in the hay with the heavy barn scents that gave some measure of comfort.

Instead, she returned to the house. The fire's calming warmth would die as soon as Hank arrived. Journey was shocked when Miss Rose had insisted he come for supper. Hank, of course, had been thrilled. He no doubt saw the invitation as a prime opportunity to endear himself to the woman.

"I've seen how people defer to her aged wisdom," Hank had announced. "And I've inquired about her, discreetly, through the town. She's rich as a troll, I tell you, and she carries a lot of weight around here. We'll seek her out first."

Zane would be coming. Journey held an uneasy hope that his presence would keep Hank from embarrassing himself, and her as well. She climbed the stairs to her room, peeled off her barn dress and washed at the basin. Her navy dress slipped over still-damp skin, and she breathed deeply, one hand at her waist to quell the jittery swirls in her stomach.

A quick knock at the door startled her. "Guests are here, dear," Miss Rose called, interrupting her anxiety.

Journey forced herself down the stairs to answer the door, stepping back as Hank's tall form filled the doorway. Zane stood behind, his broad frame edged out around Hank's. How could he be so at ease? Hank dwarfed him by a good head, yet Zane looked taller somehow.

"You look lovely," the preacher said, nodding Hank through ahead of him.

"I must agree," Hank added quickly. The words slipped over his lips, aided by the heavy oil shining his mustache. "And you, Mrs. Bishop—you're simply ravishing." He swept his hat off with one hand and grasped Miss Rose's fingers in the other, bowing over it. Journey held her breath, but Hank stopped shy of kissing her hand. Hank always knew exactly where the line was and halted short of it when it suited him.

"Your invitation to this wayfaring stranger is beyond all kindness, ma'am," he said. "I surely hope this doesn't inconvenience you."

Could his accent get any thicker?

Miss Rose's blue eyes shone with a peculiar light. "Company is never an inconvenience, Mr. Baines. Come, let's seat ourselves. Journey has everything ready, so I hope you'll forgive the break in Southern etiquette. I've never stood much on formalities."

The scent of venison mingled with smoke from the fireplace, giving the air of an intimate dinner party. If only it felt that way.

"I'm sure I'll find your social graces as refreshing as your boisterous spirit, Mrs. Bishop. Now, if I might escort you?" Hank tucked her hand into the crook of his elbow and turned toward the table.

Miss Rose nodded and allowed herself to be led. Journey watched them a moment before an elbow nudged her side. "Guess that leaves you and me," Zane said, mocking Hank's drawl. A broad smile of even teeth filled his face.

Though her arms felt like wood, Journey forced them to bend around his. Zane patted her hand with his free one and she started. The warmth of his touch gave a comfort she hadn't expected. She looked up, and he went on, his voice soft and deep.

"We'll follow your lead. Let us know what you want. He's your friend—acquaintance. But if you find he's not the man you think he is, we're here. Remember that." His voice lowered, and his gray eyes shone with care.

She looked ahead, forcing her feet to move and fighting to keep her tears at bay. He had summed up the entire problem. Hank was exactly the man she knew he was, and he was about to ruin everything.

Zane led Journey into the kitchen, which was warm and inviting with wondrous scents filling even the corners. With a sharp pang, he remembered the cozy evening meals Sarah would have waiting for him on cool fall evenings. He knew, somewhere in the far corners of his mind, that most memories of his marriage were colored a little brighter than they might have been had Sarah survived the fire. But it was no exaggeration that they had rarely fought, and it was a fact that her brightness tempered the heaviness and disappointments he faced as a minister. Often now he found himself eating something cooked to less than perfection with his own limited skills from a battered tin plate someone had donated after the fire took everything.

He glanced at Journey, her fine features puckered with tension, face pale as he helped her to her seat. How many home-cooked meals had she shared with anyone before arriving on Miss Rose's doorstep?

Sitting down beside her, he looked at Hank, calm and arrogant and shifty. He hated the feeling in his gut that told him to be wary when it came with no real proof.

Journey held herself stiffly, making herself as small as she could on the chair beside him. While Hank seated Miss Rose at her customary place at the head of the table, Zane touched Journey's elbow, running his fingers along her sleeve to end with a light squeeze to her hand.

She started, fear clouding her gaze for an instant, as if he had woken her from a deep sleep. Her fine eyebrows curled, then smoothed. She relaxed, even if it was forced, and an uncertain smile touched her lips.

He wanted to tell her everything would be fine, that they'd get through this together with the Lord's help. He wanted to keep his hand over her tiny one until she believed it.

But Miss Rose cleared her throat delicately, breaking the moment, and he felt the weight of Hank's heated glance. He smiled back, then again at Journey, hoping he conveyed the thought anyway.

He squeezed her hand again. "Let's bow our heads in thanks and ask the Lord's blessing."

* * *

Journey etched a polite smile on her face, not wanting to give Hank the satisfaction of seeing the fear she felt. She had forgotten how accomplished he was at spinning a tale.

"And so I told her, 'I beg your pardon, but I do believe that's your canary.'"

He could entertain even the dourest of souls with that story. She might have laughed herself had she not heard it so many times or had her stomach not been churning. For now, Hank mastered the conversation. And it wasn't just humor. He could compliment with all the necessary doses of sincerity and affect an attentive ear to the hostess. Yes, he made an excellent dinner guest. Hank knew his game.

"But Journey insisted we offer the poor woman a few morsels before sending her on her way. That's just how she is." Hank patted Journey's arm. "Always thinking of someone else."

She flinched and looked away. That "poor woman" lost everything to one of Hank's hustles. Journey had pleaded for him not to turn her and her young son out in the street. But he'd refused and blackened her eye for the suggestion. That's just the way *he* was.

"That comes as no surprise to us," Miss Rose said, wiping her mouth with a cloth.

Hank certainly endeared himself to her, Journey thought. Maybe she shouldn't hold it against herself for getting mixed up with him in the first place. She'd been so young then, it was no wonder she found him witty, charming and attractive. Even now, he might accomplish it if she didn't know him better.

Zane managed to laugh at all the appropriate places, but Journey sensed his stare throughout the evening. At least he wasn't buying into Hank's facade. Was he?

Miss Rose surprised her. The woman laughed until tears streamed down her wrinkled cheeks. Where had that fiery staunchness gone?

It seemed Hank's scheme would be easy, yet harder than she thought. With Miss Rose charmed by Hank, all Journey would have to do was feed her ideas. Perhaps Miss Rose wouldn't be dissuaded if she tried. From experience Journey knew that once the elderly woman took a shine to a person, she didn't give it up easily. After all, Miss Rose had taken her in without so much as a how-do-you-do and had expected so little in return. No, Hank would have an easy time of it with Miss Rose on his side.

Journey didn't realize she had sighed out loud.

Irritation sparked in Hank's eyes, but he covered it by pulling out his pocket watch. "My, my—the hour is getting late. You really must excuse my lack of manners, Mrs. Bishop. It's been so long since I've enjoyed such fine company, and the venison was cooked to perfection."

Miss Rose nudged her chair back when he stood. "Thank you, Mr. Baines. It's been an entertaining evening for me as well. I'm sorry we've monopolized your time. We left little opportunity for you to get reacquainted with Journey."

"Not to worry, ma'am. I've taken over quite a lucrative land development opportunity in Walten. I'm sure Journey and I will have plenty of occasions to revisit old times."

"Your business is in brokering land deals?" Zane asked.

"Uh—Hank managed several kinds of business ventures in Savannah," Journey said, hoping she didn't choke. At least she could say that honestly. Although Hank's victims wouldn't have seen his schemes that way.

Zane's eyebrows creased in disbelief. "That seems like a stretch for a little town like ours."

Hank's brown eyes gleamed in the lantern light of the parlor. "Now, that's small thinking, my good man. Think of the proximity to the gold strikes in and around Virginia City."

"You think we're in the same vein?" Zane asked, refolding his napkin.

"Yes, and I have maps to prove my claim, sir."

"My, that would be something," Miss Rose said.

Journey stared at her crumpled napkin. "Hank has been involved in similar projects in the past. He is experienced." Another truth, but her heart twisted. "*If* there is a strike to be made." Zane nodded, but his gaze never wavered.

"Virginia City's grown too big for its britches," Miss Rose said. "Shooting and stealing are out of control."

Hank extended his arm across the table to Miss Rose, as if to offer comfort. "I agree. That's why the townspeople need to have a say. Everyone buys in, creating one collective claim. The people elect a board to manage the mining process, and everyone takes a share in the profit."

"It sounds like a plan worthy of consideration." Miss Rose smiled as she looked around the table.

Journey glanced at each face, trying to read the thoughts behind each one.

Zane leaned forward. "And that will keep the lawless element away?"

Hank laughed as if a child had shared a joke. "It's not a difficult thing to jump a claim defended by one man. It's quite another to try with a whole town involved." He paused and gazed around the table. Journey knew he read them and was trying to decide whether to forge on or stop while he was ahead.

"Why would you want to do that for this town?" Zane asked, eyebrows furrowed over his gray eyes.

"I'd gain a share, of course, but it gives us all a great opportunity. I trust I can count on your support in this."

Zane choked on the water he'd sipped. "Whoa, hold on there. I'd have more questions I'd want answered before I endorsed this."

"Naturally," Hank said. He didn't bat an eye, but Journey saw the tension mounting in the deepening creases on his forehead. "I can provide all sorts of maps and documents for your perusal."

Zane smiled. "That'd be mighty convenient. But I prefer to check into such matters firsthand. I'm sure a businessman like yourself can appreciate that."

Journey could see Hank's face grow hot even in the waning light of evening. She'd never seen anyone put him in his place so calmly and firmly. She looked at Zane, his thick hair blocking a full view of his eyes, but she could tell by the set of his jaw and shoulders that the matter was settled.

"You must forgive me." Hank leaned forward in his chair. "I get a bit overzealous when I see such potential. I won't spoil our time with all this talk of business. I'd hate to wear my welcome too thin. After all, it's been such a lovely evening." His words were for Miss Rose, but his fiery gaze bored into Zane.

"Then we must do this again sometime," Miss Rose said. "Maybe when business is not quite so prevalent in your mind."

Journey moved to begin clearing the table. Relief washed through her, allowing a small smile to ease her face. If Hank expected Miss Rose to jump into an investment opportunity right away, maybe he'd lose patience and look for an easier mark.

But Hank was not to be cut off so quickly. "I'd be happy

Dear Reader,

Because you've chosen to read
one of our fine Love Inspired®
Historical romance novels,
we'd like to say "thank you!"
And, as a **special** way to thank
you, we've selected two more
of the books you love so well,
and two surprise gifts to send
you — absolutely **FREE!**

Please enjoy them with our
compliments...

Jean Gordon

Editor,
Love Inspired
Historical

HOW TO VALIDATE YOUR
EDITOR'S FREE GIFTS!
"THANK YOU"

1 Peel off the FREE GIFTS SEAL from front cover. Place it in the space provided at right. This automatically entitles you to receive two free books and two exciting surprise gifts.

2 Send back this card and you'll get 2 Love Inspired® Historical books. These books are worth over $10, but are yours absolutely FREE!

3 There's no catch. You're under no obligation to buy anything. We charge nothing—ZERO—for your first shipment. And you don't have to make any minimum number of purchases—not even one!

4 We call this line Love Inspired Historical because every other month you'll receive books that are filled with inspirational historical romance. This is a new series filled with engaging stories of romance, adventure and faith set in historical periods from biblical times to World War II. You'll like the convenience of getting them delivered to your home well before they are in stores. And you'll love our discount prices, too!

5 We hope that after receiving your free books you'll want to remain a subscriber. But the choice is yours—to continue or cancel, anytime at all! So why not take us up on our invitation, with no risk of any kind. You'll be glad you did!

6 And remember . . . just for validating your Editor's Free Gifts Offer, we'll send you 2 books and 2 gifts, *ABSOLUTELY FREE!*

YOURS FREE!

We'll send you two fabulous surprise gifts (worth about $10) absolutely FREE, simply for accepting our no-risk offer!

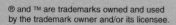

The Editor's "Thank You" Free Gifts Include:

- ● Two inspirational historical romance books
- ● Two exciting surprise gifts

▲ DETACH AND MAIL CARD TODAY! ▲

YES!

PLACE
FREE GIFTS
SEAL
HERE

I have placed my Editor's "thank you" Free Gifts seal in the space provided above. Please send me the 2 FREE books and 2 FREE gifts for which I qualify. I understand that I am under no obligation to purchase anything further, as explained on the opposite page.

302 IDL ESXN   102 IDL ESXC

Cheyenne	Kidd
FIRST NAME	LAST NAME

4240 Crocos Rd
ADDRESS

	Waterford
APT.#	CITY

Mi	48328
STATE/PROV.	ZIP/POSTAL CODE

Thank You!

Order online at:

www.LoveInspiredBooks.com

Steeple
Hill®

(LIH-EC-08)   © 2008 STEEPLE HILL BOOKS

Steeple Hill Reader Service — Here's How It Works:

to talk with you about the development at a more opportune time."

"Miss Rose could tell you a few things about this town and the land here, Mr. Baines," Zane said. "She's lived here longer than just about anyone."

"Then I will take that offer, Mrs. Bishop, to enjoy your hospitality again." Journey had underestimated Hank's persistence.

She waited for Miss Rose to extend the invitation to call her "Miss Rose," as most of the community did. But it never came. She continued stacking plates while Miss Rose and Zane led Hank to the door.

"Journey, my dear?" Hank's voice cut through her relief at his departure. "If you'd be so kind as to walk me out?"

Her throat tightened. So this was it: the next step revealed, courtesy of Hank's controlling mind. She turned and nodded, brushing imaginary crumbs from her bodice.

"Hand her my cape, Zane," Miss Rose said. "And don't be out long, dear. I want to speak with you before I retire."

Bless the woman. The departure would be quick now that Miss Rose had given her an excuse.

Zane grabbed the wrap from the peg, and Journey shivered as he settled it over her shoulders, his hands lingering a moment. She turned and saw his eyebrows creased over questioning gray eyes. She shook her head once, cutting off any voice he might put to his concern. He couldn't understand all the stakes. No matter how much she wanted him to. Besides, she was only seeing Hank off. Minutes, that's all. She'd spent years with him—what were a few moments more?

But the closing door thudded with a finality that frightened her, as if she'd just created a barrier she could never cross again.

Chapter Twenty-Two

Journey tugged the heavy wool cape around her neck, burying her hands deep within the thick folds. The wind had died, with only the cold remaining.

Hank stepped off the porch and motioned for her to follow. She avoided the hand he extended to help her down the stairs and walked behind. He didn't force the issue, and she allowed herself a deep breath. She stopped in the yard, halfway between the porch and the post by the barn where he'd tied his horse.

"You might as well get on with it, Hank," she said, mustering any scrap of bravado she could lay claim to. "I can't be out here all night."

He tightened the cinches of his saddle. "Of course not, my dear. We can't have you coming down with something now. We're at a critical juncture."

She flinched. "Which is?"

He didn't bother to face her. "I've laid the groundwork, but Mrs. Bishop is a tougher sell than I'd anticipated. You'll need to convince her to buy into this deal, Maura."

"Journey," she whispered.

Hank turned, loosening the lead and walking toward

her. "That's right—Journey. Miss Journey Smith, formerly known as Maura Sojourner Baines, formerly known as *my wife,* currently wanted for murder."

"Please, keep your voice down."

Hank swooped closer. She shivered at the icy fingers of air that pierced her cape.

"Of course, my dear. Keep things nice and quiet. We can't have your new beau finding out he's chasing after a married woman, a murderer and a two-bit—"

"Don't say it, Hank. I never was that and we both know it. And Zane's not my beau, I told you." She glanced back at the house. Warm light glowed from the windows, in stark contrast to the chill outside.

"You may not think so. He may not think so. But he's interested, Journey. A little lost lamb, you are. Pastor Thompson wants to help you find your way. And truly," Hank said, stretching his hand out to spring a curl by her cheek, "you can't blame him, darlin'. My, you are still as beautiful as the first day I saw you in that shop in Savannah."

Every muscle tensed as he touched her. Her face ached from it. She couldn't breathe. Her feet refused the command her mind screamed to run.

Hank backed off. The accent he had worked so hard to cultivate eased, too. "They weren't all bad times, Maura—Journey. Not all of them."

The moment passed, leaving Journey to wonder if she'd heard him at all.

"I'm going out of town for a few days—business, you know," he said, the accent back in place. "I should return by the end of next week, in a few days. You have until then to convince your Miss Rose to buy into this once-in-a-lifetime opportunity. And by all means, let the good reverend know he can get in on this, too. He runs a small horse trade, and there's money in that. More importantly, his congregation has to be convinced to invest as well. After all, who would attempt to dupe a minister?" He laughed and his teeth gleamed, like a wolf's.

"But what if he won't?"

"He has feelings for you. He hasn't sorted it all out yet, but he wants to trust you. Use that."

Journey shook her head. How could she take advantage that way?

Hank's clenched fist drew her attention and she ducked. He chuckled. "I see we still have an understanding."

She glanced back at the house. She'd been out too long already. "Can't you see that this will ruin me? I could have a place here, maybe even a real home. I can't do this. I— I won't."

"I'm sorry, my dear." His voice grew gruff as he swung atop his horse and edged it to stop at her side. He leaned down so close that she could smell the stench of his breath. "I didn't mean to imply you had a choice in this matter."

She pinched her lips together. "I want to be left alone. I'm not helping you anymore, Hank. Hit me if you're so inclined." She drew back. "Turn me in if you want. There's nothing you can say or do this time that will change my mind."

He straightened in the saddle and gathered the reins. "You've been many things, my dear, but never foolish. Don't ruin this."

She glanced away, looking over the snowy waves of bluffs to the west. Would the fear in her eyes give her away?

A jerk on the chin drew her eyes back to Hank's, too close and too cold, like black stones. "And don't even imagine you'll get away again, Maura. Not like the first time. I found you without even trying." He pinched her jaw in his fist. "Believe me. If I have to hunt you down, I will. And the reunion won't be nearly so joyous the next time."

She tore herself from his grip with a shake. "You do what you have to. But you'll do it without me."

"How noble you've become! Perhaps I can't force you to cooperate." He pulled his coat tighter and stared at the skyline with a faint smile. "But I can make you wish you had. Such a fine young minister. Such a shame for him to be out on his own so much, checking on his congregation, shepherding the fine people of this community." Hank clucked his tongue and his shadowed form shook in the darkness.

"Whatever would they do without him?" He paused. "Remember, I gave you a chance to protect your new friends."

He galloped off, dark coat, hair and horse blending in with the black horizon. She blinked back tears. Minutes passed before her frozen mind compelled her into the warmth of the house. Once Hank had his way, only coldness would remain.

Zane raked his fingers through his hair, peering out the window into the darkness, and chuffed out a breath.

"She's only on the other side of the door, Zane. What could happen?"

He turned to see Miss Rose hobble into the great room, having stacked the supper dishes for Journey in the kitchen. "Hard to tell. Everything's been flying like robins caught in an early snowstorm ever since she rode into town."

"You have been spending a fair amount of time keeping

your eye on her. There's no one who could fault your ministerial concern for her, but you've done what you could. You have no further obligation toward her." Miss Rose settled onto the couch. "Some folks are determined to cause themselves trouble."

"You're the last person I would've thought would ask me to forget about her problems." He sat in the rocker and pulled it closer to her side.

Miss Rose rested her head against the tall cushion, her gray hair pressed wide around it. "I'm not telling you to forget, Zane. Not about Sarah, not about Journey's problems. I just want you to see that your concern is beyond what your job as our minister requires. Journey certainly doesn't expect it. What's more, she doesn't want it."

"She's alone and needs someone to help," he insisted.

"See, even as a boy, if anyone needed someone to come to their defense, you were there. Your mother told me once you gave a boy a black eye for throwing stones at that old stray dog." She smiled. "But now that Hank is here, I would think you'd be happy to pass along the responsibility." Miss Rose closed her eyes.

"What if this is only the start of her problems? That man leaves a bitter taste in my mouth. What if I let her face this trouble alone and it turns out to be more than she can handle? What if the very thing she's running from has found her here?" He leaned forward, tugging his hair and resting his elbows on his knees. "How can I let her stand against him by herself?"

"I'm glad to hear you say that. I wouldn't expect anything less." Miss Rose smiled without opening her eyes.

"You don't trust him either?" He raised his head in surprise.

"Not further than I can throw him."

"But—"

"He's entertaining, I'll give him that." She wiggled down into the cushion. "There was nothing false in enjoying his tales. But it doesn't mean I think we should sell the ranch and give him the proceeds. The whole deal smells too sweet—like fruit when it's starting to rot."

Zane rocked back in the chair and boosted himself up, resting his hands at his waist. "I agree. I'm taking a trip to Virginia City the first of next week to see what I can dig up."

Miss Rose opened her eyes and leaned forward, tapping her cane on the floor. "What if you get snowed in? Can't this whole business wait until spring? Mr. Baines won't be pushing anything before Christmas, surely."

"That's the trouble. We need to know what we're dealing with so we can protect Jour—protect the town, before he starts pushing." He stood and walked to the window.

"There's no shame in wanting to protect her," Miss Rose said.

"It's not only her. There's a whole town to consider. What if we're wrong and this is a legitimate offer? Folks around here—"

He turned at the feel of a warm hand on his shoulder. Soft blue eyes met his. "You've been thinking about me, about Sarah, about everybody else but yourself for too long, Zane."

He grasped Miss Rose's hand. "I couldn't help Sarah the night she died. She cried for me, Miss Rose. She cried for me to get out of that house without her, and I did…and she died."

Miss Rose stretched a bony arm around him. "We've gone over this before. You were hurt, too. We could've lost you both. The Lord had other plans."

His breath caught on the hard knot in his chest. "I know that. It's taken a lot of time and a lot of prayers. I still don't understand it, but I know it. But maybe this is my chance. Maybe the Lord needed me here to help Journey, to keep whatever mess Baines is set on bringing to Walten from happening."

Miss Rose gasped, a soft puff of indrawn air. "You think the Lord took Sarah so you'd be more focused on Him, don't you? I wondered why all those young gals at church never caught your eye before now."

"I'm willing to live life as a bachelor if that's what the Lord requires," he said, his voice straining. Surely Miss Rose understood that. But the ache he never had been able to dismiss entirely burned around his heart. "If I had only known before we married, I would've spared her." His breath caught on the ache in his chest, and he rubbed his hand over his face.

"Oh, honey," Miss Rose said, draping a warm arm around him. "I didn't realize. You have to know that God planned that man and woman would help each other to get through this old world together. If ever a woman was created for a man, it was Sarah for you.

"Now, I'm not saying Journey can't fill that job. She's not a suitable choice at the moment, but I don't know what the Lord has in store for the two of you ahead. All I'm saying is you need to let your heart open to the possibilities, not close yourself off because you're afraid."

He faced the window. The two shadowed forms outside drew closer, then suddenly apart. He wondered about their conversation. "All I know is that I have to follow this trail until it forks or flat out stops. I'm not being stubborn. I've prayed and I believe I'm where God would have me."

"In that case, my boy," Miss Rose said, pushing herself away with a firm grip on his forearm, "let me pack some biscuits for you to take along. I'll send a wire to Reed so he knows to expect you. Whatever storm's brewing, I'll feel better knowing both of my boys are working it out together. And I'll be praying for you both."

He focused on the window, watching Journey's shadow pull away from the other. Fear seemed very real any time she was near Hank. Zane knew she needed help.

But the question never stopped nagging at the back of his mind: what if she was fooling them all?

Chapter Twenty-Three

Zane nudged his horse closer to the wooden boards along the wide street. Buildings rose up and pressed in on him, blocking his view of the mountains surrounding Virginia City.

A stiff wind blew through him, but the sun shone overhead, trying its best to offer a little heat. He pulled his sheepskin coat closer around his neck and drew a slow breath. After two frigid nights on the trail, he wanted nothing more than to stretch out in a soft bed and sleep until the light of day woke him.

Virginia City had grown more civilized in the years since the gold strike in 1862. The town had sprung up overnight, but there had been over a hundred murders in the first two years. Now, Wallace Street's main thoroughfare boasted three churches, a fine courthouse and several good hotels. The town had tamed considerably.

Two cowboys slammed out from a saloon, trading blows and rolling from the sidewalk. Zane sidestepped the men and crossed to the other side of the road. *Well, maybe it's not totally tamed yet.*

First things first, he thought. Let Reed know he'd arrived, then stable his horse.

Moving along the mile-long street toward the courthouse, he stopped at the sturdy building of stone that sat next to it. Reed met him outside, the word SHERIFF inscribed in block letters above the door where he stood.

"Well, what brings you out this way, Pastor?" Reed slid his hat back with one hand. The other held a rolled wad of handbills. "Or should I say, 'horse trader'? I'm guessing it's only one or the other that would bring you to town in this weather."

Zane joined the older man on the open porch. "Guess you could say neither this time. Or maybe a little of both."

"Come on in and set yourself by the stove a bit, then."

Zane tramped into the warm office, guided by Reed's handshake and a welcoming clasp on the shoulder. "I trust Aunt Rose is well."

"Fit as a fiddle. She'll outlive us all."

"If spunk will do it, then I'm sure she will. Have a seat," he offered.

Zane pulled his hat down and drew his fingers through his matted hair. "I need to find somewhere to stay, get settled in. But I figured I'd talk to you first, let you know I was in town."

"Aunt Rose sent a telegram." He reached into the narrow front drawer of his desk and pulled out a pale yellow paper. "Zane arrives Wednesday STOP Watch for him STOP Love Aunt Rose STOP."

Zane laughed and tugged his gloves from his frozen hands. "That's like her." His fingers soaked up the heat, making them tingle.

"I figure this must be pretty significant if you're coming here this time of year." Reed handed him a steaming mug of coffee from the stove. The scent roused Zane from the drowsiness that'd crept up after the long, cold ride. The sheriff pulled up a chair and propped his boots on the low stool at his feet, tipping back and clasping his hands behind his head. "How long are you planning to stay?"

"I head back tomorrow if I'm to make it for Sunday service." Zane gulped the rich coffee, melting his insides. He hunched over the steaming mug, digging his toes into his boots as they began to thaw and burn.

"So this must be some kind of important," Reed said again. He tilted back a little farther and scratched his jaw. "What's on your mind?"

"What have you heard about more gold strikes along Alder Gulch?"

"The stories turn out better than the strikes, for the most part. But I suppose the luck is still fair. More folks are arriving down along the way. Especially since we've settled down a mite. But I'm guessing you're looking for something more specific."

"Have you heard about the likelihood of a strike near Walten?"

Reed laughed, a deep, rich sound. "Wouldn't that be something? So many folks moved out to get away from all the trouble gold's caused here. I guess stranger things have happened, but I'd be surprised if the line played out that far. Why do you ask? You figuring on going into prospecting?"

Zane shook his head. "Not hardly. We had a visitor come to town who claims he has maps that prove there's gold right near Walten. He's talking of selling shares to the people to set up a gold-mining company of sorts. Everyone pays in, everyone shares in the profits." He followed Reed's gaze to the fire, watching him consider the information.

"Do the people seem inclined to buy in?"

"It hasn't been set out before everyone yet. I know he wants to get a few of us on board first. Me, your aunt, people who have been around long enough to have some say."

Reed straightened in his seat. "He picked the wrong crowd then. Gold nuggets have never been what you've searched for."

"But what if it's there? Word's bound to get out. The man says if the town sets up as one big claim, it'll keep lawlessness from taking over our town." Zane rubbed his tired eyes with the heel of his hand. "You remember what this place was like a few years ago, Reed. I'd hate to see that come to Walten."

The sheriff stared at the fire. "Not much better now," he murmured. "No, I'd hate to see that, too. But do you think his plan would stop it?"

"Let's just say, I don't think the man would have a problem with a criminal element coming into the town. In fact, I get the feeling he would be the forerunner."

A pause lengthened before Reed spoke. "Are you going to give me a name?"

He stretched, feeling each ripple of his spine, and cracked his knuckles, absentmindedly thumbing an old rope burn.

Reed cleared his throat and his boots pounded the floor as he stood. "Does this have something to do with Journey?"

Zane jerked his head up. "What makes you say that?"

"Never mind. You just answered my question. Aunt Rose has been concerned," Reed said, walking over to fill his mug from the coffeepot on the stove. Zane waved off the offer of a refill.

The sheriff sank to his seat and curled his lips over the

bitter drink. "It doesn't surprise me that she'd make a difference. Listen, Zane, I can't help you if you don't tell me what you know. Especially if Journey's involved."

"I don't know that she is."

"But you suspect—"

"I suspect she could be in danger if she is. She's been acting peculiar lately. Ever since this Baines fellow found her."

"Found her?" Reed asked.

"Remember the stranger from Thanksgiving? Turns out Journey knows him. I knew she was running from something. Turns out it's a someone. They claim he's an old family friend. Well, he claims that and she doesn't correct him. She isn't very excited about him being there. I've had colts that had been whipped before I got them that didn't act as skittish as she does." He bent low in his chair, rubbing his temple.

"So she's asking for your help?"

He scratched his eyebrow and grinned. "Not exactly. She'd be happier if I signed up for foreign missions."

Reed laughed and stood to stoke the fire. "I was there, Zane. I saw her, and I don't think you could be further from the truth." He took another gulp of coffee. "What can I do to help?"

"I thought we could look through some old posters."

"You came all this way to look through posters? Why not send a wire?"

"I've seen this guy. I thought it might move things along a bit, in case he hasn't always gone with the same name."

Reed eased back into his seat, rubbing his thick fingers along his lip. "This isn't like you to be so suspicious."

"I know. That makes me even more sure that something's up. I've prayed about this. I believe the Lord sent me here."

"I've never known you to miss on something like this, Zane. But you look done in. Why don't you settle in over at the hotel? Get some hot food in you and come back over after supper to look through the posters."

Zane stretched and stood, swirling the last of the coffee in his cup before draining it down. "You won't get an argument from me. If you could point me in the direction of the livery, I'll untack my horse and get him settled in."

"You'll find it down a piece from the hotel. Tell Beans I sent you."

Zane pulled his heavy coat back on, now toasty from its placement near the roaring fire. His fingers felt stiff as he tugged on his still-damp gloves. Supper sounded good. Sleep sounded better. But too many questions still rumbled in his head, and he'd come for answers. A pale, freckled face framed by tight rings of ruby-brown hair came to mind. Yes, the sooner he figured out her story, the sooner he could put Journey out of his mind.

The wind grew stronger as the sun set. Clouds billowed in overhead, promising more snow. As he walked toward the courthouse, Zane was thankful for the muffler Miss Rose had forced on him before he'd left. The sidewalk changed its width and rise seemingly at will but was easier to walk on than the snowy street.

Passing up the nap for a bath had been a good choice, he decided. The hot water had eased aches he'd gotten from sleeping on the ground that the lumpy bed would not have. *I'm getting soft,* he thought.

The streetlamps had not been lit yet, but inside the jail-house Reed had lanterns burning brightly. They'd need the light if they were going to search through the stack of wanted posters Reed had pulled—an entire year's worth.

His friend turned as he walked in, a pile of papers in one hand, a cup of coffee in the other. "Have a seat, Zane. I figure we might as well start with the most recent posters and work our way back."

Zane took the offered seat with a nod and tipped it back, pulling the first poster closer to the light to study the face drawn on it.

"It might be helpful if I knew what we were looking for," Reed said. "Does this guy have any distinguishing marks?"

"He has really dark hair. Wears it longish, with a mustache to match. He's tall. I suppose some ladies might consider him handsome." Zane flipped to the next poster.

"I'll warn you, the likenesses usually aren't as helpful as the written description, and even then you probably know ten other folks who'd match it."

"I see that," Zane muttered. "But I still think we need to try. It could prove important to a lot of people. My parishioners could lose everything."

Reed slid into the chair across the narrow table. Zane looked up when he cleared his throat. "Your only concern is your congregation?"

"Walten is a good town. I want what's best for it and the people who live there."

"And that's all there is to this?"

"You're fishing."

Reed harrumphed. "A devout bachelor like myself?"

Zane settled back and flipped to another yellowed leaflet.

"But no one would blame you if you happened to notice how pretty she is."

He shook his head, never lifting his attention from the papers in his hand. "Journey needs me to get her away from this guy."

"Are you so sure she wants to get away from him? And what makes you think I'm talking about her?" Reed slid closer to the heat of the stove.

He snapped his glance to his friend. "Because no one likes to live in fear." He grinned. "And because I know you."

Reed nodded, his expression sober. "I reckon you're right, Zane. Reckon you're right. Can you use some more coffee?"

He nodded and turned his full concentration back to the papers on the table.

A few hours later, night had taken a firm hold over the city, and Reed turned up the lanterns. Zane rubbed his eyes.

Reed's voice broke the silence. "You want to finish up tomorrow?"

He tilted his head, holding out his mug for a refill. "Are you kicking me out?"

"No," he said. "Just checking."

"So make yourself useful." He laid the last of his posters on the pile at the table while the sheriff disappeared down a narrow hall.

"You want to go back another six months?" Reed called from the back room of the office.

"We might as well." He stretched his legs, pacing around the dusky outer room.

Reed returned with a smaller stack. They settled in to search the ink pictures. Zane feared they were all melting together in his mind. One big criminal. He wondered how Reed dealt with it all.

"Zane? Look at this."

He stood and looked over Reed's shoulder at the poster he held, pulling it from the sheriff's hand to ease it under

the light. The hair was drawn loose, but the curls were unmistakable. The lines were harsh but the composite utterly
recognizable.

And under that familiar face, he read the words:

"WANTED: Maura Sojourner Baines."

Chapter Twenty-Four

"Name's different, Zane. It could be someone else. What do you make of it?"

"It's her." He barely recognized his own voice. *What kind of trouble are you in, Journey?*

Reed smacked his shoulder. "We don't know the whole story. What else does it say?"

"Wanted for murder, arson and theft. In the state of Georgia," Zane read. "There has to be some mistake. She wouldn't do those things."

"It's hard to say what some folks will do under the right circumstances. You have to admit it yourself, Zane, she's awfully skittish for someone with nothing to hide."

"But murder? Tell me you think she's capable of killing someone. Even physically—she's so small." He laid the poster on the table but couldn't tear his attention from it. He didn't want to remember the gun she'd drawn on him in the barn.

Reed peered out the window, shaking his head. "No. No, I don't think she's capable of it. But that's not the point. She's a suspect at the very least, and I think it's best if we bring her in and get this settled."

"You can't arrest her. She's finally starting to trust us."

Reed read the poster again. "Maybe we have reason to not trust *her.*"

Zane locked a fist in his hair and blew out a heavy breath. "Does it have to be right away? If she were going to run, she would've done it before now. She's stuck in Walten until spring breaks. That gives us time to find out what happened. Besides, it'll soon be Christmas. I get the feeling she hasn't had many nice ones."

The sheriff scratched his mustache. "If she's convicted of murder, she won't have any more Christmases, nice or otherwise. But it isn't her name. And it would explain the connection between her and this Baines fellow. They must be related somehow. Maybe a brother or something. I agree it's not likely she'll run for a few months yet."

"Thanks, Reed. You don't know what this means to me." Zane rubbed a hand over his face.

"I expect you don't know what it means to yourself."

Zane thought he would elaborate, but Reed turned back to the fire and sat in the closest chair.

Zane stood to go, pulling his muffler around his neck. "I appreciate your help with this. I'll stop by in the morning on my way out of town."

Reed looked up, coffee cup midway to his mouth. "You're leaving now?"

"I already found out more than I wanted to know. I need to turn in early so I can start fresh tomorrow. I have a congregation to get home to."

"What about Baines? You want me to keep hunting for more on him? It would help to know Journey's connection to him. Until we know more, we can't count her out."

Zane pushed his hair back under his hat. "I'd appreciate it. You'll wire me if you learn more?"

"Sure enough. But remember, this could have nothing to do with the gold maps," Reed said.

"I think we're both too skeptical now for that." Zane grinned and pulled on his gloves. "But I'll keep my eyes and ears open, and I'll be in touch. Pray about it, won't you? I don't want to force Baines's hand, I don't want my judgment clouded about Journey's involvement and I don't want to put the town at risk by holding on to what I know for too long." What if they were working together?

He pulled on his warm coat. "But, if this man's claims are true, many people could benefit from the money a mine could generate, even if there's a fraction of the gold in Walten that's been found here. It's going to take more discernment than I have."

"Deciding when to come in out of the cold takes more discernment than you have," Reed joked, then sobered. "I'm always praying for you and Walten. I grew up there, you know."

Zane nodded and moved to the window. "Looks like the wind has picked up."

"You'll have a hard ride ahead if you want to miss the next snowfall."

Zane moved to the door. "Should I head out tonight?"

"I think if you don't get some sleep you'll fall off your horse before you hit the trail." Reed leaned back in his chair. "You'll make it. It won't do to take the scenic route, is all."

"Thanks, Reed. For everything."

"You stop by in the morning. I'll have a letter for Aunt Rose."

"Will do. See you bright and early." He stepped out into the night. The wind pierced through his heavy coat. Its howl silenced all other sounds around him.

Street fires burned low and at wide intervals, providing little light and even less heat. Zane expected they would soon be smoldered to prevent the risk of spreading to nearby buildings as the night winds picked up.

A noisy shuffle came from the left as he passed a narrow alley. He felt the crack of a heavy board across his back before he could turn. Surprise forced the air from his lungs. He twisted, trying to get away, but only felt himself dragged farther and farther from the dim fires.

A flash of pain at the back of his head, and his feet became useless. Blackness threatened to blow in with the storm, but stones cut into his cheek, rousing him again.

An arm pinned him to the wall. He sensed that his attacker was at least a head taller. The voice that rumbled down to him confirmed it. "If you were as smart a man as you think you are, Pastor, you wouldn't have been digging around where you have no business."

He tried to pull his scattered thoughts together, to make sense of it all.

"Come, come, now—has the cat got your tongue?" Another jolt knocked his head into the wall. Something solid pressed against his throat, making it hard to breathe. "I'll make it real simple, real simple. Let this alone, and stay away from Maura."

He heard a mumbled response, then realized it was his own.

"All you need to know is your precious Journey isn't so innocent. Or do you know that already? Stay away from her. Mind your own business, and you stay alive. I'm sure we understand one another," the voice said. Zane tried again to identify the tone, but the echo resounded in his head, tinny and far away as he spun around into the harsh wall again.

Zane swung out, determined to get away. Reed…Reed could help. One fist found only air, but the other clipped a shoulder—at least, he thought it was a shoulder. The way the light and darkness danced around in his head, he couldn't tell for sure.

A fist in his gut doubled him over, leaving him unable to recover before a slash of pain cut across his head once more. This time, he fell down through the darkness, into something cold and wet.

Lord, he prayed. But his thoughts went no further and the darkness consumed him.

Chapter Twenty-Five

Journey stared out the window above the kitchen sink and scrubbed furiously at a pot. A cold sliver of ice sank to the pit of her stomach, despite the dishwater that steamed around her. The snow blew white on the horizon, blending with the sheeted clouds in the sky.

Where was Zane? Tucked in somewhere warm, she hoped. She'd been surprised at his sudden decision to make a trip to Virginia City. Even more worrisome was the fact that Hank had left on his business trip the day before him.

She couldn't bring herself to ask questions. Not knowing for sure was easier. If Hank tried to work another angle, she'd have to tell others of her involvement with him, especially Zane. Could he help? What would Hank do? Best not to think about it.

Miss Rose had insisted on a rare Monday-afternoon trip into town. She seemed her spunky self but a mite quieter than usual. Something had her worried, too. Journey wiped the last plate and stacked it, then grabbed the dishpan to throw out the lukewarm water.

"Oh!"

Miss Rose stood behind her. The mucky water sloshed over the kitchen floor.

"I didn't mean to scare you. I was just going to get another log for the fire. That wind is blowing right through the cracks."

"I'll get it. You should stay bundled up and close to the heat. It's drafty out here."

Miss Rose smiled. "I'll tell Zane you were dutiful in hovering over me in his absence."

Journey swallowed and bobbed her head, setting the pan of water back into the sink. "It's the least I can do. Will he be back for Sunday's service?"

"Oh, yes. He expects to be back Friday evening, late."

She walked behind Miss Rose, carrying a few extra logs into the sitting room. "I'm sure you'll be relieved to see him."

The woman paused, adjusting her shawl over her shoulders.

"Oh, I miss him, but I'm not worried about him. The Lord will watch out for him, and He can do the job much better than I could. I notice your friend Mr. Baines hasn't been around, either. I hope there's nothing wrong."

Journey concentrated on stoking the fire, wanting to protest the use of the word *friend*. But better not to draw more attention to it. "He's out of town this week."

Miss Rose settled back in her rocker, adjusting a pillow under her head. "It is a funny coincidence, you meeting up with him again all the way out here."

Journey swallowed hard and brushed her hands on her apron. "I suppose so."

"Don't worry. They'll both be back before you know it, itching to be around underfoot." Miss Rose closed her eyes for a nap.

Journey slipped into the kitchen. She didn't know which bothered her more, the fact that Miss Rose was probably right or the fact that deep down she didn't believe it could be that simple.

A blinding white…

Cold. Darkness. Each registered in his mind as separate ideas, but he thought no further than that.

Someone rolled him over. Light stabbed his eyes and he tried to raise both hands to block it but only one responded. Someone lifted him by his coat lapels, and he swung at his attacker. But his feet slipped, unable to support him.

"Zane! What happened?" He knew the voice that echoed in his head. "It's me, Reed."

Zane swung his head up and leaned forward, determined to balance himself. The bleary form of Reed Knox swam before him, and he wondered what he was doing.

"Cold out here." His words slurred together, like his tongue had grown too large for his mouth.

"I know, buddy. Come on, let's—"

He dropped again into the cold darkness.

He waved to Sarah, sitting by the fireplace. She smiled at him but didn't say a thing.

Suddenly, fire slithered along the floorboards, creeping up the rockers of her chair, and he darted forward. But as he fought the burning heat, a scream rang out. He looked through the flames to see Journey falling into their grasp.

"Whoa! Whoa, there."

Zane felt a weight at his shoulder, pinning him down. He gasped when he tried to throw off the heaviness, and pain ripped through his head and side. He opened his eyes and found Reed staring, his eyebrows curled together and mustache scrunched tight. He looked to be in need of a shave, too.

"Do you really look that bad, or is my vision that blurry?" It sounded like someone else's voice saying his thoughts.

"What kind of fool question is that? I've been up all night with you carrying on. Do you remember what happened?"

Zane glanced around the room, having learned not to make any sudden moves. He was in the sheriff's office; they were looking for something here last night. Wasn't it last night?

"How long have I been out?"

Reed pulled up a chair and sat. "You kind of roused when I dragged you in here, I think. I found you halfway down the street, half covered in snow in the alley by the bank. If it weren't that I keep an eye out for Old Petey, I might've missed you."

"Old Petey?"

"Let's say he's a regular. He's sleeping off a drunk in the back right now. He walked in on his own not long after I dragged you in here. How do you feel?" Reed gave him a scrutinizing look.

"Like I ran into a wall."

"From the looks of it, you did—a couple times. What happened?"

"What time is it?"

"It must be getting close to noon. Why?"

Zane shifted up on the bed, not easy with one arm in a sling. "Last thing I remember, we were looking at wanted posters. Then I woke all trussed up like a turkey." He managed a smile. "So what'd you do to me?"

"You go around smiling like that in the shape you're in, folks will think you've lost every plum in your pie."

Zane swung his feet out to the floor and cradled his head in his hand. "Honestly, Reed, I don't remember. You didn't hear anything?"

"Lie back down. You wouldn't be going anywhere now even if you were right as rain. The snowstorm's raging out there," Reed said, nodding toward the front windows.

"I guess that's a no, then?"

Reed shook his head. "I'm just glad I found you when I did. It's a wonder you didn't freeze to death."

Zane eased to his feet, swinging his good arm out as his view got shaky.

"Sit down!"

He shook his head. "I'll be fine. I need to move around some."

"I knew I should've had the doctor take your pants. That'd keep you in place."

"You'll know better next time," Zane said with a grin. He shuffled to the window, ignoring the stitch in his side. "How long do you reckon this storm will last?"

"Not long. It's moving fast. But then I don't imagine you'll feel much like sitting on a horse for a couple of days, anyway."

Reed stepped over and set a chair by the window. Zane sank into it, lips curled together. "I'll have to wire Miss Rose."

"I figured I'd wait until you roused before I sent word."

"Good. Don't tell her anything that will worry her. It's probably just a thief looking for money."

Reed laid a heavy hand on Zane's shoulder. "I'll tell her you'll be home sometime next week, and not to worry. She'll figure the storm delayed you. But we both know this isn't about robbing a preacher."

Zane turned back to stare at the driving snow through the windowpane. "Reckon you're right. Maybe I did get hit harder than I thought, because I'm thinking someone didn't want me to make it home too fast."

"Who knew you were coming?"

"Miss Rose, Sam and Abby, Journey…"

Reed looked at him.

Zane leaned back in the chair, trying to ease the ache in his ribs. "It wasn't Journey."

"So tell me how you know this."

"Because," he said, rubbing his temple with his thumb. "Because it was a deep voice."

"You remember now?" Reed slid forward on his seat, waiting.

"Not much. Just that the voice was deep and came from above me."

"Like the voice of God?"

Zane grinned. "Real funny when you're not the one wearing the sling."

"Sorry. But we know it was a man taller than you with a deep voice. Strong, too, I'd say, by the looks of you."

"I wasn't exactly expecting a fight. Besides, we don't know what *he* looks like this morning," Zane said.

"True, but we do know he walked away." Reed walked over to his desk in the corner of the dim room and opened a drawer. "Anyway, I think I'll search back a little further in the posters. Where's Hank from?"

"Georgia. Abby said Journey had lived there, too."

Reed scratched his mustache with his thumb. "I'll send a wire and see if anyone's heard of Baines. It's worth a try."

Zane nodded and smothered a yawn. It stretched his ribs too much. "Think it's time for a nap."

"Terrible to get old," Reed said, giving him a hand up.

He stood without help, caught his balance and wavered back to the bed. "I reckon you're the one who'd know."

Chapter Twenty-Six

Journey peered through the frosted glass at the swirling snow from the rocking chair where she sat.

"I don't know that he'll get back today," Miss Rose said.

"Who?" She let the curtain slide from her hand.

"Zane. It could be more like late Saturday night, I'd expect, what with the storm and all."

"I wasn't—I mean, I didn't… He never said when he'd be back or even that he'd be going. You don't suppose he's caught out in this?" She focused on the tiny stitches of the suit she was sewing.

Miss Rose rocked, head back, the rest of her buried in quilts. "No, he'd miss it, or at least the worst of it, if he left when he planned. But it could slow him down some."

Journey watched Miss Rose close her eyes. Another nap. She had been so tired lately that Journey thought Doc Ferris should stop in and check on her.

The creak of the rocker stopped, leaving only the tick of the mantel clock and the crackle of the fire inside the snug house. Journey looked up from her work to see Miss Rose sleeping and eased off her own chair, walking to the window to draw the curtain aside.

The sun rested behind the saddle of mountains in the west. The cold, flat disk radiated light from the fresh snow through the day but provided little warmth. Something moved and caught her eye.

"Rider coming," she whispered, glancing at Miss Rose, who hadn't stirred.

Pulling her cloak from the hook, Journey slipped outside. The wind had calmed through the day but seemed to be picking up with the setting sun.

She peered into the dimness. The rider blended in with the shadowed mountains, almost invisible. But still, she watched. It could be Zane. She shivered, trying to shake the uneasiness.

The figure rode close to the window, and she drew back as horse and rider emerged into the faint light. "Hank."

He swept his hat off. The balance of light from the house and the remaining rays of the sun mixed to give him an eerie glow. His eyes glittered black and tiny. *Snake.*

"Hello, my dear. I wanted to drop by and let you know I've returned. Please forgive the lateness of the hour." His accent lacked smoothness, as if he were very tired.

"Where were you?" she whispered, her heart pounding.

Hank shook his head. "Oh, but, Maura, you're my wife even yet. It's good to hear your concern."

"It's Journey. And please answer the question."

He chuckled but it ended in a cough. "My, my, I admire this new spunk you've acquired here in Montana, *Journey.* I've been looking after our interests in Virginia City."

"*We* have no interests there." *Keep your voice steady,* she thought. "*We* have no interests anywhere."

"Oh, but we do. Roy has come to help us with all the details of the little investment we're going to make available to the fine people of Walten," he said.

Any fight she'd gathered evaporated from her.

Hank didn't seem to notice, but surely he felt it. "Roy found me lying on the floor after you'd belted me with that flatiron the night you left. He'd come to warn me our fine sheriff was about to appear at our door with a warrant for my arrest."

She hoped Hank could not make out her expressions in the darkness. She knew he'd been up to no good when she was with him in Georgia.

"The sheriff would have caught me good," he continued. "Then Roy concocted the plan to get out and set fire to the place. He testified as witness to your part in my murder and in the blaze that harmed all those dear neighbors." He paused to clear his throat.

"You should have stuck around for the trial. The community was quite irate. Quite ironic, isn't it? If you hadn't tried to kill me, you would have been rid of me anyway. Rather amusing, don't you agree?"

Could it be that she had found her way out when true escape had lain so close at hand? Stupid, stupid woman! But then, she'd had little choice at the time. Kill or be killed. If she'd been better at it, she wouldn't be in this predicament now.

Hank paused. He'd always been a master at effect. She waited, drawing her arms around herself under the cape.

"Roy and I were able to make our way out before the whole place burned to the ground. Pity about the place. We had some good times there, Maura."

"If you consider beating me a good time," she said, her voice quiet and blending with the night.

"Can't you just once remember something good?" His voice flared. "I loved you, Maura. I still do, you know. I miss your fire. It's only that you made me so—"

"As I recall, it was the whiskey that made you so…"

He smiled, faint light glistening from his teeth. "Either way, the fact is now we're together for as long as I say. Turn me in, and you'll be tried for attempted murder, at the very least. There's the little matter of the arson, too. Not to mention the fact that a good sum of money went missing. You'll be sent back to Georgia, where we'll still be married."

"Turn me in. I don't care anymore. I'm tired of living in your grasp."

"Perhaps I will." He swiped a hand over his mustache. "Perhaps you'll have no reason to stay regardless. I think you'll find your new beau not quite so attentive as before."

The coldness around her was nothing compared with the chill that shot through her. She cleared her tight throat. "What have you done?"

"Don't count on the help of your young Pastor Thompson any time in the near future."

Her heart dropped.

"Hank, if you—"

He cut her off with a laugh. "I don't think you're in any position to finish that thought. I'll be in touch."

Journey called to him as he turned to go. "Hank, you didn't…" She couldn't say it, but she knew he'd done as much before.

"Let's not raise a fuss, Maura. It would be a shame to disturb the delightful Miss Rose." He turned, an envelope offered by his shadowed hand. "I almost forgot. Telegram from Virginia City, dear. Addressed to Mrs. Rose Bishop. From her darling nephew, I'd suppose. I picked it up in town." He clucked his tongue. "I do hope it's nothing serious."

Her eyes felt wet and frozen, like her breath. She clasped the envelope to her. By the time she drew her gaze from it, Hank was gone.

Chapter Twenty-Seven

Journey swept through the warm room. Miss Rose slept, her face turned toward the fire's heat. Journey moved up the stairway, straining over the creaking fourth step.

A sliver of moon shone through her bedroom window. She grabbed her satchel and tugged the latches open, coins jangling inside the pockets. Precious few. Still not enough for a horse of any kind, and how far could she get on foot?

She threw in her navy dress and jerked the straps tight. Miss Rose's horses would get her anywhere she needed to go. The thought ripped through her head before she could quell it. She padded back down the stairway, her mind racing. Take the horses, ride off and never look back. And the money Miss Rose kept in her rosewood box on the mantel would go a long way in helping her get lost once again. She could…

The sight of Miss Rose asleep on the rocker stopped her. Miss Rose would want to help, would understand. And once she settled again, she'd pay everything back.

Walking over to the fireplace, she pulled the money from the box. She couldn't stop to count it but knew from the thickness it would take her far.

Stuffing the wad of bills into her coat pocket, she passed Miss Rose's chair and out the door, easing it closed behind her. The bitter wind kicked in her face and made it hard to breathe as she ran across the yard to the barn.

Puffs of air clouded her view. Hank would never let her go if she didn't do it this way. He'd already hurt Zane; he—

Zane. How far had Hank gone to get what he wanted? He had never displayed too many limitations before. Gambling, stealing, pursuing the magnificent plan—whatever struck him at any given time as the best way to make the most money in the least time with the least amount of effort. And yet, how many months behind on the rent had they been when she left Georgia?

Zane had to be fine. Surely Hank had only meant to frighten her. She patted the money in her pocket. Maybe she could give Hank the money he craved, and he would leave everyone alone. Could it be so simple?

"What will she do when she finds out Zane's hurt and I'm to blame?" she muttered. Her fingers froze, her harsh breath echoing in the quiet of the barn.

She grasped Homer's dark mane, pulled her fingers into it and rested her forehead against his neck. "What will we do if he's worse than hurt?"

The image of Zane lying cold and in pain somewhere along the empty trail crushed her heart. She'd look for him and find Reed. Reed could help. But would he help a woman who had tricked his aunt, taken advantage of her hospitality and fallen in love with his friend only to endanger his life?

Wait. She didn't love Zane. She didn't. He invaded places in her life he had no business being. She told him to stay out of her way and stay out of her life. He hadn't listened to her. And now he paid the price.

"Journey?"

The sound drifted through the thick barn walls. Miss Rose must be awake, and calling her. Would the darkness hide her if she sneaked out the side door? What if Miss Rose tried to find her?

She wiped a tear with the back of her hand and walked outside. She'd stay, just a little longer, until they had word from Zane. It would give her time to think things through, to lay tracks that Hank couldn't follow.

Nothing mattered beyond that. No one would care what happened to her once they knew about her past. A past that Hank knew all about: being raised in a cathouse with no father to speak of. Selling herself into Hank's service at fifteen. Had it really been worth the trade to avoid the life her mother had led up until the week before she died? When she turned seventeen and Hank married her, she thought her chance at a respectable future had finally arrived. But that was all lost now.

"Journey? Are you out there?" Miss Rose called again, her voice wavering in the wind. Her shadowed form stood in the open doorway of the house.

"Yes, Miss Rose. I'm coming."

Journey drew the bills from her pocket and, with a glance back at the house, slid them into the edge of the carrot bin inside the barn door.

She walked across the yard. The wind whispered through the porch eaves as she stamped snow from her boots and shook it from her skirt hem. She hung her coat on a peg, her gaze catching the box on the mantel. The heat of shame burned her face.

Miss Rose sank into her rocker, wiggling closer to the fire. "Whatever were you doing out there, Journey? You'll catch your death of cold out on a night like this."

She swiped a stray curl from her forehead and tucked

it behind her ear. "A messenger delivered a telegram for you, Miss Rose." Her voice felt trapped in her throat.

The woman coughed and leaned back in her chair, sending it to motion as she closed her eyes. "Read it to me."

Her voice sounded calm, but the blue-veined fingers tightened over the arms of the chair. Journey's hand trembled as she opened the seal and scanned the brief message.

"Zane delayed STOP Be home early next week STOP Don't worry STOP Delay gold mine STOP Reed," she read. "Oh, Miss Rose!"

"Don't fret now, child."

How could she be so calm? Journey blinked a hot tear away. "But if Zane were truly fine, he'd send his own telegram. What if—"

"The only thing we can do now is to pray. Will you do that with me?" Miss Rose stared at her, no longer rocking.

Journey sank into the closest chair and forced the thin paper into the envelope with shaking hands. "But God won't listen to me. He's never listened to me. He'll answer your prayers. You do it."

"Zane needs us both. Please." Her voice was gentle but raspy, and a soft smile graced her face. "What can it hurt to try? God never stops listening. Never."

She nodded. If it made Miss Rose feel better, she'd try it. She felt her hands engulfed in the too-warm grasp of the other woman and watched as she bowed her head. The smile never broke as Miss Rose talked to the Lord as if He was sitting next to her.

Journey bowed her head and remembered to close her eyes. Her thoughts didn't form a prayer, exactly, but she wished with all her heart that God would listen to Miss Rose's prayers, given on behalf of a man who certainly deserved His mercy.

Chapter Twenty-Eight

Zane held his arm stiffly at his side. He didn't need the doctor from Virginia City to tell him how fortunate he'd been. A broken arm. Ribs bruised, wrapped tight but not busted. His headache had hung on through the better part of Sunday, but he'd been kicked by horses and hurt worse. He smiled, knowing Doc Ferris would not favor his decision to head back to Walten. Or Miss Rose, he supposed. But it felt as if he'd been away for a month, instead of a week.

Had Journey missed him? He thought of the poster and the telegram from Georgia folded carefully in his pocket. Everything came down to questions only she could answer.

The modest steeple of the church rose over the final ridge and above the other buildings that made up the little town of Walten. His town, his church. He longed to be there but had other stops to make first.

Pulling up to the post in front of Sam and Abby's store, he slid from the horse and dusted snow from his coat with one hand.

"Zane!" Abby flew from the porch, grabbing his good arm in both hands. "Are you just getting back? We've been wondering about you. When Reed sent the telegram, we thought… Well, he didn't tell much. What happened to your arm? To your face?"

He lifted a hand to the bruise at his eye. He thought it looked remarkably better when he'd shaved the morning before leaving Virginia City. "Never mind that now. You'd better get in from the cold. Is Sam around?"

"Around back. Go on, and I'll make coffee."

Moving around to the storage shed, he found Sam stacking crates of supplies. "Hello!" he said, not wanting to startle his friend.

Sam didn't turn. "Grab a crate and join the party."

"Not today, I'm afraid." He smiled and lifted his broken arm a little when Sam faced him.

"What happened?"

"Have you heard anything about investing in a gold claim in Walten? From that Baines fellow Journey knows?"

Sam sat on a crate, pushing his hat back and slipping his gloves off. He kicked another crate over and motioned for Zane to sit.

"Some. Most folks around here don't have the money for that kind of thing, though. There's talk Mr. Baines will take land as collateral if people are willing to sign over, but I haven't heard of anyone who's taken him up on that offer. I'd imagine some will."

Sam sighed and scratched his jaw. "He seems awful sure there's enough gold to make us all rich as trolls. Some folks are worried about what could happen to the town if word gets out before we have a plan in place. Baines has everyone shook up with tales of 'crime and avarice' to follow."

"A lot of these people lived through those early days in

Virginia City. They know he's right on that count." Zane passed on the seat, not willing to subject his stiff side to getting up from it later.

"How busted up are you?" Sam asked.

"Bruised ribs, broken arm. Had a little run-in with a wall or two one night. Baines wanted my stamp of approval on this deal. I told him I'd want to check things out for myself first." He leaned against the doorway of the shanty. "I'm thinking he took exception to my doubts. And he wants me to stay away from Journey."

"He's been out of town himself."

"How long?"

Sam rubbed his neck. "He left same day as you, maybe the day before. I guess he was back in town sometime Saturday. He ended up delivering Reed's telegram. I heard he headed back to Virginia City, though. I'm surprised you didn't see him on the trail."

"He and I wouldn't ride the same path."

"What do you mean?"

"I mean, if he left right away, he'd have made it back in time to—"

"You think he's the one who beat you?"

"I found out enough to know that if we were sitting on a gold mine, Hank wouldn't be looking to cut the town in for the profits."

"So how can I help?" Sam asked.

"Right now I have pieces, but nothing fits together yet. Keep your ears open, see what folks are saying and tell them to hold off until we can get a town meeting together. I'll let you know when I find out anything for certain."

Zane cocked his head toward the main building. "Abby promised coffee, and I could sure use some."

"Right. But the minute you need me, I'm there."

"Thanks, Sam." He shifted, then winced as the pain grabbed his side. "Could have used your help in that alley-way," he said with a grin.

An hour later, warmed inside out by the coffee, Zane rode out to Miss Rose's. Abby's fresh bread with preserves hadn't hurt his outlook, either.

He slowed his pace as he drew near the ranch. As much as he wanted Journey to answer his questions, he didn't relish the confrontation.

"Dear Lord, show me how to talk to her. She's scared, and I reckon she has every reason to be. Show her, Jesus, that she has no reason to fear me. She hasn't exactly been happy with my help to this point. But, Father, I have the town to think of, too. I think— God, I'm asking you to work this out because I know You can and I know I can't. You've said that when we seek Your will, we'll find it. Help us all. In Jesus' name I ask. Amen."

He scanned the rolling mounds of snow, knowing the whiff of smoke rising from over the next hill belonged to Miss Rose's chimney. He nudged his horse onward.

It's good she has Journey this winter, especially since she's been down with that cold, he thought. How would she feel when she discovered her boarder was mixed up with Baines?

Zane made his way into the frozen yard. The wind had swept a path between the house and the barn. The sky, wide and gray, promised another dose of snow. Maybe they'd have a fresh coat for Christmas, if this weather held. He went into the barn and tied Malachi to a post.

"Here, boy," he said, reaching into the carrot bin. His fingers swept over soft paper, and he pulled it out. Instead of the knobby carrot, he held a stack of bills.

Hundreds of possibilities swarmed, but only one lodged in his mind. He tucked the bills into his sling and stroked the horse's face. "We could get kicked out mighty quick, if Journey has anything to say about it. But she has a lot of explaining to do herself."

The door slid open, and he turned to see her slip through it. "Journey," he said, hoping not to startle her.

"Zane." He couldn't decipher the tone in her voice. She sounded almost relieved, but maybe the surprise of finding him in the barn brought the lilt to her voice.

She stood still for a moment. Then, drawing a deep breath, she said, "Oh, Zane, I'm so glad you're here."

He stepped forward, grasping her arm with his good hand. "What is it?"

"Miss Rose—she's sick, been sick, but today, I have to get Doc Ferris." She pulled herself away, stumbling toward the stalls.

The importance of any questions he had paled. "I'll go. You go back to Miss Rose, make her comfortable. I'll fetch him."

She sagged with relief and drew closer as he slid his hand up to caress her cheek. It felt damp and soft.

He almost lost his balance as she leaned toward him, resting her cheek against his chest. He brought his free arm around her and patted her shoulder, almost out of instinct. He soaked in her warmth, rubbing his fingers in small circles at her shoulder. A dam inside him cracked, and a wave of protectiveness surged through.

She shuddered in his arms, as if trying to compose herself. "I'm sorry. I didn't know what to do. I've made such a mess of things. I never meant to—"

"We'll talk about that later. I'll go for Doc." He felt her draw away. He pulled himself into the saddle with one arm.

She opened the door for him to ride out. Light filtered down, casting a glow over her face. She looked younger with her freckles more pronounced against her pale skin. Her brown eyes were wide, frightened.

"It's only to town and back. I'll be here with Doc before you know it. Then we can talk, all right?"

She nodded, looking up at him with wet trails marring her cheeks. "She's so hot. I'm afraid for her."

"It'll be all right." He hoped his words assured her. With a squeeze of his legs and a duck of his head, the horse took off across the cold terrain.

Zane prayed.

Chapter Twenty-Nine

Miss Rose rested under a mound of quilts, her breath so shallow they didn't stir. Journey threw another log onto the fire, where it crackled and popped. The sound of a fast-moving buggy drew her to the sitting room. How long had Zane been gone?

The men brushed snow from their pant legs and dusted it from their hats as they stepped through the door.

"Where is she?" Doc Ferris asked.

She led him to Miss Rose's room, off the sitting room in the front part of the house. "I'm sorry to call you out so late, Doc. I didn't know what else to do."

"You did right, sending for me. I'll take a check on her. Wait here with Zane."

"Can't I help?"

He patted her arm and smiled. "Could I bother you for some coffee? I surely could use a cup."

She nodded but didn't move until he went in to Miss Rose's room and slid the door partially closed. She put the kettle of coffee on in the kitchen and then returned to pace the floor in front of the couch. Zane sat, almost swallowed in the cushions, eyes partially closed.

"Sit down, Journey," he said. "You must be exhausted. I had no idea she was so ill."

"What took you so long?" She stopped in the middle of the braided rug, hugging her waist.

"Doc was out at the Andersons'. I told him about Miss Rose and he came right away. Said it sounds like the same thing Mr. Anderson has, and Mrs. Hamler, and the Wilsons' son, Jimmy. Influenza."

She sank to the end of the couch, opposite Zane, and rocked forward, unable to hold back any more tears. She was too tired to try.

He shifted and she heard his muffled gasp. "Zane?"

She wiped her face, noticing his. "What happened to you?" she asked, thumbing the bruise near his eye. How had she missed it when she'd first seen him standing in the barn?

"We have to talk."

She drew her hand back. His gray eyes held her focus. He knew. She slid from the cushion and backed away. "Please, don't—"

"I have to, Journey. I have questions and there's too much at stake. It's not just about you or me." Slowly he stood, his bound arm pressed tightly against his side. He drew a page from his coat pocket with his free hand, unfolded it and held it out to her. Waiting.

She peered at the wrinkled paper, afraid to touch it. Hank's sketchy face stared back. The likeness was rather good, though he wore his hair much longer now. She choked. "The law did know about him in Savannah. If I had only realized."

Doc Ferris stepped out from the bedroom, cutting off all but thoughts of Miss Rose. Journey pulled the poster from Zane's fingers and slid it behind her. "How is she?"

Doc shrugged into his coat before answering. "It looks like influenza. Tricky thing. I'm thinking of pulling everyone who's come down with it into one place, so I can treat them all at the same time. It's too hard to keep up with everyone spread out as they are."

"How many are there?" she asked, her voice shaky.

"Maybe ten. Mostly children and older folks, but it'll spread. We'll need someone to take word out to some of the outlying farms, tell them what to look for, and what to do if they come down with it. We'll need blankets and buckets, food and water, cots and mats." He adjusted his glasses.

"I'll talk to Abby. Where should we tell folks to go?" she asked.

"How about the church?" Zane offered.

The doctor gripped his chin in his hand and nodded. "It *is* the largest place. We'll need wood for a fire out back and someone to tend it. We'll need hot water."

"I'll ride out and check on the families farther out, then Sam and I can get a fire going," Zane said. "I don't know medicine, Doc, but I'll help any way I can."

"I'd be obliged," Doc Ferris said. "I'll go back to town, start getting supplies together. Let Miss Rose rest a few hours, then bundle her up and bring her to town at dawn. Rest as much as you can until then, and I'll send some telegrams, see where we can find more quinine should we need it. It's going to be a long few weeks before this runs its course, I'm afraid. We'll need all the help the Almighty can give us."

He clamped his hat tighter and tapped the brim toward her. "It was good you sent for me, miss. You both take care, now. And, Zane, take it easy on those ribs. Once people start coming into town, we'll need all the able hands we can find."

Journey closed the door behind him. Thick flakes of snow fell, the lazy kind of shower that signaled a break in the storm.

Zane grabbed her shoulder as she passed him, moving toward Miss Rose's room. She ducked with a gasp, her heart pounding.

He released her as if she'd burned him. She focused on the fire glowing in the hearth, embarrassed by her snap reaction.

"I'd never hurt you. Never." He stepped back. "But we need to sort this all out before we get to town. How do you know Baines? And why is he here?"

She whipped her coat from the peg, punching her arms through the sleeves and tugging her hair out from the collar. She grabbed her saddle pack, which was leaning against the wall near the door.

"Where are you going?"

"I'm leaving before I cause more trouble. I should've gone a long time ago," she said, clamping her hat down on her head.

He stepped in front of her before she could reach the door latch. "Don't you think you owe us an explanation?" A handful of bills waved before her eyes, swirling in time with her thoughts. "You're going to leave now, like this, after all Miss Rose has done for you?"

She looked away and swiped back her tears. "I would have paid it back. I swear it. I've brought nothing but problems for this town, and I need to get away before things get worse. Look at you. You never answered my question. What happened to you in Virginia City? How do you explain that welt by your eye? The sore ribs?"

Zane stood back, his lips drawn into a tight line.

"Never mind. I already know. Hank came by. You're

lucky you got off so easily. He could have killed you. I thought…"

"Thought what?"

"I thought he had." She palmed the rough warmth of the fireplace stones behind her. "I thought he killed you and left you lying out on the trail." Each word squeezed from her throat. "But you're safe. We prayed—that is, Miss Rose prayed—and here you are. I can't take a chance of you getting hurt again."

"How will your leaving make everything right?" He made no move toward her, but she moved another pace away from him.

"Hank won't have any hold over me if he doesn't know where I am."

"What hold does he have on you, Journey?" His voice softened and he stepped toward her. She felt his hand on her shoulder, drawing her to him. She felt safe in his arms, holding her strong and warm.

"Tell me about that poster." His jaw rubbed her head as he spoke.

She looked up at him. This would be easier if he were angry. Hank had trained her to face that. Instead, his gaze held, firm but compassionate. His eyes crinkled at the edges, eyebrows furrowed.

She looked away and pulled from his hold. "I can't."

He moved away a moment, and she fumbled with the lashings on her pack. She looked at him again when he blocked the light from the lantern in the window.

"Then maybe you can explain this one."

Her own likeness greeted her. Not a very flattering one, but hers nonetheless, staring from the wrinkled parchment.

She closed her eyes and fought to draw a breath. "It's not how it looks. Please, let me leave."

"So it is you," he said. "I figured, but I've been wrong before. Hoped this was one of those times."

She opened her eyes to see his outstretched arm. Glancing toward the door, she allowed him to guide her to a chair by the fireplace. She knew she owed him an explanation.

He wasn't demanding that she leave. He hadn't hauled the law in to come and take her away. Was he really giving her the benefit of the doubt?

She sat down, picking at the brim of her hat. "How much do you want to know?"

"Everything."

Tell him, a silent voice pleaded. *Tell him why you have to run.*

"Hank's my husband."

Zane would think everything had been arranged from the start, that she had tricked them all, but it was better that way. It would be easier to go if he hated her.

Zane sat in the chair beside her and smoothed out another paper. He stared at it a moment. "If Hank Baines is your husband, that makes you a widow according to this."

He laid the page on her lap as he stood. She read without touching it. "You don't know how I wish that were true."

"So tell me what is true. Let me help you sort this out."

"Does Reed know?"

"Where do you think I got the posters?"

"Are you taking me to the sheriff?" Her breath came fast and short. A year of looking over her shoulder—ended. The thought almost brought relief.

"Not unless I have to." She cried in earnest when he fingered the curls draped down her back. "I convinced Reed you deserved a chance to explain your side of things. Won't you tell me, Journey? If you leave now, there's no way I can keep you safe."

She folded over in the seat, burying her face in her skirt. "I can't be safe. Not here. Not anywhere Hank is."

"What are you saying?"

She lifted her head enough so her words weren't muffled. "I'm saying that you should call Reed and have him lock me up. Maybe jail is the only place where Hank won't be able to hurt me anymore."

"I don't think it's that simple. Is it true, what the poster says? Did you kill a man by burning down a hotel? Are you Maura Baines?"

"I am Maura Baines, but I never burned a building. And I never killed a man, but it doesn't mean I never tried. That's enough for God to punish me, I suppose."

"Tell me how you got here, Journey—Maura—whoever you are." He sounded as confused as she felt. "At least let me try to help." Zane's tone didn't plead. It sounded firm and comforting, like his arms had been moments before.

"My mother's maiden name was Sojourner. I borrowed from that when I needed to get away. And Smith could be anyone. Miss Smith would never attract attention. Being away from Hank was all that mattered."

"You didn't know they declared him dead?"

She stood and walked away, arms crossed. "I knew because I was the one who'd killed him, or at least tried to kill him."

She whirled on Zane, trying to judge his thoughts. What did it matter now? He'd have to notify the law. Bars that kept Hank away would be better than living like this, always waiting for the day he'd find her. It was too hard, and she was too tired to fight anymore.

"You must've had a reason. The judge could take that into account. Besides, if he's not really dead—"

"He's not, but apparently someone died that night. Do you think a judge will care what happened? 'Certainly, Your Honor, I'm innocent. I never intended to kill the man who died. I believed I had killed someone else.' Not only thought it, was glad of it."

She moved to the window, staring out into the blackness. Miss Rose hadn't stirred. Thank goodness she wasn't awake enough to hear this.

Zane stood beside her, looking straight ahead through the window and she tensed. "How'd it happen?"

He didn't deny her involvement, she noted. But he still tried to wrap his mind around it, still tried to understand. She touched his shoulder, ashamed that he should care.

"It's not your fault," she said. "I made bad choices after my mama died. She was a…a saloon girl. I was fifteen when she died." It seemed so long ago.

"Fifteen?"

"I was scared and Hank offered me more than the life my mother had. At least it was only him." She didn't go into details.

She remembered her mama's smile. "She seemed different, those last days. She made me promise not to go the way she did. I don't think I could've anyway, but then, look at where I am now." Her laugh sounded hollow, even to her.

She turned to Zane, sensing his gaze. The compassion she saw was more than she could bear. Her resolve faded.

"I met Hank when I was so young," she continued with a heavy breath. "But he wasn't always mean like he is now. He always had that drive for more, the fierceness to make things happen. He treated me as well as Hank knows how. I don't expect he grew up much better than me, but he never spoke of it. Then plan after plan to make things good fell through, and he started drinking more. He grew angrier at life. I was in the way, I suppose. The fierceness I thought would protect me turned against me."

"He hit you." Zane didn't ask, he knew.

She nodded. "Quite often. I stood it for three years, waiting for him to turn into the man I wanted him to be. But it only got worse. I thought he was going to kill me many times those last few months. Maybe it would've been better that way. Easier for him."

"No."

She pulled back at the anger in his voice. His hand fisted against the windowpane.

"No one deserves that."

"Most women live with being hit. My mama lived through worse and for longer than me. She was stronger."

"You're strong, too. No one deserves a life like that."

She dismissed him, moving back to the seat by the fire. "I started saving what money I could, so I could buy a ticket to someplace far away. I figured Hank would be happy to see me walk out. But he came home one night, full of plans and hope and liquor. He found my satchel with the money I'd hidden. He was furious. He would've killed me that night, but he was drunk and he tripped. When he did, I grabbed the flatiron and I—I hit him." Over and over.

She pictured the dingy room above the saloon even now, wrinkled her nose at the coppery scent of blood that flooded her memory. She would've sworn Hank was dead when she left. He certainly wasn't moving. But then, her only thought at the time had been to get away. She shivered against the chill of the memory.

She forced her mind back to the present, to the warmth that surrounded her in this room. She cleared her throat and twisted her head to look at Zane, surprised to find him sitting close.

"I've made so many mistakes in my life, never a good or right decision. But my biggest regret is that I didn't make sure Hank was dead before I left. It's haunted me ever since. I didn't want him to die, not really. But I wasn't sorry, either."

Her breath shook. How could she explain? "Things would be so much easier now if he had."

"We'll work this out, you'll see," Zane said. "But I can't help if you leave. I can't protect you out there."

"You can't protect me anywhere, Zane. That's the whole point."

"Let me try. Don't give up now."

She sank into the cushions and shook her head. Didn't he realize it was pointless? "They'd lock you in the cell beside me."

"It'd be worth it if it helped you."

A tear dripped on her hand. "I'm not worth it. And Miss Rose needs you. Just let me leave."

Zane slid to the floor before her. "You know I can't do that. Reed already knows about the posters. Do you really want to live like this, always running, always waiting to be found out?"

Wasn't he listening? Of course, she didn't want to live that way. But what else could she do? If she could just get away and rest....

"I'm tired, Zane."

"I know you are. All the more reason to stay." His gray eyes caught her attention.

"Will you give me a few days? I can help the doctor. I need to be sure Miss Rose is well." She looked at the dying fire. "Then you can wire Reed."

She strained for any sounds of discomfort coming from Miss Rose's room. But it was silent except for the whispers of wheezy breathing, the ticking clock above the mantel and the fire as it crackled.

He weighed the decision in his mind, she could sense.

"All right. Miss Rose will need you. The whole town will." His voice was low but determined. "Then we'll contact Reed. He can help us sort this out. He could talk to Hank. Maybe he'd help to clear you—"

"No." She shook. "Hank won't help me. Not without a higher price than prison. Jail would be better."

Zane opened his eyes, as if he had been praying. Then he pushed her hair back, searching her face. What did he expect to see? She relaxed into the warmth of his touch in spite of herself.

"We'll do it your way." He took the satchel from her grasp. She had forgotten she still held it. "We'll pray. God can work this out in ways we can't even imagine. You have to believe that. I'm praying that you will. In the meantime, you'll promise you'll not run?"

She nodded her head in agreement. What was one more broken promise?

Chapter Thirty

Journey leaned back on her knees and swiped a hand across her forehead. She hardly recognized the church sanctuary. Instead of pews facing the pulpit in neat rows, they lined the edges of the room, some with patients resting precariously on them, a few holding tired caregivers. Other patients slept or tossed on cots and piles of blankets scattered about the room.

The heat Doc Ferris ordered to keep the sick comfortable made the room oppressive for those trying to keep up with the continual washing, cooking and treating of those in need. The odors of sickness and the smell of turpentine the doctor had used as an antiseptic mingled in the air.

She heard the outer door open and turned toward the entryway. Where could they fit another person or find the energy to care for another patient?

Zane tapped snow from his hat with his free hand as he entered. She stretched to her feet, grateful to see he came alone. A three-day growth of beard darkened his face, and she could see the sag of his eyes from across the room. With a weary smile, he wound his way through those lying on the floor.

"How are you holding up?" he asked. He clasped her warm hand in his cool one.

"I could ask you the same. Have you rested at all?"

He grinned. "Guess that's a 'no' for us both."

"I slept after you left this morning. We've been taking turns between us."

"But there're fewer workers than we started with." He glanced around the room. "You have to take care of yourself, too." He squeezed her arm lightly and heaved a deep sigh. "How's Miss Rose?"

She looked over to the cot in front of the pulpit. Under the high pile of covers, Miss Rose's pale form lay. "She's been awful quiet. Too quiet, but Doc says she's no worse."

"Let's go outside and see how Sam's coming with the bonfire. You could use the fresh air," Zane said.

She hesitated. The patients seemed to be settled for a moment, or at the very least were being cared for by another attendant. But Miss Rose, what if…?

"C'mon." He squeezed her arm. "We'll be right outside. Doc will call us if there's any change." His voice grew louder as he looked toward the doctor, stooped over a patient in the back corner.

"Sue Anderson isn't doing well," she whispered.

Journey thought of the day they'd quilted together. She couldn't help but think that Sue's notions of romance might thrill at the idea of having her fevered brow mopped by some handsome benefactor. Instead, she had a kindly old doctor who likely was as poor as a church mouse for her attendant. The influenza hadn't taken note of her privileged status nor held any illusions of romance.

"Go on," Doc Ferris said. "Rose'll rest easy for a while. Bring in more hot water when you return." He nodded them out the back door.

The cold air felt clean and fresh after the heat of the church. She slipped into the coat Zane handed her. Sam poked at the fire blazing under a large kettle, boiling bed linens and cleaning cloths. Both the chill of the air and the warmth of the fire reddened his face.

"How you holding up?" Zane asked him.

Sam greeted them with a nod. "Tending fire's the easy part. Journey's the one that's got to tend the folks inside."

"How's Abby? I haven't seen her lately," she asked.

He wiped the sweat from his brow and replaced his hat. "She's tired this morning—been busy keeping the store open, making sure folks can get what they need. And she's been cooking and baking up a storm in that kitchen. But she misses you and wishes she could help here. I let her sleep this morning."

"She deserves it," Journey said.

"We're all in this together." Sam rubbed his hand over his face. "If you can take over the fire, Zane, I'm heading out for Virginia City. Doc needs more quinine."

"You want some company? That's a lot of snow to get through on your own."

"It'll be faster sending one man, I think. Besides, you shouldn't be out gallivanting around the country with that arm busted and all. I'm packed for the trail already. Just wanted to give Doc a hand before I left."

Zane took his fire prod and nudged his friend's shoulder with his own. "Then by all means, get going. We'll take it from here. You take it easy out on that trail."

"Will do," Sam said, clamping his hat down. He walked to the tree where he'd tied his horse and mounted. "I'm riding straight through, so I aim to be back late Thursday night, no later than Friday morning."

"We'll be expecting you." The men shook hands and Sam headed out.

Journey watched him nudge his horse into a trot back through town and off to the north and west. "How long have you known him?"

"Sam?" Zane stopped poking logs to toss another one onto the fire. He took his time brushing his glove off on his denim pants, as if his mind couldn't remember that far back. "We've been friends a long time. Our families came west together during the gold rush in California and then moved to Montana when that played out and things got crowded. He's like my own family. He even introduced me to Sarah. She and Abby were best friends."

For a moment, all was silent save the water bubbling in the large basin perched over the fire. His eyes took on a faraway look, and a smile appeared on his face—Journey found herself wondering about his wife.

Everyone had loved her. Just hearing them say her name made that plain. She imagined what Sarah must have looked like, pretty and tall, with sleek brown waves falling around a porcelain face. Miss Rose and Abby had mentioned Sarah's beauty both of face and spirit many times.

Journey poked a loose hairpin into place. When had she brushed her hair last? She must look a sight. And likely smelled worse. She wiped the smoke and grime from her face.

"You have a smudge," he said, pulling her from her reverie. The pad of his thumb brushed against her cheek, and something in his gaze changed. He leaned forward, his hand cupping her cheek.

Then he blinked and his lips parted in a gasp. He turned back to the fire, clearing his throat.

"What about you?"

Her heart jumped. "What about me?"

"Do you have any family?" He concentrated on the glowing blaze, but she sensed her answer mattered.

"No, not really. There was a woman who…worked with my mother. She helped me to leave that place. I always thought she must be what an aunt was like. I don't know much about Mama's family." She hugged her arms around herself. "After she died, Hank became the closest I had, until—"

Until Walten? When had she started thinking of them all as family?

She turned back to the church. "I need to tend Miss Rose, make sure she's warm enough."

Zane turned also. "Didn't we just come out to cool off from that heat?"

"To see that she's not too heated, then—"

"Why not stop over and see if Abby can use a hand? Let her know how Miss Rose is doing?" Zane tipped his head to look under the brim of her hat, with a hand on her shoulder to still her. He leaned the tree limb he used to stir the fire against his bound arm. "I'm sure she'd like the company."

She glanced across the snow to the mercantile, squinting against the sun's reflection. Abby had done so much over the past few days to make sure food and supplies were on hand. "I could run over for just a few minutes."

She headed off without a backward glance. The packed snow under her feet marked the path worn by many trips between the two buildings. Her feet felt like lead as she pulled herself up the few back steps to the mercantile.

"Abby?" she called out, easing her way through the door. Hearing no response, she moved into the tiny kitchen in back of the store, which connected the business to Sam and Abby's home. A small pile of wood lay scattered near the low flames. Rags littered every flat surface. Abby certainly had been busy to let this mess happen. She couldn't remember a time when Abby's home wasn't meticulously clean. She walked into the shop, coming in behind the counter.

"Abby!"

Her long form lay on the floor, stretched on her side in an odd slump. Journey knelt down and shook her shoulder.

"Abby, can you hear me?" Her skin felt hot, even through her woolen dress.

She grabbed a heavy blanket from the shelf and spread it over her. "I'll be right back." She ran her hand over Abby's clammy face. "I'm going for help." Abby sighed but Journey sensed she didn't realize anyone was there.

"Zane! Zane, where's Doc?" Journey called, running from the store to the church.

She found him pushing a wad of sheets into a steaming pot.

"Zane, it's Abby! She's sick."

He abandoned the boiling pot and met her halfway up the path.

Together they moved back to the shop. Abby hadn't shifted. Zane bent down on one knee, grasping the blanket to pull under her as he scooped Abby up from the floor.

"Get another blanket to throw over her, Journey. We'll get her to the church."

"You can't, Zane. You're hurt."

His head snapped back. "I can if you help me. Lean her up."

Journey pulled Abby's arms carefully, holding her head as it lolled to the right. Zane braced in behind her and clutched Abby around the waist with one arm so that her upper body balanced against his broad chest.

"Grab her legs."

She obeyed, biting the inside of her cheek as she struggled to balance under Abby's long form.

Lurching and stumbling, they made their way down the steps and across the yard to the church's back door. She heaved a sigh of relief when Doc Ferris appeared at the corner and took a firmer grip on Abby.

She raced ahead of them into the church, tripping up the steps into the sanctuary that seemed to shrink with every new patient.

Doc and Zane followed close behind. Zane's labored breathing echoed above the pounding in her ears.

The doctor's chin jutted toward the pulpit. "Set up a cot over near Miss Rose. It'll save you from running between them."

She swallowed over the tight knot in her throat. Her eyes washed with tears, and she couldn't tear her attention away from Miss Rose's tiny, hidden form. The doctor's hand grasped her shoulder.

"Come on, now," he said gently. "We need to stay focused. They need us."

She nodded yet couldn't seem to make her feet move, until Zane sank onto the floor by the door, Abby limp in his arm. She scrambled to the pile of blankets the women of the community had brought in and traipsed back through the patients to set up the last available bed. Unfolding one blanket only partially made for a thick pad to soften the rough fabric of the cot. She helped Zane and Doc slide Abby onto it.

"I found her lying on the floor," Journey said, her voice low. "She's so hot, Doc. Burning up."

She nudged Zane aside to lay a heavy quilt over Abby, then stood back, wiping sweat from her forehead.

Restless movements from around the corner of the

pulpit drew her to Miss Rose's side. The woman shivered; her eyes opened a slit but remained unfocused. Journey grabbed a cup half full of tepid water and held it to her lips, supporting her head with her other hand. Only a few dribbles made their way down Miss Rose's throat before leaking from her lips over her cheeks.

Tucking the blanket closer to Miss Rose's chin, she moved back to help with Abby. She seemed paler, if that were possible, except for bright spots of color on each cheek.

Doc Ferris handed her a bottle of white powder. "Mix one spoonful of this into a tin of water for her."

"I'll do it, Doc," Zane said, pushing up from Abby's side with one arm.

Doc looked at her, then back to Zane. "No, right now I need you to rest a minute so you can go for Sam. He can't have gotten far."

Zane moved to get his coat, before realizing he still had it on. "I'll be back quick as I can," he said, pausing at the door.

Journey stepped over to him. She sensed his urgency. The thought that his best friend could lose his wife, as he had, brought a flicker of something to his soft gray eyes. Was it fear? She put her hand on the arm of his coat to stall him.

"You'll pray, won't you?" She pulled back and wrapped her arms around herself. Why did he look at her like that? Like she'd lost her mind? He prayed all the time, didn't he?

"I mean," she stammered, "when you were gone and then Hank said… Well, Miss Rose prayed for you and you came back. A little worse for wear, maybe, but all right." Still, he stared. "Zane?"

"Right," he said. His voice sounded dry, far away.

"You're right. I will be praying. I have been. And when I get back, maybe we can pray together."

She looked around the shadowed room filled with fevered bodies and weary workers. Could her prayers help at all? God never stops listening, Miss Rose had said. "Go on," she said, turning him around and all but shoving him from the room. "Catch Sam. Abby needs to know he's here. Besides, we need you here. Go on, now. Hurry."

She shut the door behind him. If her prayers worked, he'd find Sam before he got out of town.

Chapter Thirty-One

Zane picked his way along the path, surrounded by ghostly figures of snow-covered rock as he moved into the mountains. When Sam said he'd be moving quickly, he wasn't kidding. He'd covered a lot of ground in an hour, but Zane expected to reach him soon, if the tracks gave any indication. Though he'd only been a fair tracker, his friend had left an easy trail to follow.

Despite the drive to push on and get back, the beauty of the land never failed to calm him. The land rose up to the west, the valley rolled out toward the east. The skies, clearing from the heavy snow clouds of the past few days, were brushed blue and white, sweeping along with the wind that blew, a little warmer than it had been. But the snow would keep the ground white for months to come. It promised to be a beautiful Christmas, though little thought had been given to it over the past few days.

C'mon, Sam. Where are you?

A thud and a groan answered him from ahead. Sliding from his horse with one hand, he headed into the scrub pines up the knoll on foot.

One shot rang out. Zane ducked and heard the bullet whistle through the tree behind him.

"I believe you've come far enough, sir." Hank's voice wheezed from behind snow-covered shrubs.

He slipped back and raised his arm slowly.

"I'm not carrying a gun, Baines, and I have no intent to hurt you. I'm looking for Sam. He's on his way to Virginia City, but his wife took sick and needs him. Has he passed through?"

Hank shook his head, his face glistening in the streams of light. "I haven't seen him. An' I'm tired of seeing you, Preacher. I should have finished you off when I had the chance."

Zane watched Hank stumble into the shrubs, gasping for air, and moved forward to catch him.

"Don't you come any closer, I say." Hank's revolver bobbed a little before his grip steadied. "I got plans for you, Preacher. Plans for you, for Maura, for this whole little town of yours. As soon as Roy gets here, you'll see."

He forced his muscles to relax, easing away. Hank didn't appear too focused, yet he held the gun.

"Let me help you, Hank. You're sick."

"Ah, you'd like that, wouldn't you?" He laughed. "I wouldn't imagine that act of kindness would endear you to our darlin' Journey, now, would it?"

A glimpse of deep blue fabric caught Zane's attention. Sam was out there. Baines made no sign that he'd noticed. *Keep him talking.*

"You know it was Roy that found her in the first place? He tried taking up honest work, riding herd up here when he spied her. I understand there was a little trouble that night. Roy didn't take so kindly to the good parson cozying up to his buddy's wife."

Hank's mustache drooped and his eyes glazed over. He slumped toward a tree to support himself, but the revolver barrel seemed plenty steady.

Zane caught Sam's attention as he appeared through the trees. He lifted his chin a little, signaling Sam to move in.

"You know that's not how it is, Hank. Besides, it seems to me she wants to be left alone—"

Hank's head snapped up. "She told you that?" He took several slow steps forward.

Zane held his ground. "I can see for myself she's afraid of you."

"That was before. We were in a bind—things were tight. It'll all be different this time." Hank's voice grew louder, more insistent.

He ducked his head and shuffled his feet, hoping to distract Hank as Sam edged closer. "I don't reckon she'll be going anywhere with you."

The storm that smoldered in Hank's eyes washed over his pale face. "I daresay she will. She'll recall how good things were, soon as we are away from here. Away from you!"

Hank lunged forward on unsteady feet, finger tightening on the trigger. From the corner of his eye, Zane watched Sam's dash, and he tucked his arm in close to dive at Hank's feet.

Strange how the quietness of the snow magnified the echo of the gunshot. It was Zane's last thought as he fell into the unmarked snow.

Chapter Thirty-Two

Journey jolted, startled from her sleep by unfocused dreams. She glanced around, finding herself at the church, and eased back against the pew.

So many were sick. Evie Wilson, looking pale, spooned water into her son, Jimmy. The first day they brought people into the church to set up the makeshift hospital, the boy had thrown up until she wondered what could be left. Now she found his stillness unsettling. She would try to get Evie to rest a little—as soon as she could force her own limbs to move.

Abby's quivering form caused Journey to cast aside all weariness. She got up and brushed her palm against her friend's face and found it scorching. Grabbing the cloth from a fresh bucket of snow, she laid it over Abby's forehead. Pale green eyes, fever-bright, blinked open.

"Sam?" Her voice cracked and she struggled to sit up. "Sam!"

Journey pulled the covers higher and tried to settle her. "It's me, Journey. Sam's on his way, Abby. Zane went after him, and they'll be back soon. You need to rest."

Abby didn't seem to hear but fell back with a sigh.

Journey hadn't thought to get her to drink some water. Doc Ferris said that was important.

"Journey? Journey, are you there, dear?"

She grabbed the corner of the heavy wooden pulpit to drag herself around to Miss Rose's side. The woman's blue eyes opened only a slit but appeared clear. "Let me get Doc," she said.

Miss Rose grasped her arm with bony fingers. "In a minute. Where's Zane?"

"Sam went for more quinine, but when we found Abby collapsed in the store, Zane set out to fetch him. They should be back any time."

She could almost feel Miss Rose's exhaustion as she rubbed the woman's head. *Any time now, Zane. Please, please get back here. Miss Rose needs you.*

She almost missed the weak voice. "Miss Rose?"

A cough with a tight, dry rattle answered. "Tell Zane I said to take care of you."

Journey shook her head. "You concentrate on getting yourself well. I'm not telling him anything."

The warm hand stroked her sleeve. "Don't be stubborn. He'll be stubborn enough for both of you. He cares for you, Journey. Let him."

Forcing a smile on her face, she rose with a squeeze on her arm. Miss Rose couldn't know all that had happened since Zane's trip to Virginia City. "I'll get some tea for you. We'll see how it sits."

"Fine, dear. I'll be here a while yet." Her eyes closed and a smile eased the lines on her face. At least she seemed peaceful.

Lengthening rays from a cold disk of sun cast an eerie light through the window. She went for her coat and headed outside for some hot water to make the tea. The weight in her pocket reminded her of the pistol she'd started keeping there since Hank's last visit.

She searched the path Zane would have taken and then looked toward town. The whole community seemed to hold its breath, waiting in the quiet to see how the epidemic played out. Looking west, the jagged spines of the hills lay under a blanket of white, rising to blue-toned mountains farther back. It struck her as odd that she hadn't thought of the land that lay beyond them in quite some time. The urgent plan to get as far west as solid land allowed no longer drove her.

The calmness of Walten had crept in on her, and she found herself wishing that she could belong there.

She shook her head. Where were Zane and Sam? Shouldn't they have returned by now?

God... she began. She concentrated on the fire. What could she say? That she wanted to stay? It seemed too big a miracle to ask. For Hank to leave her alone? That was more than she deserved. She had brought this mess on herself, after all.

God, please be with Zane and get him back here soon. I wouldn't ask it for myself. But Miss Rose needs him around, and Abby needs Sam. She paused, wondering how to end her prayer. *And if I could stay until I know they'll be all right, I'd consider it a real gift. I appreciate it, God.* The name sounded strange coming from her lips. Who was she to call on God?

Journey threw another log onto the bonfire. The need for hot water for cleaning the sick, boiling cloths and making tea never ended.

Dipping into the kettle of water warming over the fire, she poured it over the willow bark powder at the bottom of the mug and set it on the pile of wood to steep. She leaned back and rubbed the tired muscles in her lower back. She'd gotten more sleep those cold nights on the ground coming west than she did on the hard pews these past few nights.

Motion caught her eye, and she turned to find three riders trotting into the far end of town. She ran around to the front of the church for a better view. The figures looked tiny, framed by the buildings on either side of the street, the sky wide and blue-gray overhead. Two men rode upright, the third lay over the back of his horse. Her throat tightened. Then her feet pounded forward, until she met the riders in the middle of the road.

She looked up at Sam, who didn't seem to notice her as he traveled on to the church. His mustache twitched, and his eyes blinked in rapid succession.

Zane, on the other hand, stared down at her, looking like he had in his cabin the night Gypsy had gone wild, crashing through the trees, leaving both her and the horse with broken legs. The night he'd had to shoot Gypsy. His jaw worked in and out with tension under the shadows of his hat brim.

"What's happened?" She craned her head, trying to see around him and his horse. Who else had fallen sick?

Zane slid from the saddle and stood in front of her. Only then did she see the fresh bruise forming over his eye. She reached up to brush his thick brown hair away. "Zane?"

"It's nothing. I fell, is all." He cocked his head in the direction of the other horse that trailed beside and slightly behind, out of her view. "Journey, it's Hank."

She narrowed her eyes and stepped away, arms stiff at her sides. He reached out to grasp her, but she jerked back, freeing herself. Could he hear her heart pounding?

"How could you? How could you bring him here, Zane? After I told you—"

"Listen to me. He's sick. I couldn't leave him out there in the hills to die."

"I trusted you. And now you've brought the fox to the henhouse!"

"We'll keep a close watch on him. He won't be able to hurt you or anyone else anymore, I promise. But he's burning up with influenza, like the others. He needs a doctor."

"If this God you're always telling me about is truly just, he'd have died out there."

"We're better off with him here, where we can keep an eye on him. He won't be turning you in to the law anytime soon, and he won't be trying to sell shares in some non-existent mine."

"No!" She tried to catch her breath. Miss Rose had said he would take care of her. Thankfully, she knew better than to rely on him. It seemed only right that his concern lie with the town. She understood that.

She couldn't blame him for not trusting her, but at the same time something heavy settled over her. The fear that slipped away when Zane held her close and safe that night in the barn returned with a vengeance.

She shook until she thought she'd rattle apart. Hank couldn't win. She fumbled in her coat pocket and touched cold, sharp metal. She lunged forward, holding the revolver steady in her hands.

Zane watched Journey's expression change in an instant. Fear aged her more than mere years would show.

A flash of metal appeared as she darted forward, hands withdrawn. Her fingers shook from the weight of the pistol in her tiny hands.

He stepped close, thankful that the deserted street kept them from prying eyes. Hank's eyes blinked open, looking like muddy puddles. They focused on the barrel pointed high at his chest.

Zane's heart hammered. He laid a hand on Journey's arm, grateful when she didn't flinch at his touch.

"Leave me be," she said, her voice deep and tight. She never looked away from Hank, whose mustache trembled and throat convulsed.

"You know it can't end this way." He kept his voice low, stretching his other arm around her.

"It can end any way I want. You're the one who reminded me to watch my back. That's exactly what I'm doing."

"Not this way."

"Once Hank's gone, I'll never have to worry about him again. You'll never have to be bothered with *me* again. I'm already wanted for his murder. For once in my life the stories about me will be true."

Zane shifted his weight and nodded Sam off when he turned back toward them. "If you do this, you'll never be free of him. He's here, Journey, but he can't hurt you. Look at him. He isn't going anywhere. We'll contact Reed—get him to come and tell us how to handle this. We'll get a lawyer from Virginia City to come if you need one. We'll—"

"No!" She thrust the barrel closer to Hank's heart.

Hank wheezed. "Listen to him, Maura—Journey. I promise you, I won't stay around to bother you anymore."

"You lie!"

Zane stretched an arm forward, pushing the barrel tip toward the sky. The jolt knocked the gun from her hand, and it fell to the ground, slowed by the thick folds of her skirt.

She turned on Zane. Her fists pounded against his chest,

and he crushed her to him. This only served to free her feet, which she dug sharply into his shins. An elbow poked his tender side, and he released her, sucking in a breath.

"Journey?" Zane edged closer. "C'mon, sweetheart, come inside. We can work this all out."

Hank silenced her response with a moan. His eyes darted like a cornered cat, and he sucked in a great breath of air and held it, bowing low over the saddle. Only the slightest movement told Zane he hadn't stopped breathing.

Zane watched Journey, her bottom lip quivering as great tears gathered in her deep brown eyes. He leaned forward, hoping to offer comfort. But she staggered back, then turned and ran before her tears made good on their threat to fall.

Chapter Thirty-Three

Zane moved to follow her, until he heard Hank tumbling from his horse. Zane went to his side but kept an eye out for Sam, who'd already made his way up the front steps of the church.

"C'mon, Baines," Zane said, nudging him with his boot. Hank didn't move.

It took several failed attempts before he managed to pull Hank to his feet. Together they wobbled to the church. The main street of Walten had never seemed so long. Finally they were met by a puff of warm air and Doc's helping hands.

Zane stomped snow from his boots before stepping into the welcoming heat of the sanctuary. His shoulder throbbed, and the ache in his ribs made it hard to breathe. Even more painful was the feeling he'd abandoned Journey. Would she ever trust him again? But how could he have done anything but bring Hank to town?

After Hank's warning shot had ricocheted off a tree to skim Zane's forehead, Hank had collapsed under the fever and ache of the grippe. Leaving him would have meant certain death out there in the snow. Journey wanted him dead, but he had brought Baines to town for help. Had he destroyed any trust Journey might have had for him? Had he taken mercy too far?

Sam knelt at Abby's side, brushing her long hair back from her damp face. Doc Ferris held Miss Rose's head up, coaxing something steamy into her cracked lips. *Jesus, be with all these things going round in my head. Help us, each one, to focus on the task at hand, and give us wisdom to know just what that should be at any given time.*

"Sit down, Zane," Doc called over to him. "You look like you've been ridden hard and put away wet yourself. I'll check your arm and that wrap on your ribs in a minute."

He obeyed, finding a spot in the corner and struggling with the buttons on his coat.

The room was an odd balance of quiet and chaos. The heavy steps of tired workers echoed across the floors. An underlying drone of raspy breathing filled the room. Strange how a church that seemed plenty large every Sunday morning when he stood before all those peering eyes could shrink so much. He closed his eyes and leaned his head back.

Doc Ferris roused him. He darted up, cradling his side when he felt a stitch.

"Hold on there," Doc said. "You slipped off a bit. You're entitled." He frowned, looking at the welt Zane felt above his eye. "Trouble on the trail?"

"You might say that."

"I might say this looks like a bullet nicked you." Doc's eyes concentrated on the slice on his forehead, but the rest of his expression demanded an explanation.

"I ran into Baines in the little piney. He fired off a shot and I took heed, but he wasn't himself. I could see he was feverish, not thinking real clear. But then, I'm not exactly his favorite person these days, as it is. Sam came up from behind to get the pistol away, but Hank shot again. I ducked and slipped on a patch of snow, but the bullet ricocheted off a branch and creased me."

"Did you lose consciousness?"

"No. Things got a little blurry there for a minute, but I didn't pass out."

Doc stood and turned back to a pile of bandages behind him. "You're fortunate. It'll be sore, but no stitches. Take off that shirt and I'll check those ribs. They'll need to be rebound after that fall, I'd expect."

Zane looked at all the ladies shuffling to feed broth to the patients who were awake. "Here?"

"I doubt you'll garner much notice." Zane could hear the tired smile in his voice. "Come on, now. I haven't got all day."

Zane eased his shirt off, and the undershirt beneath that, as his ears grew warm. In no time, Doc had the binding loosened off. He winced as the doctor prodded his tender side but convinced him it felt much better than it had a week and a half ago.

"I'm going to wrap you again, just the same," Doc said. "There's no sense in being hasty."

"Where's Hank?"

Doc nodded to a cot on the far side where Hank lay with his head toward the front door. "He's been quiet ever since you brought him in."

"Good. Has Journey come back?"

"Zane?" A low voice from the back of the room interrupted them.

"Miss Rose?" He stood, pulling his flannel shirt around his shoulders, and moved over to her bed. Sam sat on the floor nearby, his head leaning on Abby's shoulder, their hands entwined. Both slept.

"Zane? Are you there?" Miss Rose looked as though she were trying to sit up on the cot and failing.

"I'm right here. Settle back and tell me what you need, and I'll get it. You rest."

"Journey? Where's Journey?" she asked, lying back.

He glanced at Doc, who shook his head and continued gathering his supplies. Zane pulled the blanket up under Miss Rose's chin.

"She stepped out for a while to clear her head some. Sam and I, we brought Hank in. He's sick, too."

"And Journey?"

"I haven't seen her since," he said. "She wasn't happy to see Hank and not pleased with me for bringing him here. She said I should have let him die out there."

"And maybe you should have, Lord forgive me," Miss Rose said, her voice sounding much like his grandmother's had, but she had smoked cigars. Zane tilted her head to give her some water.

"I know," she said, rolling her eyes a little at him.

He leaned back. "I didn't say anything."

She coughed and her face scrunched up, making her wrinkles even more pronounced than usual. "You've been my pastor…long enough. I know what you'd say."

He grinned as she closed her eyes again. For a moment he thought she'd fallen asleep. But she slid her hand over his and squirmed under her blankets.

"Go after her, Zane. Look out for her. She needs you."

"What about you?" He brushed wiry gray wisps from her face.

"I need to know you're both fine and looking out for each other. The Lord has something in store for you both, Zane. Don't be afraid of it. I don't know when she'll be ready for you. But let yourself be ready for her if the Lord allows it."

He stood, finding her blue eyes focused on him. "I'll find her. We'll help her through this, whatever happens. Don't worry. Just rest." He moved to get his coat and hat.

Her fragile voice followed him over the growing din of the room. The light through the windows slanted, casting a reddish tone over the golden wood of the sanctuary walls. It lit Miss Rose's face.

"Go on," she said. "Like I told Journey, I'll be here a while yet."

He pulled his shirt closed and fumbled through the buttons, managing to slide most of them through by the second try, even with his fingers moving stiffly from their sling. He grabbed his coat.

"Preacher?" A quiet drawl caught his attention, and he turned to see Hank's foggy eyes focused on him.

Anger flared within him, to his surprise, but he went to the man's side. *Lord,* he thought, *give me the right words to say—and keep me from thrashing him myself.*

He pulled a chair up to the low cot. Hank's breath came in shallow gasps that didn't rustle the blanket over him.

Where was Journey? He shifted in his seat. The sun would soon set. His knee bounced and he looked toward the door. But he sensed the Spirit wanted him here.

A low voice called his attention back to the bed.

"I would suppose," Hank said, "that you're happy to see me here. Rather fitting, right?" His eyes remained closed, as if he hadn't the energy to open them.

"Fitting, no. Believe me, Baines, I take no pleasure in you being here." He rocked in his seat. *Where was Journey?*

"You don't find the least satisfaction in my illness?" Shallow breaths interrupted his speech. "After I lied, tried to cheat your town, and am married to the woman you're in love with?"

"Don't forget our little meeting in Virginia City, Hank. And I care for her, but I'm not *in love with* Journey."

"So you say. And I'm to believe you forgive me for all that? No one has that capacity to forgive."

The flames that took Sarah came to mind. The rescue he should have been able to make. "I've had to forgive things a lot worse than anything you've done. But what I do isn't what matters here." *Maybe Journey had only gone back to Miss Rose's to think things through.*

Hank licked his lips. "I didn't intend for things to turn out this way. My ma took me to church when I was a boy. I know about God."

Zane glanced at his pocket watch and leaned close to Hank's pasty face. He sure looked worse than the other patients. Where was Doc? "But do you know His Son?"

The dark eyes widened. "It's too late to feed me that line, Preacher. I always meant to get my life together, to make things right. It never seemed the proper time, though."

Doc Ferris came over and placed his hand on Hank's head. Then he dug Hank's hand from under the covers and checked his wrist against his pocket watch.

"Anything I can get you?" he asked. Hank shook his head. Zane cleared his throat and looked at the doctor.

Doc nodded him over to the dim corner before answering. "He's not going to make it, Zane. He's too hot and drying out. His pulse is weak and out of beat, and there's nothing more I can do. If we had more quinine, maybe. But I think he was too far gone when you found him. Sounds like pneumonia has settled in his lungs."

Rubbing a hand over his face, Zane looked back over at the patient. "Hard to figure how a man gets to the place where he is."

He let his gaze wander around the sanctuary. "I was heading out to Miss Rose's, figured Journey might have gone that way. But if you think he hasn't got long, maybe I'll sit with him a bit, try to talk to him again."

Doc nodded. "I know you'd rather be with her. But you won't have another chance at Hank, unless I miss my guess. I'll say a prayer for him."

"Throw one in for me, too, Doc," he said. "I'm afraid my compassion's about to run out."

He patted the doctor's stooped shoulder and moved back to the seat by the bed where Hank lay.

Chapter Thirty-Four

Journey slipped into the church entry without a sound, pausing at the door to the sanctuary. Her breath clouded before her, but she felt warmed by the shame that burned her face. Why did she always make everything worse by her actions?

She rested her forehead on the rough door frame, then pushed the door open. Lanterns had been lit but not enough of them to conquer the growing darkness. Most patients seemed to be resting, with workers waiting to attend any need that might arise. The room was quiet, and only Doc Ferris seemed to notice her. Still, she couldn't force herself through the door.

She spotted Zane's broad back, sitting next to a cot by the wall. He blocked the view of the patient, but she could tell from the size of the feet hanging off the edge that it was a man. And she could well guess which man, even before she heard him.

"You still here, Preacher?"

"Thought maybe you'd like to talk some more." She heard Zane's low reply.

"There's nothing more to say. You think I don't know

how this is going to end? You expect me to come blithering to the Lord's feet, begging Him to take me now, when I know I can't do a thing to earn my keep?"

"It's not about 'earning' anything, Hank," Zane said.

Did he really think he was dying? Or was this some unexpected trouble that he planned to turn to his advantage?

"That sounds very well, but that's not the way life works," Hank said.

"No, but that's how God works. There's still time for a change, if you want it."

Could he change? Journey wondered. Could God forgive someone like Hank? Would He?

"The only thing I want, Preacher, is to be left to myself."

She caught a glimpse of Hank's face, which held a grayish cast in the waning light, as Zane shifted and lowered his head.

"Let me sit awhile and pray for you. I won't say a word. But just in case you change your mind—"

"Suit yourself, Preacher. I expect you have a job to do." He chuckled, but it came out in a gasp. "At times like this, I'd imagine you'd rather have found another line of work."

She watched Zane raise his head and detected a grin from the dimple on his cheek. The thought must have crossed his mind. He stood and walked over behind the pulpit, pulling out a worn Bible and returning to his seat. He opened the book over his knee with one hand. She watched his lips move silently in profile.

Hank shifted, turning to draw in more air. He seemed to have trouble with that. Would the same happen to Miss Rose and Abby as the illness lingered?

"One thing, Preacher."

"Yes?" Zane held the Bible closed with his finger marking the place.

"Tell Journey…" She leaned forward to catch every raspy word. "Tell Journey I'm sorry. She's a wonderful woman, kind and full of life. At least, she was before I changed that in her. She deserved someone good." Hank's dry cough interrupted him.

She slipped a step back with surprise. Her mother had been a prostitute. She'd grown up in a saloon and taken up with Hank before she'd married him at seventeen. Even now, with the mess she'd made of her life, she'd never thought it wasn't all she deserved.

"It's not about deserving. God forgives us in spite of what we deserve. That's what I'm trying to tell you," Zane said.

"Too late for me. I won't come groveling to the Lord this way. But Maura…maybe Maura. Journey deserves someone like you, Preacher."

Zane slid his chair forward, but Hank waved him off with a finger that barely moved. "I believe I'll sleep for a while now. You'll be sure and tell her what I said?"

She didn't stay long enough to hear Zane's response. She couldn't face him, not now.

Shutting the door without a sound, she left the church. The cold fresh air would clear her head. The last thin rays of sunset clung to the snow-sculpted hills and peaks.

Did Zane truly believe Hank could be forgiven? She wanted to scream her denial of the thought. But what if there was hope for someone like Hank? For someone like her?

She stepped down to the ground and headed for the shed, where she'd left the horse. She needed to feel the cold on her face, needed to breathe in the open air, away from town. She needed to think. She needed—

But all thoughts flew from her mind as hands clamped around her waist and over her mouth, stifling her scream. Then light burst behind her eyes, and darkness fell.

Chapter Thirty-Five

Icy cold seeped in, drawing Journey awake. Shivering overtook her and her teeth chattered. She blinked her eyes open but only darkness greeted her. Rough wood bit into her cheek as she shifted on a lumpy pillow. She couldn't feel her hands, couldn't tell if they were in front of or behind her.

She struggled to keep her breathing slow and even, but her gasps echoed around her, unnaturally loud in the hollow air. Where was she?

Hearing no sounds that would indicate another's presence, she shifted to her side until her back met with solid wall, and muffled a groan as sensation returned to her hands with jagged tingles. Only then did she realize they were bound, along with her feet. It took several tries before she managed to rock herself upright.

Not even the barest flicker of light could be seen. Maybe it was night outside. How long had she been unconscious? Would whoever brought her come back for her?

It couldn't be Hank. He was too sick, wasn't he?

Roy! All control left her at the thought, and she blinked, trying to dispel the darkness. The air wafting by smelled dank and seeped through cracks around her. The walls around were close, leaving her boxed in where she felt suffocated by the darkness. She drew her legs up, trying to conserve any heat her shaking could muster. What did Roy want with her?

Hank's kindnesses had been few and far between, but at least they had existed before he'd met Roy. Hank became cruel, but Roy truly frightened her. Hank's temper ruled him, especially once he began drinking more. Roy never lost control; every cruel act sprung fully planned from his mind to be carried out. And that made him terrifying.

Tears spilled down her face in icy trails. She hugged her knees to her chest, rocking to and fro in the narrow space. *Think!* She commanded her pounding head. What would Miss Rose do?

Pray? Come sniveling to the Lord when she found herself between a wall and, well, the blinding blackness that lay beyond?

"You expect me to come blithering to the Lord's feet, begging Him to take me now, when I know I can't do a thing to earn my keep?" Hank's words echoed in her mind.

Zane said it wasn't about earning anything, that God would forgive, that it wasn't too late for change.

She thought back to the week before her mama died. The owner of the tavern where her mother worked had been furious when Mama refused to take any more gentlemen callers. Not gentlemen, she corrected herself. Not men like Zane and Sam. Those men had been like Hank and Roy, taking only for themselves.

Mama had been sick, but she'd never have returned to that business. She had tried to explain why, but somehow those lessons had been lost in Journey's efforts to get away after Mama died. Within that week, when she was hungry and cold and tired of living in the streets, Hank had befriended her and taken her to live with him. Could God forgive all that she'd done since that time? So many deceptions.

There's always a chance, she reminded herself. She pushed into the wall at her back as the darkness crushed in tighter.

She buried her head in her bound hands. "Oh, Lord," she whispered, her voice unnaturally loud as it cut through the overwhelming silence. "I've made such a sorry mess of my life. Then I tried to hide it, and that's only made it worse."

Rocking harder in the enclosed space, she paused to catch her breath. "Jesus, I don't know You, not really. I only know I've made so many wrong choices that I can't make any right ones anymore if You don't help me."

She stopped, listening, arms trembling around her knees. Her breath caught. Was that a creak she heard? But if there'd been anything unusual, it made no other sound.

"I know You can forgive me, Jesus, if You only would. And whether I make it out of here or not—" she gulped, hoping the latter would not be the case "—but even if not, Lord, I want to be Yours, and to know Your forgiveness. Uh, thank You, and…amen."

She lifted her face. The throbbing in her head moved from the back where she'd been struck to a point behind her eyes. Sniffling, she managed to fish a handkerchief from her pocket with her hands tied.

Cold air still wafted around her. No light threaded its way into the blackness in which she was submerged. A rescue didn't appear any closer at hand than it had a few moments before. But the cold knot of fear and confusion and sorrow that had gripped her heart began to loosen...and soften...and grow warm. Peace filled her as the happy tears fell.

Chapter Thirty-Six

Zane jerked his head up at the sound of feet stomping in the door. How long had he dozed? He needed to find Journey.

"Reed?" Zane watched him make a beeline from the entry to his aunt's side and followed. The sheriff sat at Miss Rose's side and held her hand, his gaze resting on her tiny form. He swallowed hard and blinked several times.

"How's she doing?"

"She's resting. How'd you hear?" He adjusted the sling around his arm.

"I met a man on the trail who said there's been sickness and that you had everyone holed up at the church. When I didn't find anyone at Aunt Rose's, I thought—"

"I'm sorry. I should have wired before."

But Reed waved him off. "No matter now. I'm glad you were with her." Zane caught his glance. "Besides, I'm here on business. I had a visitor. A man came in by the name of Roy Clemson. He claimed to be a lawman from Georgia investigating the case of Maura Baines, otherwise known as Journey Smith."

"He came all that way to find her?"

Reed shook his head. "Something didn't sit right with me, either, so I did some checking of my own. He's no lawman and I have a poster on him."

"He's looking for Journey?"

"She ever mention him? Do you recognize the name?"

"No, but Hank may. He's sick and Doc says he doesn't have long, but we could ask." Something clicked in his mind. "You said no one was at Miss Rose's place? You checked the barn?"

"I looked around a bit, hoping. But I didn't see anyone. Why?"

Zane shook his head and scratched his eyebrow. "Journey was none too happy with me for bringing Baines here. She ran off, and I thought she'd go there."

"Preacher?"

He glanced over his shoulder at Hank and stood, looking at Reed.

"I'm sure she'll turn up, soon as she's had a chance to think things through," Reed said.

Zane watched him pull his seat closer to Miss Rose's side. Sam knelt near Abby. Both women were still and asleep, but Abby's color had already improved since they'd found her. He wished the same for Miss Rose.

"Preacher? Are you there?"

He shuffled to his chair beside Hank. A lantern flickered its light over his gray face. "I'm here, Baines. What can I do for you?"

"Maura," he gasped. "Where is she? I have to talk to her." Hank kicked his blankets off.

"She's not here. You have to settle down." He held the man with a hand at his shoulder. "Doc?"

The man appeared at his side, with Reed right behind. Doc grabbed Hank's wrist with one hand and pulled out his pocket watch with the other. "You can't carry on like this, Mr. Baines. What can I get you?"

"Maura. I have to tell her—Roy's coming. He said he—could persuade her—to help us."

"Help you how?" Zane's voice sounded unnaturally loud to his own ears in the quiet room.

"Mining deal. We had maps, drawn up special." Hank puffed. "Never had a chance to use them."

He leaned forward, clenching his hand in the blankets covering Baines. "What will he do?"

Doc Ferris nodded him off with a furrowed brow. "Take it easy, son. She was here earlier."

"When?"

"You were talking with Hank. She didn't stay long."

His fingers tightened into a fist. "Where would he be, Baines? What will he do if he finds her?"

"Don't know." Hank coughed hard and fell back, his breath shallow. "But he'll find her, unless you do…first." Air gurgled in the back of his throat and his face grew dark as he tried to inflate his lungs. "Tell her I—tried." He choked and his lips went white. He brought a trembling hand to his chest and his eyes rolled back. He struggled again with the blankets. "Too hot…"

Zane tried to pull the man upright, awkward with one arm in a sling, but lost his leverage as Hank grew heavier and slumped to the bed, eyes closed. He looked to Reed and then Doc, who shook his head and replaced Hank's hand at his side. "He's gone, Zane."

He wanted to kick the cot and make Hank tell him more. He blew out a frustrated breath. His muscles tensed, and he felt Reed's hand on his shoulder.

"You might as well rest yourself. There's no way we

could pick up any trail tonight," Reed said, stretching to his feet. "You know that."

He fell into a chair by the window, cradling his ribs. "All I know is that she's out there. What if this Clemson guy has found her? We have to do something."

"And she could be tucked in at Aunt Rose's place by now for all we know."

He gave a ragged sigh. "I know. I should've gone out to check myself. Maybe she—"

"Look at yourself. When's the last you slept?" Reed asked. "Your ribs must be killing you."

"Not so bad that I can't ride."

"Ride where? Unless you know right where she'd be, we could mark up any tracks we might find if we wait until daylight." Reed eased into the seat by his side in the corner.

Zane remembered Journey's fury as she had stormed off, thought about Hank's warning about Roy Clemson. Somehow he didn't hold out hope that she could be sleeping, safe and sound. Wind rattled the window.

"I know," he whispered. "But something's not right. I feel it. Tell me you believe she's fine."

Reed cast his gaze toward his aunt, shielding his eyes in the shadows of the room. He kept his voice low. "I believe we can only trust the Lord to take care of her until He guides us to find her. But we can't head out until daybreak. You get some sleep, and we'll leave at first light."

Miss Rose's voice barely crossed the room. "Zane? Zane, are you there?"

He moved to her side and knelt. "Right here, Miss Rose. What can I do for you?"

"You can settle yourself. You're no good to Journey or anyone else if you go off half-cocked." Her weak voice was painful to Zane's ears.

"I have to find her. I hate to think she's out there and I can't—" His chest burned and he swallowed over the knot in his throat.

Miss Rose slipped her hand over his. "She's not Sarah."

He focused his gaze on the lantern on the far window-sill. "I know that. I don't want her to be."

"You think if she's not Sarah, you can't love her," she said. "But that's the one thing they have in common."

He looked down at her pale face, blending in with the pillow slip. "I only want to help her. She needs me."

Miss Rose managed a dry laugh. "You need her. She's the only woman to get any of your attention since Sarah died." She shifted under the covers. "Besides me, that is."

He leaned down and smiled. "No one deserves the attention more than you."

"I won't always be here to look out for you. You need someone, Zane. Journey loves you, you know."

"She'll be gone the minute the snow melts."

Her blue eyes blazed with fever and irritation. "Only if you don't give her a reason not to. You love her. Or you're starting to. Don't let Sarah's memory blind you to a future she'd want you to have. Go after Journey."

"She's not even a believer. I can't just— She's not—"

"Trust God. He's working on her. Trust Him and go after her."

"I will," he said. He looked at her pasty skin and heard her shallow breathing. He leaned down to kiss her cheek. "I will."

Morning couldn't come soon enough.

Chapter Thirty-Seven

"Journey!"

Sunlight had only begun to kiss the horizon when Zane and Reed were saddled and ready to head out. The night air still hung cold and frosty, and he wondered, not for the first time, if Journey was somewhere warm. They pushed the horses hard on the ride out to Miss Rose's place, but the careful search of the ground for even the barest of tracks garnered no leads.

"Journey! Can you hear me?"

Reed reined in beside him. "She's not here."

"Jour—"

"Zane!" He felt Reed grab his coat sleeve and pull him around, carefully because of his ribs. "We're wasting time. We need to backtrack this Clemson guy and see who's talked to him, where he'd go if he did have her, where he'd be now if he doesn't. Maybe if we talk to him, we could at least take out some possibilities. We can't go out searching all over creation and hope to find her," Reed said. "It'd be like looking for a needle in a haystack."

"Your way could take days." He kept his voice low and tight. "That's time Journey might not have."

"Do you have a better idea?"

He swiped a knuckle over his forehead. *Dear Lord, where is she? Guide us, please, Father. Why, if she were mine, I'd—*

Mine.

"Zane? You feeling all right?" Reed shook him out of his daze.

"I will be when we find her," he said with a nod. "And I think I know where we can look. Listen, you go ahead into town, ask around and see what you can learn about Clemson. Baines has been stirring up interest in the old mine. He's been staying out there. Maybe Clemson is, too, and if so, maybe he's taken Journey there."

Reed shifted in his saddle. "I don't know, you with that arm? What if you meet up with Clemson without me?"

"I'm not looking for trouble. I only want to find Journey, make sure she's not hurt. I'll be careful."

His friend still looked doubtful. "You're sure? Aunt Rose'll kill me if anything happens to you."

"I'm sure. I'll see you back at the church."

Journey shivered and felt her stomach flop, shaking to stay alert. She blinked and tried to stretch before remembering her bound hands. The darkness prevented her from seeing anything more than shapes, but the impenetrable black lightened with streaks of sunlight winding through the loose boards in the walls. It must be morning.

What was that noise?

The wind moaned, piercing the cracks at her back, but she could have sworn there was something else. *Lord, am I losing my mind?* Day and night all tumbled together. She slid until she felt the press of boards at her shoulder.

Again she heard it. A voice. Maybe voices.

Would someone be looking for her? Would they even notice she was missing after the way she'd run off? What if Roy came back for her? What if—

Wait a minute, she told herself. What about faith? Wasn't part of believing in God remembering that He had control over everything?

Her hands no longer had any sensation, but she clenched them to bring the feeling of pins and needles back at least. If someone came, she'd need to attract attention. If Roy returned, he already knew where she was, and calling out would do no harm, she reasoned.

"I'm here!" Her voice filled the space around her, sounding raspy and weak to her own ears. She coughed as the chill air suffocated her. "I'm in here!" she called again, louder.

She strained to hear over the odd moans and creaks of the closet. Weren't the voices getting closer?

Rocking back and forth, she tried to stop the trembling that chased down her spine. "Zane!" She couldn't stop the tears that rolled down her face. "Please, Jesus! Let it be Zane!"

Zane pulled his horse back into the stand of trees near the old mine. He squinted across the clearing to the mine shack standing in all its dilapidated glory near the mine entrance. *Please, Lord, let Journey be there.*

Steps sounded closer, and Journey held her breath. "Zane?"

The closet door creaked open and a match flared. She screamed.

"'Fraid not, Maura," Roy said, his face eerie in the soft glow. "By the time your preacher man figures out where to look for you, we'll be long gone."

Cold dread formed a lump that sank to her stomach when he drew closer, settling back onto his haunches and blocking the doorway. The glimpse she had of the room that lay beyond told her little.

He grinned without a single tooth showing. "Your prince won't be arriving anytime soon."

"What do you want?" She struggled to catch a deep breath.

"You. You're going to straighten out this whole mess.", He leaned closer until she could smell a strong lack of soap on him.

"There wasn't a problem until you told Hank where I was."

"No problem at all," Roy said. "You flitting about with your new beau under your husband's nose. And Hank was still going to cut you in on the deal."

"It wasn't like that. I didn't want to be a part of any deal. And Zane—"

"That's not the point, is it?" He struck another match and watched it add its glow to the first as it burned out, then used it to light a cheroot held between his teeth. "The money you took from Hank that night you left belonged to me. So I figure it's me you owe, after all."

"I don't owe you anything," she insisted.

A third match lit the lantern that rested at his feet, still necessary in the morning grayness. He drew a long puff and let the smoke swirl slowly from his lips and nose.

He continued talking then, as if he'd never heard her. "You'll come with me. I'm sure we can find something for you to do until you pay your debt." She felt his gaze on her, moving from her boots to her face, lingering longer than it should. "I'm sure we can come to some kind of agreement." His tone showed he didn't care about being agreeable.

"I'm not going with you, Roy. We'll settle this here."

"Hmm…that might have worked if you had helped Hank like he said you would. As it stands, maybe it'd be best for you and me to move on, head to California. Some towns are starting to get right civilized—makes the folks more willing to be fooled. With looks like yours, they'll fall in well enough." He stretched a stubby finger and stuck it into one curl. "Yes, Hank certainly knew what he was doing when he took up with you."

She stiffened, her heart pounding in her throat in the pattern of her uneven breaths.

"Yep, you're a fine-looking woman, Maura." He drew forward, eyelids heavy.

He caught her bound wrists and pulled her up close. The scent of tobacco gagged her.

He leaned closer. She squirmed, moving her arms between them, and pushed him away, scrambling to her feet in the tiny closet. She slipped down on her tingling feet. Roy moved closer and yanked her back up. She staggered as he shoved her away, managing to right herself against the wooden doorjamb before she toppled over completely.

"You could do worse than taking up with me." His lips brushed her ear as he spoke. Bile rose to her throat.

Sparks of panic flew behind her eyelids, which were squeezed shut as his hand slid around her waist and up her back. The other hand trailed through her loose hair brushing either side of her face. She panted and thrashed, striking out with her bound hands.

Roy grabbed her waist again and thrust her away. Sharp pain gouged her back and forced air from her. She cringed when he stepped forward, beefy fist raised.

She ducked and rolled against the wallboards to the

floor. He grabbed the hem of her dress and yanked her back over the uneven floor, pulling her upright against him despite her kicks. *Lord...*

"Let her go, Roy."

A voice boomed against the unnatural light as she struggled free. Zane! His shadowed form blocked most of the morning light as he stood in the outside doorway.

Journey squirmed and thrashed until Roy's grasp loosened and she felt him pull away. She dropped to the cold dirt floor of the cabin and rolled to her knees, squeezing into the corner.

Roy spun free of Zane's grasp on his collar and whirled, shoving him against a rickety table. He gasped as his bound arm twisted.

Then Roy stepped in, wielding a board at his head. She squealed and Zane managed to avoid the swing. The sickening crunch of wood against wood muffled his groan as his tender ribs battered the rough edge of the stand.

Roy swung again, this time catching the side of the preacher's head. "Zane!" Journey yelled as he slumped to the floor.

But he kicked out, knocking Roy's legs from under him. The man fell to the floor and scrambled to some dark corner.

Zane pulled toward her, and she reached out to help him lean against the wall beside her.

"Did he hurt you?" he asked, panting and trying to stand.

She helped him up, holding her bound hands over his side to check for further damage. He worked to catch his breath, swaying slightly. "No, he— I'm fine. Zane!"

Roy swung the wooden club again. This time it connected with the end of Zane's chin, forcing his head back and into the rough wall. He dropped to the floor, unmoving.

Journey wobbled to his side on her knees. She ran her fingers over his face, hoping to rouse him. "Zane?"

But a cold, hard grasp jerked her to her feet. Roy pinched her jaw in his grimy hand, bringing tears to her eyes.

"Don't bother. You'll be a lovely memory for him, if he has a memory after that hit. Now, you're coming with me."

"No!" She pulled away, moving to Zane's side. "Please! Please, you have to let me help him. I'm no good to you, I'd only slow you down."

"I said—"

"They'll follow if I'm with you, Roy. They came this far. If you go now, you'll be in the clear. They'll never catch you, they'll—"

Roy slapped her and she sank to the floor. "Fine. You make a good point. But if you say a word about me to a soul, I'll be back and I'll kill you and your darling pastor— and anyone else who means anything to you. And you know I can."

She shook, unable to speak.

"I see we have an understanding." Roy grabbed the lantern and moved to the edge of the waning shadows. "Be sure it stays that way."

He left her in gray silence.

Chapter Thirty-Eight

Zane roused as pain seared through his head. He opened his eyes, his vision murky at best. Gentle hands smoothed his face.

He sat up carefully, leaning against the rough board behind him. Where were they again? He moved his good arm around to push himself up and away from the wall.

"Journey? You there?"

The soft sound of crying echoed between the walls of the almost empty cabin. He brushed her shoulder and pulled her into the crook of his arm. She curled against him without any argument. He leaned his head back with a deep sigh.

He breathed deeply, choking with the staleness of the air in the shack.

"Journey?" He nudged her. "Journey, where'd Roy go?"

She continued crying and he shook her. "Journey! Where is he?"

"He said if I sent the law after him he'd come back and kill us. Then he took the lantern and left. How badly are you hurt?"

"Never mind me. We have to go now if we want a chance to catch up to Roy. Come on!"

He pulled himself upright, using the sturdy beam at his back for leverage, and dragged Journey up behind. "Let's get out of here."

Her head nodded against his chest, and he wrapped an arm around her shoulders. She followed a few paces, then stopped short. Her wide eyes gleamed in sudden panic.

"What if we don't find him?"

He ran his fingers down her arm to clasp her hand. "We will. We have to, or you'll be looking over your shoulder for him every day for the rest of your life." He tried to calm her with slow, even tones. "We have to move now. Maybe he headed back to town for Hank, or maybe he's camping somewhere close, but we can't know until we get out, all right?"

"What about Hank?"

Her warm arms trembled and tightened around his waist. She didn't falter, but he sensed she wanted the truth.

"One thing at a time, right? Let's get out of here and get help. Reed's in town. Then we'll talk. There are a lot of things I need to tell you." He felt strength grow in her and wondered at it.

"Oh, Zane. You haven't any idea."

Journey felt Zane's arm wrap around her shoulders and relaxed into his embrace. His muscles tensed under his coat sleeve, but she couldn't tell if this was from pain or something else.

She watched Zane carefully, saw his struggle to stand upright and not crash to the floor. She tried to support him, but a night of sleeping bound in the cold had caught up with her. Her legs cramped fiercely.

"Zane—"

She cringed, rubbing her legs with frustration. He tugged her onward and she skidded to her knees, gasping as tears streamed down her cheeks.

"Journey! We have to—"

"I'm trying. Give me…a moment."

They wouldn't get anywhere at this rate. He'd move faster alone. "Go," she said, exhaustion sweeping over her. "Go on without me."

He drew closer and she heard his voice in her ear, soft yet firm, as he stooped on one knee, wavering at her side. "No! We have to stay together."

He helped her to her feet and again they stumbled on. The distance seemed to grow as he staggered and turned without pattern. Only his determination kept him upright as he tugged her along.

Zane pulled Journey closer as they stepped onto the porch, where the roof lowered above them, sunken near the entrance. He motioned for her to follow behind, and she nodded her understanding, unable to read his eyes anymore. They appeared as two black caverns in his face.

Two turns around the corners and the glow from a lantern shone in the still-darkened woods ahead. Roy must be waiting for them.

"Zane?" Where would they go now?

He muffled a cough and clutched his side. How much farther could he manage? "This way!" he whispered.

She followed. Where was he going? The path narrowed and she glanced back. In the early morning mist she could make out the outline of the cabin where Hank had been staying. Roy, too, most likely.

A crack sounded up ahead. Gunshot? She started, feeling Zane drag her behind a tree.

Then another crack, this one a sound breaking in her ears from much closer. Zane's arms shook around her and loosened as he slipped to the ground.

Zane whipped around at the sound, dropping to the ground. "Journey!" He grabbed her hand and dragged her down beside him.

He heard her scream, a shrill echo in his pounding head, and swayed to his knees behind the tree. Holding her down with a hand at her head, he peered into the dim array of trees, searching for Roy's location. The growing light sliced through his head. He turned back, a finger to his lips to tell Journey to be quiet.

"I know you're out there, and I know you're listening." His mouth dried up, making it hard to swallow. "This has to end here, Roy. Hank's dead." The roaring in his head distorted all other sounds. "Turn yourself in and help Journey clear her name. Hank would've wanted that, and things'll go easier with you if you talk to the judge."

Journey struggled to her knees in spite of his warnings. He managed to grasp her waist and hold her tightly, edging around the tree that hid them. He squeezed Journey closer, black dots swarming his vision between them. She squirmed from his grasp, and the sound seemed to explode around them.

He peered out again, hoping for a glimpse of the man, but instead the sound of a gun being cocked met his ears. He froze, keeping his arms up and away from his sides as he turned to face the end of Roy's gun.

Close. They were so close. But Roy drew back, smashing the pistol at his head again, and Zane's vision grew black, the sparse light slowly overtaken by gray dots that obliterated all else.

I'm so sorry, Journey, he thought. *I couldn't save you, either.*

Chapter Thirty-Nine

Several moments passed before it registered in Journey's brain that Zane hadn't followed her. The sun had replaced the blackness overhead, but no movement of shadow behind her could be seen. She dropped back to her knees, scanning the trees for any sign of motion.

Zane. She spotted him now, lying at the tree where she had left him, unmoving. His wide eyes stayed closed, their long, dark lashes brushing his dirt-streaked face. His shirt and free hand showed torn patches, and a scrape along his chin bled readily. She worked her way back to him, darting tree to tree until she collapsed at his side. Another gash caught her attention on the other side of his head, one she hadn't noticed before.

Exhaustion weighed on her and her eyelids drooped. They needed help. Once she rested, maybe she could—

Her eyelids snapped open. She had to stay alert. *Oh, Zane. Wake up!* She wanted to scream at him, wanted to see those gray eyes. Instead, she rubbed a smudge from his cheek and tried to jostle him awake.

If Zane had come looking for her, maybe he wasn't alone. He wouldn't come himself in his condition, would he?

"Help." The word came out soft and weak and raspy from her dry throat. She drew in fresh air for long moments and tried again. "Help!"

Trees rustled and footsteps rushed from the surrounding brush. She twisted around to find the source of the noise as it drew closer.

One last scrape of limbs and she shrieked as Roy stepped out into the flat where she and Zane lay sprawled.

Her heart pounded in her ears as he stopped short. His lips drew into a sneer. "I knew you wouldn't let well enough alone. Stirring things up in this charming little town, too, eh, Maura?"

"Stop it, Roy. You know I haven't done anything. You know I didn't kill anyone. It wasn't me that set that fire. Please, we need to get him help."

He stepped closer and she trembled. If only Zane would wake up. His chest lifted and breath puffed shallowly, but his face remained lax. She tried shifting her legs to rouse him. *Please, Zane.*

Roy stood over her. His hand ripped through her ragged hair and jerked her head, tilting her face to his. He pulled his stump of cheroot from yellow teeth and breathed more smoke into her face. "I know you didn't set any fire. That's part of the fun for me, you see. You didn't kill Hank, but he's dead now. You didn't start that fire, but a man was burned to death in it. You'll never be able to prove—"

"Clemson! Put your hands up and step away."

Reed? Reed! *Thank You, Lord!*

Roy's hand gripped her even tighter and yanked her up, which sent Zane rolling to the ground with a muffled moan.

Reed stepped into the path. A gun flashed in his hands. She struggled, feeling Roy's grip loosen with surprise.

He shoved her and she sprawled against Zane. Landing on her side, she saw Roy's own pistol draw upward in his hand, cocked and ready. She heard the thundering echo at her ear as she tried to reach him in time to thrust him away, saw the puff of smoke drift from the end.

"No!"

Roy smiled and lowered his gun to her face and she felt an instant cold streak settle in her stomach. No time to pray, no words to fill the instant of time that seemed to hang frozen. Roy's hand continued to drop and he slipped a step, falling over a tree root to land on his back. His eyes closed, but that evil smile held for a moment before easing away with the slump of death that took him. Only then did Journey notice the dark stain of blood growing in the center of his chest.

And then Reed was there, squeezing heat into her arms and lifting her to her feet once again. She hovered as he knelt by Zane, who still hadn't opened his eyes, and watched him lay an ear to his chest. Her breath caught, unable to draw in or release. Zane had to be all right. Dear Lord, nothing else mattered, so long as Zane lived.

Warmth. A cool hand. Each sensation made itself known slowly in his foggy head.

Sarah waved to him from where she sat by the fireplace. Zane waved back and she smiled. She stood then and drew her rocker closer to the flame, pulling another chair beside her own. She pulled a tiny pistol from Journey's saddle pack and threw it into the fire. Then she lifted the pack to the chair.

Journey appeared and sat with her. He moved forward to join them….

"Doc, he's awake."

A cool hand held him down as he struggled to turn.

"Let him up. He's likely queasy after that knock to the head." Doc Ferris's voice punched through the throbbing walls of his head.

He lost the contents of his stomach and felt the hands guiding him back into bed. His eyelids felt like wagon wheels as he shifted them open.

Journey's smile greeted him. He thought he managed a smile back and patted the hand that rested over his chest. "We're all right," he said.

She must not have understood, because she leaned closer and said, "You rest. We can talk about this all later, when you're feeling better. You're going to be fine, Zane. We're both going to be just fine."

When Zane roused again, his stomach still felt wobbly, but he did open his eyes without getting sick. Journey sat in a chair at the foot of his bed, asleep with her head tilted against the wall, one arm resting over his foot. She looked like he felt.

"You awake, Zane?" Reed stepped into his line of sight.

He managed a small nod. "Reckon I am." He paused to think, which seemed a lot more difficult than usual. "'Cause surely something prettier than you will be there to meet me at Heaven's gates."

Reed managed a chuckle and sat down. "What do you remember?"

He searched his foggy memory. "We were looking for Journey this morning." He stopped to draw in a slow, shaky breath. "So what'd you do to me this time?"

"You do an awful lot of talking for a man in your condition," Reed said. "Do you remember the mine?"

He closed his eyes and tried to think. "You mean Hank's

mine? Wait, he's dead, isn't he?" He pushed his brain to recall more. "Roy! Roy Clemson—"

"He's dead, too. There was nothing I could do."

Zane nodded his understanding.

"The pieces will fill in later, Doc says. You'll feel fine in a week or so, be up and around before that."

"What about Journey?"

She had slipped around to sit next to Reed before he realized she was awake. "It's all going to work out. I have a lot of things to tell you once you're feeling up to it." Her voice was quiet but her smile spoke loudly.

"Reed?" he asked, not taking his gaze away from her almond-brown eyes.

"She's a free woman. Both her accusers are dead, and I heard enough from Clemson and Hank to clear her name. I expect the fact that she ran will be forgiven by the courts, under the circumstances."

Zane smiled, his eyelids feeling heavier by the moment until he could no longer keep them pried open. "How are the others?"

"Abby's feeling better. Doc says she had a mild case, but it was good you brought her in when you did. Sam's with her now. Jimmy Wilson still has a long row to hoe, but Doc thinks he'll pull through. We haven't had a new case in over a day, since you found Abby. Doc thinks we may be through the worst of it." Journey's quiet voice soothed his aching head.

"And Miss Rose?"

Silence. He opened his eyes to catch the tail end of a look Journey and Reed exchanged. He struggled to his elbows. "How is she?"

"Not good." Reed didn't mince words. "She's developed pneumonia. She's weak. Doc Ferris says it's out of his hands. She's been asking to see you. She said she wants to talk to you and Journey both."

"She awake?"

Reed glanced to his aunt's cot and nodded.

Zane struggled to sit, in spite of Journey's and Reed's hands trying to hold him back. "No, let me see her, let her know I'm well."

He thought he held steady but must have wavered, because Journey's strong arms drew around to support him. Together with Reed, they helped him move to a chair beside Miss Rose's cot. He managed the short distance and sat with a heavy thud.

"'Bout time…you got here," Miss Rose whispered. Her skin tinged with blue and her blankets barely moved as she panted. "You had us scared silly."

"Sounds like you've been doing the same," he said. Journey settled on one side of him, and Reed on the other, sitting on the end of Miss Rose's cot.

"Nothing to be afraid of, Zane. You know that better than anybody, I suppose." She puffed several times before she could speak again and her legs shifted restlessly. "Journey knows that now, too."

He stared in confusion a moment before understanding flooded him along with surprise. He turned to Journey. "You believe?"

"I heard you with Hank, saying there's nothing God can't forgive, even with all he had done."

"But Hank didn't believe, Journey. He hardened his heart and wouldn't accept God's forgiveness." Zane ran a thumb over her hand.

Journey placed her other hand over his with a light squeeze. "Reed told me. I'm glad you tried, though. I guessed if Jesus' death could cover Hank's sins, that maybe there was a chance for me, too. I prayed, in that mine shaft when I woke up. I prayed, Zane," she said, her eyes growing damp as the deep joy he'd just now noticed shone from them. "I prayed and God forgave me. I know what you were talking about now. And, oh, I have so much more to learn."

Miss Rose gasped, her face scrunching with pain as she turned to Zane. "And you'll be around to teach her. I believed the Lord had something special in mind when He brought you here, Journey. This one's about as special as they come. You've both been given an early Christmas gift."

She grew paler and her eyes closed. Zane wondered if she'd fallen asleep, but she forced them open again. "I won't be around…to see how…things progress. But…you can be sure…I'll be keeping an eye…on you all. So long as the Lord…allows it."

He leaned forward and stroked her cheek, ready to deny that this was her time. He glanced at the tears pouring down Journey's face with disbelief, then watched Reed take his aunt's hand in his own.

"I've had a life far better…than I deserved," she continued. "But I'm ready to see my Lord…in person. And see my Wallace again, my family."

Her eyes drifted closed and Zane leaned forward even farther, cupping her cheek in his hand. "No, Miss Rose—"

"Yes. You've been…like a son to me, Zane," she said. "But don't you…ruin this. It's a time…to have joy."

She shifted enough to peer up at Reed. "And you…have been…a wonderful…nephew…so strong and bright…true to God's calling…brave." She paused again, her eyes drooping. "I love you—both my boys."

Journey lost control then, weeping openly and loud in

the tiny sanctuary that seemed hollow in its emptiness. He gripped Miss Rose's knotted hands in his own, stroking the fingers.

"And you…missy. Only just met you…but you're to me…all I fancied…a daughter of…my own…would be…"

Journey choked out a "Thank you" on broken sobs.

"Don't go…thanking me. You want to say…thanks, you take…care of my boy." Miss Rose pushed her head back into her pillow, arching slightly as she tried to draw in enough air. "You all…take care of…each other…"

A sudden slump and an easy smile across her face announced her passing. Reed drew his aunt into a final embrace as Journey sobbed, rocking in her seat.

Zane drew Journey close and shed a few tears of his own.

Chapter Forty

Journey stepped from the lukewarm water and toweled herself dry. She donned her dressing gown and brushed her damp hair back to dry in the heat of the fireplace. Tomorrow would be Christmas Eve, and the last of the patients had been sent home a couple of days ago. The epidemic had hit the town hard, but Doc Ferris thought it might have been worse. Another note of praise in the joyous season.

Curling onto the rocking chair—Miss Rose's rocking chair—she thumbed her Bible open to read. She'd been working through the Gospel of John on Zane's suggestion.

There was so much to learn, so much she didn't understand. But each week she'd take her questions to Zane. And each week he'd shed more light.

She read for an hour, maybe more judging from the way the fire's flames had subsided. She stood and stretched, then pulled on her long coat and twisted her hair under her shapeless hat. The bathwater would be cool enough by now to dump.

Dragging the metal tub through the back door, she tilted it into the snow. Her gaze scanned along the moonlit ridge as a shadowed form of horse and rider appeared on the rise above the kitchen. Zane.

She returned the tub to the pantry and buttoned her coat over her robe, then moved to meet him at the front door.

He pulled up short next to the porch, and she saw another horse tethered behind Malachi when Zane dismounted. He nudged his Stetson from his head just enough to peer up at her. "Evening, Journey," he said.

"What brings you out this time of night?"

"I apologize for the hour. I meant to get by earlier but got called over to the Hamlers' to help shore up the barn roof. Can we talk?"

"Do you want to come in?"

His eyes caught the light and a grin tugged on his lips. "'Avoid every appearance of evil,' Journey. I can't. You come here."

Her cheeks grew warm as she moved down the steps. She fished a crumbling lump of sugar from her pocket and offered it to Malachi, scratching his nose as he ate it. "I'm sorry I don't have any for your friend," she told the horse. "What's her name?"

"Actually, she hasn't been named yet," Zane said, speaking of the mare. "That's up to you."

She turned to face him, almost knocking into his broad chest. She stepped back to a more comfortable distance. "What do you mean?"

"Merry Christmas, Journey. The mare is yours, if you want her."

She looked at the sturdy little horse with surprise. "For me?"

He nodded. "I didn't have anything ready at the time,

but I do feel kind of responsible for your horse. I mean, there's not a thing I could've done different to save it, but I felt bad that it had to be done, just the same."

"I was angry at you for a long time because of that, you know." She smiled, moving toward the tethered horse. Her honey-gold coat shone, brushed carefully over sleek muscles.

"Even yet?"

"No. There have been a lot of changes in me since September. But you didn't have to do this. Homer's mine now, I guess." She shook her head, blowing softly on the mare's nose. "I still can't believe Miss Rose left this whole place to me. She was a good woman."

Zane looked toward the barn and nodded in agreement. "That she was." A moment passed. "I wanted to talk with you, Journey, about your plans."

"Plans?"

"You know, now that you've been cleared of charges. Now that you're free to come and go as you please without watching over your shoulder." He shrugged. "I know you've been waiting for spring so you could move on. I guess it's…well, is that still the case?"

She stroked the horse's tawny hide. "I hadn't really considered it much. I've been sorting through things, trying to move on without Miss Rose here. Learning more about God and what He wants from me. I've spent most of my life running from something or other, Zane. I guess I'm trying to learn how to sit still."

"So you're staying?"

She concentrated on the horse's dark mane. "How important is it to you?"

His hand on her shoulder turned her to face him. He stared hard a moment, his gray eyes looking almost black in the darkness, then drew her close. Sweeping the hat from his head allowed the moon to create a halo of light on his brown hair. He ducked, tilting her chin so he could slip under the wide brim of her hat.

She closed her eyes as the warmth of his lips melted hers. Their pressure brushed along her cheek to her ear, into her hair as her hat slipped back, letting several heavy curls escape. He smelled of leather and wintergreen, filling her senses. Her body relaxed and she leaned toward him only an instant before he pulled away.

"I'm sorry," he whispered, but somehow he didn't sound completely sincere. "This isn't the order I meant to take."

She squeezed his arms, pulling him in to kiss his cheek. "What are you saying?"

He smiled and placed his hat back on his head, adjusting hers as well. "I learned a lot since September, too. I learned that I love you more than I wanted to admit. I learned that I can do that without forgetting Sarah. I want—that is, what I'm trying to say is—"

"I love you, too." She smiled, happy tears blurring her vision.

Zane laughed, a deep, rolling sound. "So now, for my Christmas present—will you marry me?"

Joy filled her. But… "What about my past? There'll be those who aren't so willing to forgive as you. What will Mrs. Decker say? She's had you picked for her son-in-law for a long time."

"It doesn't matter. I'll preach a series of sermons on gossip and forgiveness, and we'll work through it. Just say you'll have me and that you won't leave." He gathered her in his arms and held her close. She heard his heart pounding at her ear, strong and true.

It felt like home.

"Yes," she said. "Yes, I'll marry you."

His arms drew her tighter, his chin caressing her head. Would she ever begin to comprehend God's goodness?

She stood with him in the moonlight, happy in the love she felt. Never had Christmas meant more, knowing Christ's heart, and that of this wonderful man. A sudden thought brought her back to peer into his eyes, teasing. "Why bring the horse? Is it a bribe?"

"Not exactly." He sighed. "I didn't want your not having transportation away from Walten to be an excuse for marrying me."

She giggled. "You're saying taking this horse and heading west might be a smarter option?"

"That could well be." He laughed. "But she won't love you like I do."

His arms slid from her and she shivered in the sudden chill. His hand gripped hers. "So have you come up with a name for your mare?"

She hugged his arm, leaning against him as they looked the horse over together, standing under the light of the Christmas moon shining down over the crests of snow on the ridges around the ranch.

"I think I'll call her Dweller, Zane. Because we're both here to stay."

Dear Reader,

Thanks so much for taking time during this busy, joyous season to read *The Parson's Christmas Gift*. I hope you've been blessed by the reading, as I have been in the writing of it.

Journey and Zane both had to surrender their pasts to the Lord in order to find a new beginning with each other. What a blessing to serve the God of Second Chances (and Third, and Fourth…).

This is my first journey into the world of publishing, and I pray there is a long road ahead. I'd love to hear from you at mountainwriter7@yahoo.com.

In Christ,
Kerri Mountain

QUESTIONS FOR DISCUSSION

1. Fear is a big motivation for Journey. In what ways is fear helpful to her? How does fear hinder her? Is there a place for fear in a Christian's life?

2. What evidence do we see that Zane's faith has grown through the death of his wife and child? How does this prepare him for the test of his faith with Journey?

3. Journey's accident changes her very general plans of heading as far west as possible to a very specific set of circumstances that are unwanted. Can you think of a time where a bad situation focused your choices toward a better path?

4. How does Zane's need to protect Journey initiate his attraction to her? How does that same protective nature cause him conflict when it is directed toward the town?

5. Journey agrees to help Hank because she feels she has no choice if she wants to protect her friends from her secret past. Is this true? How does she come to see that the Lord's way is always best?

6. Zane is suspicious of Hank and his relationship with Journey. What place does a skeptical attitude have in a believer's life?

7. Contrast Zane with Hank. How do they exemplify the two worlds Journey is caught between?

7. How do Zane's dealings with Hank during his illness show not only his Christian compassion, but also his love for Journey?

9. How does Miss Rose's influence serve to lead Journey toward a decision for salvation? What can we learn from her methods to help us bring others to Christ?

10. What are Hank's redeeming qualities? What keeps him from accepting Christ? What do we learn about Zane in his decision to stay with Hank rather than follow after Journey?

12. How do Miss Rose's final words serve God's purpose for Journey and Zane?

13. What motivates Zane to give Journey a horse for Christmas? How does this deepen their relationship?

Love Inspired
HISTORICAL
INSPIRATIONAL HISTORICAL ROMANCE

Widowed father Boothe Powers has lost his faith—until he meets dedicated nurse Emma Spencer. She could love his boy and heal his own heart. Yet how can he trust a profession he blames for his greatest loss? Emma has her own secret anguish. But if God would grant her one miracle, He knows exactly what her heart is yearning for.

Look for

The Path to Her Heart

by

LINDA FORD

Available January wherever books are sold.

Steeple Hill®

www.SteepleHill.com

LIH82804

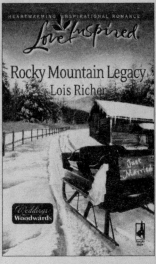

REQUEST YOUR FREE BOOKS!

2 FREE INSPIRATIONAL NOVELS
PLUS 2
FREE
MYSTERY GIFTS

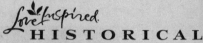

Love Inspired.
HISTORICAL
INSPIRATIONAL HISTORICAL ROMANCE

YES! Please send me 2 FREE Love Inspired® Historical novels and my 2 FREE mystery gifts (gifts are worth about $10). After receiving them, if I don't wish to receive any more books, I can return the shipping statement marked "cancel". If I don't cancel, I will receive 4 brand-new novels every other month and be billed just $4.24 per book in the U.S. or $4.74 per book in Canada, plus 25¢ shipping and handling per book and applicable taxes, if any*. That's a savings of over 20% off the cover price! I understand that accepting the 2 free books and gifts places me under no obligation to buy anything. I can always return a shipment and cancel at any time. Even if I never buy another book, the two free books and gifts are mine to keep forever. 102 IDN ERYA 302 IDN ERYM

Name	(PLEASE PRINT)
Address	Apt. #
City	State/Prov.	Zip/Postal Code

Signature (if under 18, a parent or guardian must sign)

Mail to Steeple Hill Reader Service:
IN U.S.A.: P.O. Box 1867, Buffalo, NY 14240-1867
IN CANADA: P.O. Box 609, Fort Erie, Ontario L2A 5X3

Not valid to current subscribers of Love Inspired Historical books.

**Want to try two free books from another series?
Call 1-800-873-8635 or visit www.morefreebooks.com**

* Terms and prices subject to change without notice. N.Y. residents add applicable sales tax. Canadian residents will be charged applicable provincial taxes and GST. Offer not valid in Quebec. This offer is limited to one order per household. All orders subject to approval. Credit or debit balances in a customer's account(s) may be offset by any other outstanding balance owed by or to the customer. Please allow 4 to 6 weeks for delivery. Offer available while quantities last.

Your Privacy: Steeple Hill Books is committed to protecting your privacy. Our Privacy Policy is available online at www.SteepleHill.com or upon request from the Reader Service. From time to time we make our lists of customers available to reputable third parties who may have a product or service of interest to you. If you would prefer we not share your name and address, please check here. ☐

LIH08R

A SECRET PAST, A PRESENT DANGER...

HANNAH ALEXANDER

A terrible secret haunts Dr. Jama Keith. But she must return to her past—her hometown of River Dance, Missouri—and risk exposure. She owes a debt to the town for financing her dreams. If only she can avoid old flame Tyrell Mercer—but River Dance is too small for that.

When Tyrell's niece is abducted by two of the FBI's most wanted, Jama can't refuse to help—Tyrell's family were like kin to her for many years. The search for young Doriann could cost Tyrell and Jama their lives. But revealing her secret shame to the man she loves scares Jama more than the approaching danger....

A KILLING FROST

Love Inspired.
HISTORICAL

TITLES AVAILABLE NEXT MONTH

Don't miss these two stories in January

SECOND CHANCE BRIDE by Jane Myers Perrine
On the run from a shameful past, Annie MacAllister plans
to act as the new schoolteacher in Trail's End. At least until
she's saved up enough money to start her life over. Soon
Annie catches the eye of John Sullivan, upstanding citizen,
the father of one of her students and a man capable of
exposing her troubled past. Together they will need
some divine forgiveness to rekindle their faith and find a
future together.

THE PATH TO HER HEART by Linda Ford
Widowed father Boothe Wallace has a hard time trusting
the medical profession, which he blames for his greatest
loss. Until he meets sweet, beautiful nurse Emma Spencer.
Emma's own secret pain leads her to think her dreams of a
family will never come true. But when Boothe asks her to
play his temporary fiancée to protect his son, she knows
God can see exactly what her heart is yearning for....

LIHCNM1208BPA